BERNADETTE BARRYMORE

DIANE COIA-RAMSAY

This is a work of fiction. All of the characters, names, incidents,
organizations, and dialogue in this novel are either the products
of the author's imagination or are used fictitiously.

Archway Publishing books may be ordered
through booksellers or by contacting:

Archway Publishing
1663 Liberty Drive
Bloomington, IN 47403
www.archwaypublishing.com
844-669-3957

Because of the dynamic nature of the Internet, any web addresses or
links contained in this book may have changed since publication and
may no longer be valid. The views expressed in this work are solely those
of the author and do not necessarily reflect the views of the publisher,
and the publisher hereby disclaims any responsibility for them.

Any people depicted in stock imagery provided by Getty Images are
models, and such images are being used for illustrative purposes only.
Certain stock imagery © Getty Images.

ISBN: 978-1-6657-3838-5 (sc)
ISBN: 978-1-6657-3837-8 (hc)
ISBN: 978-1-6657-3836-1 (e)

Library of Congress Control Number: 2023902000

Print information available on the last page.

Archway Publishing rev. date: 02/07/2023

CONTENTS

CHAPTER 1

Armistice day—November 11, 1918. The Great War to end all wars was finally over. Amid the celebrations in the streets of London, Bernadette Barrymore—as she was known to her friends and colleagues—hoped but doubted that her husband would be home for Christmas. However, he had survived! And as her heart rejoiced, she wondered if she would receive the chance to begin her marriage anew. So she danced in the streets with the others who were celebrating being alive and prayed for a happy life ahead.

Her husband, Lord Anthony Devereux—Tony to his family and friends—had survived four long years without injury when millions of other brave soldiers had perished. He was an officer in the Royal Horse Artillery and had risen through the ranks to become Major Anthony Devereux. Bernadette was immensely proud of him, even despite his lack of correspondence, which had dwindled so long ago until it eventually ceased altogether. He didn't write to thank her for the red socks that she knitted him for Christmas in 1916, the ones she thought would cheer him and make him laugh. Her friend Margaret had to help her with the heels since her knitting was just plain awful, although she did her best to make them nice. She had included warm socks and thermal underwear that she bought at Harrods with her staff discount, as well as sweets and biscuits that she had saved up her ration coupons to buy. The staff lunches at Harrods were tasty and wholesome, and Bernadette hardly ever ate dinner anyway, other than a slice of bread and butter and a cup of tea.

Major Devereux's mother continued to receive the occasional letter; therefore, confused and heartbroken by this turn of events, Bernadette ceased to write her husband letters of her love. She could no longer remember his voice or his laugh, and had she not had their wedding photograph, and one with him looking so handsome in his army uniform, she might not even remember his face. His smile was lost to her, his black hair and vivid blue eyes, since these traits were not appreciable in either of her two photographs. Still, she hoped and prayed that there had been a misunderstanding, probably created by his mother, and that everything would be different upon his return home.

The last time Bernadette saw her husband was in December 1915. He had several days' leave, and they made love again and again, but she didn't know she had conceived until after he returned to France. His mother, Arabella, moved back into the main house from the dower house upon hearing this news and persuaded her daughter-in-law not to write of it until she was past three months. However, Bernadette was never to reach that milestone, so in the end, Major Devereux never heard about his lost baby, and the dowager viscountess never moved back out. She retook her position as mistress of her son's home. Saddened and desperately alone, with her father's approval and Michael O'Connor's assistance, Bernadette began another life in England, awaiting her eventual return to the United States as the memory of her short marriage began to fade into a distant dream. She was aided and abetted by her father, Mr. James Barrymore, who wanted her back, and her mother-in-law who wanted her gone. Bernadette's mother, Mrs. Eugenie Barrymore, was against the proposed annulment, but her husband was a man of strong opinions, so she said a prayer each week at Sunday mass that all would come out right in the end.

Lady Arabella Devereux was a vindictive woman whose cutting remarks made toward Bernadette were hurtful and cruel, especially after she lost the baby. Arabella strongly disapproved of her son's marriage to an Irish American girl despite her mother's fine French lineage. The dowager viscountess referred to Bernadette's father as the "Irish bricklayer." However, in the end, after much persuasion and consideration, the Irish bricklayer provided a handsome dowry to his daughter, which helped to soften the blow to the widow, who was very much reliant upon her son's benevolence.

Bernadette assumed her maiden name when she finally left the dowager viscountess and her husband's family home in Hampshire in September 1916.

Once again, her mother-in-law persuaded her, "I understand that there isn't much to interest you here in the country, especially after your disappointing miscarriage, but why worry Tony? He has enough responsibility on his shoulders in France. Why not have him continue to write to you at Devereux House? You may call to collect his letters and give your letters to me. That way, they will be postmarked here in Hampshire rather than London."

Bernadette went along with this advice. She didn't particularly relish telling her husband that her father had purchased a flat for her in Knightsbridge or that she had taken up employment as a "shop girl," as her mother-in-law called female sales assistants.

Bernadette was, in reality, Viscountess Devereux, Lady Bernadette Devereux, wife of Lord Anthony Devereux—Tony to his family and friends. However, very few in her acquaintance knew this to be true. Her employer, Harrods Department Store, was aware of it, or at least senior management was aware. However, she was always addressed as Miss Barrymore—a fact that made her life in England so much easier to bear, especially following her husband's apparent desertion of her.

Bernadette's father, Mr. James Barrymore, was much affected by the tragic sinking of the *Lusitania* in May 1915 when it was torpedoed by a German U-boat off the south coast of Ireland and where more than a thousand souls perished. Although he could undoubtedly have arranged her passage back to the States, the tragedy played on his mind, and in the end, he couldn't risk placing his precious daughter in such peril. Therefore, he sent his agent, Mr. Michael O'Connor, to London to find and arrange living accommodation and employment for his willful daughter to occupy her time until he finally felt it was safe to bring her home to her family. He could never have expected that it would be more than two years before that was even possible. He wasn't too pleased about the employment, but she had insisted that she would not be sitting in her flat the day long, and neither would she be returning to Devereux House with her mother-in-law in residence. He knew she would be working long hours, but he also knew this would keep her out of mischief. However, with all of his financial success, he could never have imagined that his only daughter, a married woman of some consequence, would be working side by side with shop girls, selling perfume to Englishwomen, in the department store in which he had spent a fortune on her just a few years previously.

Mr. Barrymore had to obtain approval from the bishop for the annulment of his daughter's unfortunate and ill-advised marriage to Anthony Devereux, a titled Englishman—a viscount no less—who had broken his daughter's heart and left her stranded in a foreign land. His mother was a most disagreeable woman, and his daughter hated her for many reasons, as did Mr. Barrymore, almost as much as he hated her son, Lord Anthony Devereux.

CHAPTER 2

The Barrymores had sailed to Europe in the early summer of 1912 for their daughter's eighteenth birthday. They were to take a grand tour of England, France, and Italy. Mr. Barrymore had decided against going to Ireland, although he had hesitated upon his decision not to do so. However, his father and mother had left during the great potato famine, and it was all too recent to him—the tales he heard and their stories of hunger and poverty, which necessitated them sailing to America to start a new life.

The Barrymores had done well. They worked hard, and their only surviving son, James, was by the time of his marriage to Eugenie a wealthy and respected businessman who had made his money in construction, initially building affordable housing for many Irish immigrants living in Boston. However, he had greatly expanded his operation and business since then. He was a hero to many and feared by many more, and Bernadette was his only daughter, a surprise to her parents since there were more than ten years between her and her older brothers, Sean and James Jr.

Eugenie's family was French and Boston high society. Still, they had overlooked her intended's Irish descent due to the fine house and comfortable life that he could provide for their daughter. Thus, the couple was married in the Cathedral of the

Holy Cross in Boston, Massachusetts, and many years later, they took their only and beloved daughter to London that fateful summer of 1912, where she met and fell in love with a member of the English nobility.

The meeting was sheer chance. The family, newly arrived from America, was checking in at the beautiful, brand-new Ritz Hotel situated in the heart of Mayfair. It was very exclusive and exceedingly expensive, which is why Mr. Barrymore had chosen it. Bernadette wandered around the hotel, in awe at the beautiful surroundings, while her parents saw to the desk clerk and suitcases. She turned when she heard Englishmen's voices, still such a novelty to her. They were dressed well in white tie dinner ensembles, yet it was still just early evening. However, Bernadette noticed only one of the men. He was taller than the others and so handsome and generally well favored that Bernadette, embarrassed, felt herself blush, and he smiled at her. He looked to be somewhere in his late twenties. Bernadette shyly smiled back, until her father called out her name. The concierge greeted the gentlemen, addressing the man who smiled at her by saying, "Good evening, Lord Devereux. Several members of your party have already arrived."

In her innocence, Bernadette turned to him wide-eyed and realized he was still looking at her. She had never seen a member of the English nobility before, and from how her father had spoken of them, she never expected one to look like this man, Lord Devereux. Bernadette wondered what the celebration was for and if there were ladies in his party. She wondered if he was married and, more importantly, why was he staring at her as his companions had walked on ahead of him. She nervously straightened her dress as she stared back at him, wide-eyed and a little confused.

Her father noticed him and said, "Good day to you, sir. Fine weather for our first trip to London. We were warned that it would probably be raining. Mr. James Barrymore of Boston, Massachusetts, at your service." And her father put out his hand to shake hands with the gentleman, who immediately responded to the gesture.

Bernadette was immensely embarrassed by her father's forwardness, and just as she wondered if this Lord Devereux would speak, he did. "Not usually so much in June, Mr. Barrymore. You chose the perfect month to bring your family to London. Will you be staying long?"

"Possibly a month, depending on the weather, which you say will be fine, and then off to Paris. A grand European tour in honor of my daughter's eighteenth birthday. Please allow me to introduce you to my wife, Mrs. Eugenie Barrymore, and my daughter, Bernadette."

The gentleman responded, "Tony Devereux. Very pleased to make your acquaintance, Mrs. Barrymore, Miss Barrymore, and happy birthday."

Bernadette realized that she was still blushing since she found it most inappropriate for her father to speak so to a member of the English nobility, and she truly believed that was precisely why he did it. She found herself saying, "Oh, it was last week," and wondered why she said it—since why would this man care?

However, he asked her, "What date?"

She responded, "The seventh."

And then he surprised her. "Then we are almost twins, since mine was the eighth, although possibly a few years apart."

Bernadette Barrymore finally sensed this stranger's interest in her, fleeting as it might be, and answered with a smile, "Oh, surely more than a few, sir."

He laughed at her remark and took his leave, and the family

was shown up to their suite. Once he was out of earshot and sight, Bernadette said to her father, "I have never been so mortified, Daddy! That gentleman is a lord. How could you have been so bold! He must think we have no refinement!"

James Barrymore laughed and responded, "But, Bernadette, I had the impression that he wanted to be introduced to you, and you to him. Either you will see him again or you won't. I believe it will be the former, but first, I need to make inquiries to the concierge."

Bernadette unpacked her own suitcases. Mrs. Barrymore's maid had packed Bernadette's clothes for the trip and was looking after her mistress, but Bernadette insisted upon looking after herself, the main reason being that she had no wish to be followed around by a chaperone. The family changed and freshened up for dinner in the hotel dining room. Of course, Bernadette took special care with her toilette, all the while complaining that all of her clothes were ugly and old-fashioned compared to ladies in London, even though she hadn't actually seen any since her arrival. Her father reassured her of a brand-new wardrobe to be purchased at Harrods department store—the finest in the world. He knew she was hoping to see this English gentleman again; however, she was still so young, and it would no doubt be a passing fancy.

And they did see his party at dinner. All gentlemen, and they were laughing and talking quite loudly.

"Some sort of reunion," her father said with some interest. He was astute and noticed this Lord Devereux glancing their way more than once. His daughter appeared to be ignoring him, and he thought, *Perfect strategy, Bernadette,* as he laughed to himself and his wife gave him a disapproving look.

Lord Anthony Devereux found himself quite unsettled by the encounter, although the young girl was hardly out of the schoolroom. She was stunning—with a mass of chestnut curls that had willfully escaped her hurried coiffure. Her eyes were dark brown and almond shaped, her lips full, her complexion lovely, and her figure divine. She was the most beautiful girl he had ever seen. Girl—because at just turned eighteen, she wasn't yet the woman she would be, and he wondered about her beauty in five years, as she would then reach her full potential of womanhood.

His party was loud and boisterous, which seemed to irritate the maître d', who didn't dare express his displeasure. Lord Devereux tried but found that he couldn't dissuade himself from watching this young girl, who was purposely trying to ignore him, and he caught her glancing his way under her long eyelashes and blushing once or twice when he smiled over at her. He had already inquired about the family to the concierge and was told that Mr. Barrymore was an American millionaire who had booked one of their most expensive suites. The man had a reputation of ruthlessness in his hometown of Boston, where he was apparently in construction. Although the staff was warned that the man was intimidating, he had been generous with gratuities and so far had displayed a pleasant persona. They were nevertheless on guard and afraid to upset him.

It was as Lord Devereux expected, with the way the man was so forward in introducing his family to him. He had smiled and was about to walk away when the concierge added, "He was asking about you too, Lord Devereux. He wanted to know who you were, what you did, and your financial situation. Of course, I told him I had no idea about any of that, and perhaps he should personally ask you about it himself." The concierge stated that Mr. Barrymore responded, "Not important really—just idle curiosity."

When the Barrymores finished their meal, Bernadette and her mother left Mr. Barrymore to his port, and Lord Devereux couldn't resist the urge to ask him to join his party, who were indeed celebrating. It was a reunion of sorts of Oxford University fellow graduates—five years on—and James Barrymore talked about his education on the building sites in Boston. "I bought out or bankrupted every one of my father's past employers. He is long since gone, but I wish he could have been alive to see the success his only surviving son made of his life."

Shortly afterward, he took his leave of the Oxford graduates, and one member of the party, Lord Cecil Fallsington, cautioned his friend, "I saw you watching her and her blushes. She is charming, but I don't believe you would want him as a father-in-law. Besides, he is not truly a gentleman, and she is not of your social class, no matter how pretty she is. A beauty, I will grant you that, but surely not suitable for any serious consideration. Having said that, I wouldn't think you would want to risk anything less— not with that father of hers."

Lord Devereux verbally agreed with his friend, but his mind was in turmoil. It was just that he had never seen anyone like her, never felt such a connection or attraction. Of course, it was ludicrous, but Lord Devereux booked a couple of additional nights at the Ritz, although his original intention was to return to his country estate in Hampshire the following morning. He needed to talk to her, get to know her a little. He hoped she had brains as well as beauty; that was his desire in a wife. And then he thought, *Wife? What are you thinking about, Tony? You will make a point of meeting—speaking with her tomorrow and will find that she is as empty-headed as she is beautiful, which is just as well.* He considered his mother's reaction if he was to express these intentions to her— actually, the reaction of everyone he knew.

He decided it would be just a bit of innocent flirtation. Cecil was right. She wasn't suitable. However, he had very little sleep that night.

Lord Devereux was unexpectedly able to further his acquaintance with the young woman the following day at breakfast. She was sitting alone with a plate piled high with sausages and eggs, bacon, and toast, which she was eating while reading through brochures on London sights and excursions.

He knew he shouldn't ask but did anyway. "Do you mind if I join you, Miss Barrymore? Where are your parents? You really shouldn't be wandering around in a strange place alone. Didn't you bring a chaperone—a maid perhaps?"

Bernadette responded, "You may join me if you wish, but eating breakfast at the Ritz can hardly be considered risky behavior. I wouldn't think so anyway. I am perfectly independent, you see, being American and all that. I will absolutely not tolerate any chaperone, and I don't need a maid. I am not useless like you English. My mother is unwell from all the traveling. She has a nervous disposition, which she blames upon me, and my father has gone out. He is a very early riser. I will also be going out after breakfast."

Tony Devereux was extraordinarily amused. "I don't think it wise for a young lady to go out and about in a strange city unaccompanied. I can't imagine your father will allow that. Have you a particular destination in mind?"

"Yes," she said, smiling at him quite cheekily. Tony noticed her dimples and thought she was, beyond a doubt, the loveliest girl he had ever seen—spirited too—if she truly meant to go traipsing around London on her own. He couldn't allow that, even if her parents were quite neglectful in that regard.

"I intend to visit the Houses of Parliament. There is a ladies' gallery, and I would like to hear what goes on with the men shouting at each other down below. I shall have the concierge arrange my transportation and will leave a note for my father."

Lord Devereux was somewhat surprised at the girl's tenacity and said, "Won't he be angry? Regardless, I can't allow it. I will take you if you insist upon going there—although an odd choice, I would think, for your first excursion in London."

Bernadette was thrilled at the prospect of such a thing. *My first day in London, and a member of the House of Lords wants to take me to the Houses of Parliament! My friends back home will never believe me!* But she said, "Allow? Oh dear me, I don't believe that comes under your jurisdiction, Lord Devereux, but it occurs to me that you must be a member of the House of Lords and a Tory to boot! I'm a Democrat—the rights of the common man and that kind of thing. Forget women, common or otherwise; we have no rights whatsoever! Of course, at least in the States, we can inherit a healthy share of our father's money, which is why I have no need to ever marry, nor to be *allowed* to do anything. However, I accept your offer."

Tony Devereux had been quite astonished by her statement. Where was the empty-headed girl he imagined? The one who was blushing and smiling at him with her adorable dimples the previous evening? It seemed that Miss Bernadette Barrymore was a complete caution and must surely be an utter handful for her parents. Looking back in the years to come, he realized that that was the moment that he fell so hard for her and decided to buck the system, most especially his mother. Tony Devereux had but one month to win her over. However, from the way she was looking at him, albeit from down her nose, he knew he had an excellent fighting chance of doing so.

Bernadette relived that first day many times in her head. They spent the whole day together, and when he introduced her to several of his acquaintances as his fiancée—to their shocked amazement—she had been aghast.

"I am absolutely not your fiancée!" She had laughed. "What

will these colleagues of yours think when they find out you are such a liar!"

He was laughing at her, and she had no idea that in his heart, he meant it. They ate lunch together at an elegant café, at which he appeared well known, and Bernadette worried that her clothes were old-fashioned, or possibly her hair, since several ladies who were also lunching there were giving her strange looks. It never occurred to her that perhaps it might have been that she was alone and seated with a man who was definitely not her husband.

She asked Lord Devereux to take her to Harrods, and he told her to call him Tony. Bernadette told him to call her Miss Barrymore, but he didn't. He laughed and called her Bernadette.

A while later, when he assumed a worried expression as she started picking out a considerable sized wardrobe of new summer attire, she reassured him and said, "Daddy will pay for everything, and when he sees the bills for my new clothes, he might agree to give me an allowance. Then I will be very stingy with my money and will need to make my new clothes last—for years actually. I wonder if I should cut my hair. I have so much of it, and it is such a bother. Is that why those women in the café were looking at me?"

Lord Devereux had never gone shopping with a lady before that day and was glad of his family's wealth, which was essentially his, and that he was not one of the more impoverished of his titled friends. Even so, he was amused by the casual manner in which she spent so much of her father's money.

Mr. James Barrymore was a shrewd man of business and hardly a pushover; however, it seemed that he may have very much been so, but only with regard to his daughter. Lord Devereux responded, "No, Bernadette, I cannot *allow* you to cut your hair." He said the word deliberately, readily anticipating another rebuke, but Bernadette Barrymore asked him if he thought she was pretty and what he liked best about her. He had taken her out in his Rolls Royce Silver Ghost—a new acquisition and the principal reason for his trip to London, to pick it up. He had just driven into the darkened parking garage adjacent to the hotel.

He said, "I suppose that is an American thing, being so forward. What makes you think I like anything best about you?"

He had been joking but realized his mistake when a look of confusion crossed her lovely face. He had forgotten that she was just a young girl, fresh out of the schoolroom—she had been acting so sophisticated. So he quickly remedied his mistake and told her he liked everything best about her and that she was the loveliest girl he had ever seen. He also said that those ladies in the café were jealous of her beautiful hair. He was rewarded with a blush and embarrassed smile revealing her adorable dimples. He lifted her chin and stared into her eyes and felt an invisible force drawing them together. He knew it was wrong, but in that moment, in the darkened garage, he knew he would never want another. Her response to his kiss reassured him that she felt the same. Then they stared at each other until Bernadette broke the silence and the moment's intensity.

"I don't usually kiss boys."

Tony responded, "But I'm not a boy. I'm a man."

And she said, "I don't usually kiss men either."

He laughed—as did she—knowing that something magical had happened between them. He then helped her out of his motorcar, and, hand in hand, they walked into the hotel—only to be greeted by her father.

He didn't seem angry. He seemed almost amused as he told his daughter that there was a pile of boxes delivered that afternoon from Harrods, and she should go up to see to her mother, who had been bending his ear all day. He turned and said, "Lord Devereux, how about a drink in the bar?"

Bernadette paced the floor of her family's suite, listening out for her father, waiting to find out what had happened, but when he returned, he looked grave and told her that her viscount would be leaving in the morning.

She sat down crestfallen and accused her father of sending him away. "Daddy, what did you do? You have ruined my life! You made him go away, didn't you?"

Her father had responded, "Bernadette, this is London, not Boston, and he is not one of your high school admirers. I asked that Lord Devereux give you at least two weeks to consider the proposal he made to me this afternoon. He asked for your hand in marriage—after one day's acquaintance? I told him you were too young. I told him he also needs to take time to think about it, since you only just met. I mentioned there would be no money in it for him, no fortune, and no dowry—just in case he had that in mind."

Bernadette wasn't sure whether to be elated or furious. "Oh, Daddy, how could you? What if he changes his mind?"

Mr. Barrymore said, "Then that will be the end of it, Bernadette. If he changes his mind, it was either always about the money, or in the end, he decides that the granddaughter of a poor Irish immigrant isn't good enough for him—no matter how pretty, no matter how cheeky and smart. I won't have you taken for the money, Bernadette. Let that be the end of the matter for the present time."

Bernadette had cried and worried for over two long weeks as the family toured the sights and sounds of London Town. There was no sign of him, no word from him, and soon they would be heading for France to visit her mother's relatives who lived in Paris.

It was never about the money. Tony Devereux had hoped to see Bernadette at dinner and had leisurely taken dinner in the hotel dining room with that thought in mind. Eventually, he spoke to the concierge, who told him that the Barrymores had ordered room service and would likely not be down that evening. Tony wanted to go to their suite. He hoped that Bernadette would escape and seek him out. However, he was not to see her again until over a fortnight later, by which time he worried that being so young, she had moved on to other pursuits.

He had dreaded discussing the matter with his mother, who also brought in allies to champion her cause once she heard of his quite shocking decision—his older married sister, Charlotte, and his uncle Bertie, his father's younger brother and the man waiting in the wings should he kill himself in his new motor car. Regardless, he was the lord and master of Devereux House since his father's death many years before, and none of their contentions had any bearing in the matter or in his final decision.

He could never have reasonably expected the extent of the explosive reaction he would receive when he told them his news. One would think he had decided to marry a penniless, forty-year-old divorcée.

He had tried to console his mother that Miss Bernadette Barrymore was very young and healthy, and wasn't she concerned about heirs? His mother inquired thoughtfully about Miss Barrymore's father's financial status, and he had told her that he was stinking rich but with no intention of giving his daughter a "dime" if she married him.

"His expression, Mother, not mine. I don't believe he cares

much for the English and was not impressed by my title. At least that's what he said. He also told me that if she married a man he approved of 'back home,' he would build her the finest house in Boston with a fortune that would easily pay for every luxury her heart desired. So there you have it. He thinks he has chased me away. He thinks all English nobility are poor, with an eye out for a million-dollar American princess—which, of course, I believe Bernadette to be. However, or so it seems, one without a fortune to bestow upon an English lord."

Even his best friend had cautioned him—yet again. Cecil was engaged to be married to an English rose with a tidy fortune but quite a rotund figure. Still, her face was pretty—or pretty enough.

Tony said to his friend, "You are the only one who saw her, Cecil, and you know she is magnificent. She makes me laugh and is a frightful caution. I desire her beyond reason. In truth, I am mad with desire. I don't intend to give her time to change her mind—since she is just eighteen. I will not allow Miss Barrymore to leave London unless she marries me. God, she hates that word, *allow*, so I intend to use it daily upon her."

Lord Fallsington threw his arms up and said, "Your life, I suppose. There is no need for you to advance your cause with me. That would be quite pointless."

Nothing and no one could dissuade him, but who could imagine that his finest mare, Genevieve, would choose to give birth the morning he was to leave for London? Lord Devereux bred horses, the finest to be had in Hampshire, indeed in all of southern England. Breeding thoroughbreds was primarily how he made his money, along with the earnings from his estate, which were nowhere near what they had been a century ago. He, therefore, had to stay and see it through and to ensure that Genevieve and her foal survived the ordeal—which happily they did, and with flying colors. Mother Genevieve was in fine fettle, and her colt was flourishing by the time Lord Devereux finally set off for London. However, he should have been there at the Ritz several days earlier and was glad of his new Rolls, which was very fast, in his impatience to reach London, the Ritz, and most especially the ravishing Bernadette Barrymore.

It was raining when he arrived, and Bernadette was gazing forlornly out of the hotel window, feeling quite forsaken, when she suddenly saw the unmistakable Silver Ghost drive into the parking garage where Lord Devereux had kissed her. The car was gorgeous and expensive, so why did her father think he only wanted to marry her for money?

She shouted, "He's here!" and ran out of the room without donning her raincoat or waiting for permission.

Lord Anthony Devereux was sitting in his car, building up courage, wondering and fervently hoping that Bernadette still wanted him as he did her. They had spent just one day together, and of course, she was so very young. Then he looked into his rearview mirror, and there she was, running to him, her hair coming undone and her dress dampened by the perpetual drizzle that day. Then she stopped and stared at him, her amazing almond-shaped eyes like saucers. He got out of the car and walked up to her. She was impossibly beautiful, and he could hear his heartbeat.

She said with a petted lip, "Are you here to speak with my father? Or do you have another drunken reunion?"

Tony answered, "Neither."

And she looked as if she might burst into tears. Her innocence was so apparent to Tony, as was the knowledge that he would soon be the lucky man to teach her everything she couldn't learn in the schoolroom. She hadn't forgotten him or found other pursuits. She had been as desperate to be reunited with him as he was with her.

He clarified his response. "I'm here to steal you away and never give you back."

Bernadette then ran into his arms, and he led her into his car. He kissed her again and again and pulled down her hair as he luxuriated in the softness of it and the scent of roses. She responded passionately to his kisses and embrace, and then she started crying.

"I'm not going to stupid Paris. They can't make me. I want to stay with you." Then she stopped and pulled back, as if it only just occurred to her. "Wait a minute. You may have proposed marriage to my father but not to me. I can't kiss you anymore unless you do."

Since this was precisely what he had in mind, with his grandmother's ring in his pocket as proof that his intentions were honorable, he said, "Come on. Let's spend the day together before I have to face the music again. I might even get down on one knee if it stops raining. He can keep his money. I have enough. But I do have to caution you that I am not a millionaire like 'daddy.' Still, I can afford two or three new frocks and hats every year and some new"—he cleared his throat—"night attire."

Bernadette was delirious. "Oh, don't worry about that; I have bought so many clothes in the past two weeks as punishment for him." She smiled and looked at him quite seductively under her long eyelashes, then whispered, "I also bought night attire, as you call it, but what I bought was more along the lines of seductive negligées. Obviously, I didn't show those to Daddy."

Tony Devereux's face reddened at this remark, but he said, "I am going to enjoy your American outspokenness—but just for me, please."

Naturally, she misunderstood his meaning and declared, "I certainly have no intention of seducing anyone else ... forever actually, so I hope you are up to it ... after the wedding, of course."

She was laughing at him now since he had turned bright red. He had never met anyone like her, and she would soon be his. He was obtaining a special license from the archbishop of Canterbury, which would be easily done since his grace sat in the House of Lords, and Lord Devereux knew him well enough.

He told all of this to his soon-to-be betrothed, and she was very impressed. "Won't he mind that I'm Roman Catholic?"

Tony replied, "He will overlook that part, but will you convert to Episcopalian—Church of England? He will ask for your promise to do so—my position and all that bosh."

And her response again made him laugh. "For you, I would convert to Buddhism, and there is no reason for Monsignor O'Hurley to know a thing about it—that is, if Daddy doesn't tell him."

The following month was a whirlwind of activity, and Bernadette's brothers and Michael O'Connor were ordered to London for the wedding. James Jr. was told *not* to bring his wife, Nancy, or his daughters, simply because Mr. Barrymore couldn't abide all of their incessant chatter. James Jr. was irresponsible as a young man and had to marry Nancy, so in truth, he was happy for the break away and to leave them all behind in Boston. As for Sean, he was the family tearaway, without a serious bone in his body. There was no permanent woman in his life, nor even in the distant horizon.

Fortunately, a few of Eugenie's relatives, an aunt, and two cousins came over from Paris to add a little class to Bernadette's mostly empty side of the church, the Barrymores having had to cancel their trip to Paris, much to Eugenie's chagrin.

The couple was married in St. Margaret's, Westminster, by an Anglican bishop on August 3, 1912, much to James Barrymore's displeasure, although his beloved daughter gave him no other option. He was ruthless and a hard man of business, but his daughter could easily wrap him around her little finger. He was still somewhat shocked that she had snagged a peer of the realm within hours of her arrival in London. Still, as he walked his beautiful daughter down the aisle toward her besotted fiancé, standing impatiently awaiting her, he felt so immensely prideful, most especially with the sour faces seated on the groom's side of the Anglican church.

Lord Devereux's sister Charlotte was bridesmaid, and her two young daughters, Molly and Petula, were flower girls. Lord Cecil Fallsington was the best man, and he looked to Bernadette like he had something sour in his mouth. Actually, when she viewed Tony's side of the church, it was packed with people who all looked the same way. Bernadette did not know any of them, and since they didn't have the respect to smile at the happy bride, she wondered why they came. *Well,* Bernadette thought, *I expect their noses were bothering them. They wanted to see this Irish bricklayer's daughter.*

There were undoubtedly far fewer congregants on the bride's side of the church. The Parisians were very elegantly attired, as was the bride's mother. However, after a heavy night of drinking, the Barrymore party of men looked as sickly as the other side looked sour. Of course, Mr. Barrymore was in the peak of health since he could always hold his whiskey.

The couple was duly married, and many wedding photographs were taken. The photographs that were delivered to Devereux House when the couple was on honeymoon were unfortunately misplaced by the dowager viscountess, never to be found again.

Bernadette was later forced to take the one photograph that had somehow survived this unfortunate occurrence and was displayed upon the grand piano in the drawing room. The dowager viscountess told her to leave the frame, which was a family heirloom—although it looked recently purchased to Bernadette, who didn't want the ugly thing anyway.

On a later visit to the house, after Arabella had taken it over, Bernadette noticed that the frame now contained another photograph from her wedding day; this one was of Tony standing with his best man, Cecil. When she picked it up to look at it, she was told in no uncertain terms that the photograph belonged to her mother-in-law, who somehow still hadn't come across any of the other photographs taken on Bernadette's wedding day.

The odd assortment of guests were to gather at the Ritz for a sumptuous champagne wedding breakfast. However, Tony Devereux had other plans for his bride and him, and the wedding limousine went in the opposite direction from the others, to the Savoy Hotel, where he had booked the bridal suite. Bernadette was ecstatic when she realized his plan, especially when he told her that her valise was already at the Savoy, and her steamer chest was on its way to the ship that would be taking them on a monthlong European cruise.

She told him to go to the bar for a drink. "A quick one," she added, "to allow me to get ready."

He couldn't resist. "Ready for what, Bernadette?"

And she responded, "Isn't that what you are supposed to show me, Lord Devereux?"

Tony opened the bottle of champagne, which had been on ice awaiting the newlywed's arrival, and poured a glass each. They made a toast to their future happiness, and then Bernadette pushed him out the door of their suite and locked it behind him.

Bernadette lovingly unwrapped her exquisite peignoir and, with considerable effort, managed to unfasten her satin and lace wedding gown. As it sat in a frothy puddle at her feet, she heard a knock at the door.

She wondered who it could possibly be since Tony barely had time to go down in the lift and come back up again.

It seemed, however, that was all he did, since it was he who was standing outside the door.

She opened it a couple inches and said, "I'm not ready yet, Tony. I didn't mean that quick a drink."

She was laughing, and he said, "I was afraid you would run away."

Bernadette opened the door wider to let him back in. She was standing in her white satin underwear and silk stockings, held up with pretty lace garters adorned with pink roses.

For the briefest of moments, he just stood there, beguiled and in disbelief that this vision was his wife. Then Bernadette giggled, and he said, "Please allow me to assist you in undressing, your ladyship."

Bernadette felt every inch of her body blush as her handsome viscount went about his task, kissing every inch of her body as he did so, and soon, in the passion he had awakened in her, she was undressing him too. They fell onto the bridal bed, which was festooned with pink rose petals, and Bernadette was forced to save her new wedding night peignoir for the following morning, when they were to be served breakfast in bed.

Tony and Bernadette would relive that afternoon and night many times in their heads, as well as the romantic sea voyage that followed. They kissed and made love, laughed and danced, and couldn't get enough of each other. The connection between them was magical, and they each marveled how such mutual and intense passion could be real; but it was real, as each of them would reflect upon during the difficult and sad years that were so soon to follow, years that were to bend and twist their magical bond until at last it broke and tore them apart.

Almost exactly two years after Tony and Bernadette's wedding, on August 4, 1914, Britain declared war on Germany, and one month later, Lord Anthony Devereux joined the Royal Horse Artillery division of the British army as Second Lieutenant Anthony Devereux, thereby breaking his young wife's heart. He told her the war would be over by Christmas—most everyone was saying the same thing—but when Bernadette watched as his captain drove him away from Devereux House, she found she just couldn't believe that to be true.

CHAPTER 3

The dancing in the street began to wind down around midnight. Bernadette and her best friend, Margaret Walker, returned to Bernadette's Knightsbridge flat, where Margaret would often stay overnight—both women having so much in common. Margaret knew all about Bernadette's marriage and her American family. Margaret had a husband who had also survived, Sergeant Thomas Walker, a former sales associate at Harrods department store, where he and Margaret had met. They married right before he joined the army back in 1914. The major difference between their husbands, besides rank, was that he had kept in touch with his wife throughout the war and had been home on leave the previous year.

The following day was a holiday, and both women were up most of the night, talking and dreaming about the future, with Margaret imagining a clear path of marital bliss and children, and Bernadette having no idea what to think or to imagine.

"You have every right to walk up to the front door of your husband's house—your house too, Bernadette—and demand to know when he's expected back! She'll know—his mother—and he's a bloody major and viscount to boot. He'll be on one of the first trains to London."

"Will you come with me, Margaret? You know she hates me. She might refuse to tell me, even if she already knows."

"In that case, we'll ask the butler or the housekeeper. They will be getting ready for his return. I'm sure of it. We'll make one of them tell us."

Bernadette and Margaret were whispering to each other behind the ladies' fragrance counter in Harrods. Margaret was Irish, although her husband was English, another bond between the women.

They had become instant friends when Bernadette was shown to her department that Christmas season of 1916. Margaret, Miss Walker, was told to show Miss Barrymore the ropes. The salesgirls were all called Miss, because before the war, all the women who worked there were unmarried. However, most of the young male employees had gone off to war, some of whom had sadly been killed in action, and thus it wasn't quite the same Harrods as the one Bernadette had visited in 1912. Of course, nothing was the same, not with so much grief and devastation all around. Consequently, it followed that many young widows and married women, with men at the front, were seeking employment.

It felt as if almost every day, the name of one of Harrods' employees who had fallen in battle was posted in the lunchroom, and everyone dreaded what news the next day might bring. However, it was still Christmastime, and affluent ladies were still buying perfume, and the perfume counter was busy enough.

෴

The upper management were aware of Bernadette's true identity and had been persuaded to employ her by Michael O'Connor, who had been sent to England to see to Bernadette's welfare. However,

Bernadette was so utterly charming and with such confidence and class that Harrods was happy to snap her up with minimal persuasion. Michael was Mr. Barrymore's right-hand man, and James Barrymore trusted him implicitly. He relied upon him, since neither of his sons had shown much aptitude as his successor. James Barrymore felt Bernadette might have made a better go of it than his sons. He considered her the brightest of his children, and she was most assuredly his favorite. He had long cherished the hope that she would marry Michael O'Connor, and she would have done so with his blessing, had that English lord of the manor not turned her head and stolen her heart—only to leave her two years later in the hands of his wicked mother.

Mr. Barrymore wrote to his daughter of his plans to have her marriage annulled and to bring her back to Boston. So many men had perished, including his son James Jr. He was only two months into action, leaving his wife, Nancy, a widow with three young daughters to raise on her own. But not Major Devereux. He was a survivor—or else Bernadette might have been a titled widow who would be relieved to return to the States, away from the death and destruction in Europe.

The death of his oldest son, fighting on the side of the English, had further hardened James Barrymore and broken his mother's heart. Thus, he saw an annulment as the only proper course of action, and as soon as the war ended, he was looking into passage for him and his right-hand man—a man he still had hopes of marrying his daughter. Michael O'Connor loved Bernadette before they left on that accursed trip to London in 1912, and James Barrymore was convinced that he still did. He had never married, although he had plenty of opportunities, and a man of his age and position should have a wife.

Mr. Barrymore was glad there were no children since that would have complicated the matter. As it was, and as things stood with his daughter—working long hours throughout most of the war, her husband estranged from her—he saw no obstacle to them both agreeing that this was the best solution to end their ill-advised marriage.

Anthony Devereux had survived four long years in battle—but not without injury and not without a heavy heart, watching so many other men fall.

He had performed his duty with valor and had risen quickly up the ranks from second lieutenant to major. The thought of his beautiful young wife, so loving in her letters, which he read repeatedly, sustained him, as did her photograph that he wore next to his heart, along with the silver cigarette case she had given him that last Christmas before the war. It was engraved with their initials and the words *Forever Yours*.

Major Devereux was given leave in December 1915 and was pleased that the weather in Hampshire that year was atrocious; with heavy, wind-driven rain, every day he was home. He spent most of his time in bed with his lovely Bernadette. When he had to leave, it broke her heart once again, and he was grateful that she loved him so much.

Her letters continued for a while afterward, but they were somehow different from before, and gradually they began to lessen, and eventually they ceased altogether. Tony wrote and begged her to write to him. He asked her why she had stopped loving him, because it seemed to him that she must have done so. In the foul and putrid trenches, stinking of death and decay, he could find no other reason for such dispassion and cruelty.

He finally wrote to his mother at the dower house, to find out if she knew any reason why Bernadette had abandoned him. He was shocked at the letter he received several weeks later in his mother's hand.

April 5, 1917

My dearest son Anthony,

I am glad to hear you are safe and well. I pray for you daily, the most exemplary son a mother could ever wish for, and I am so very proud of you.

It is difficult for me to put this in writing—knowing the misery and danger that you face each morning. In fact, I hesitated in so doing since it breaks my heart to explain, but you asked for the truth.

Your wife, Bernadette, has moved out of Devereux House. She moved to a flat in Knightsbridge as far as I know, but I do not know her address. I assume her father is paying for it, since what money does she have? I also understand that she works in some shop and has adopted her maiden name. For that, at least, I am grateful, since I can hardly bear to imagine the shame it would bring upon our good family name had she done otherwise.

She just up and left a few months ago without a by your leave, and I honestly thought she would have written to you. I felt it was not my place to do so. I believe the Irish bricklayer is planning an annulment of your marriage, and although I am almost ashamed to admit this—I am glad of it. I chanced to read one of her mother's letters, which she carelessly left on the grand piano, informing her of the plan—should you survive!

I could hardly believe my eyes! Such callousness! Shameful lot! And I wish I had been more forceful in my objection to your marriage!

At least rest assured that your army wages are safe in the bank. She cannot touch a penny of anything you own. I have seen to that!

I agree that this annulment he plans might be the best thing for you, my precious son, since how can you take her back now? Also, it would seem the girl is barren since, although I am sad to say it, she had more than enough time to conceive and provide you with a son during your two years together!

I hope you received my Christmas parcel. I sent you some warm socks and sweets. I was so disappointed that you couldn't make it home for Christmas, and now it will soon be Easter, another holiday without my son. I pray daily for your safe return when we can celebrate all the holidays you have missed together and with roast goose and plum pudding and all of your favorite things to eat.

My love always,
Mother

This news devastated Major Devereux, and at first, he couldn't believe it, but as time passed, he realized that the unthinkable must be true. Bernadette had left him. She was so young, and he felt so tired and old. He was thirty-two but felt a hundred. Bernadette was just twenty-two and beautiful—too lovely to be holed up in his house in Hampshire with only his mother as a neighbor.

 from me

Tony's mother had sent him a parcel that Christmas—further proof if he needed it that Bernadette was gone. He handed out the sweets she sent and put a pair of ridiculous red hand-knitted socks up for auction among his men, and the highest bidder won them for two cigarettes. Tony thought it was a strange thing for his mother to include along with some store-bought others, but she mentioned that one of the maids had knitted them for him. He would need to tell his mother to thank the young woman and no need to say that he had given them away.

Major Devereux may have let his guard down, having survived unharmed this long, but he was losing his will to live—to go on—in the wretched trenches in that unending war, surrounded by the mutilated corpses of young men, blown to pieces and left to rot in the rain and mud in the killing fields of France. So many of his men were just boys who should be home with their families and getting on with their lives instead of dying in the muddy fields of a foreign land. He was still reeling from the contents of his mother's letter when a hand grenade exploded up ahead of him and blew a young soldier in his unit to pieces. He was one of his brightest infantrymen, Private Edward Smith—just nineteen years of age. Major Devereux stood in shock, struck by the thought of the young man's sweetheart and the photograph he showed to his fellow soldiers and the officers when he received it no more than a month ago. Another grenade exploded up ahead, and the major hesitated a few seconds before he ran away from it, but he suddenly decided that he didn't want to die this way, so far from home. However, he couldn't avoid the shrapnel that caught his face and back and right shoulder as he ran away.

Lord Devereux was treated and sent back to England to recuperate in a country manor in Sussex, where they took in many of his fellow officers. His mother and sister Charlotte visited him as soon as they got word of it, but Bernadette did not. He was fortunate—the injury was minor compared to many. He was bandaged up and grateful that he was left-handed. The scar on his face wasn't terrible, and his sister told him it would suit him.

He asked her straight out—he felt his mother knew but was choosing not to tell him.

"Where is she, Charlotte? This whole thing—I can't quite take it in. Why is she working as a shop girl? No matter what everyone has in their heads, there will be no annulment because I will never sign it, and if I survive this damned war, I am bringing her home."

Charlotte seemed nervous, and her brother concluded that she was sworn to secrecy. He winced in pain, and she finally broke her silence. "I don't know exactly where her flat is, but I know that she can walk to her place of employment. I saw her once at the perfume counter in Harrods. She was chatting on a male customer to make him spend too much on some lucky lady."

"Well," he said flippantly, "at least she's not working at the corner tea shop." However, inwardly he thought, *Five years ago, she was spending a fortune of her father's money in that same shop—a spoiled eighteen-year-old. I wonder if she is still wearing those same dresses since she doesn't have access to her husband's army pay. Still, I am confident that "daddy" and his sidekick O'Connor are seeing that she is not short of a shilling or two.*

Then he said, almost casually, "I am certain that Mr. James Barrymore hates me, and I can't say I blame him."

It was two weeks before Christmas 1917, and Major Anthony Devereux was being sent back to France. He was to take the train from London Kings Cross station, and he had to stop himself from crying when he boarded it with other soldiers and officers, who like him were being sent back to the front. If only things were different. If only he could have spent just one night with his lovely wife.

He had gone into Harrods that afternoon. The first time since the day he fell in love with her so long ago. He thought to confront her, and perhaps she would explain everything away.

The store was crowded due to the time of year, and he thought how lucky were the civilians he saw shopping there—almost as if there wasn't a war on. There were other officers too, and he asked for directions to the perfume counter.

She didn't see him as he stood and watched her. She was more beautiful than he remembered, even in her black and white uniform. She was serving an RAF officer, a pilot, and his heart was sore with jealousy when he watched her smile at the pilot with her dimples that belonged only to him and that he so adored. She was spraying perfume onto a handkerchief, and the man was clearly flirting with her, although she didn't appear to be taking him seriously. The pilot made his purchase, and as he left, he walked past Major Devereux and greeted him as a fellow officer would, but then added, "If you are shopping for your lady, try the perfume counter. Ravishing. Made me want to be single again."

Tony Devereux wanted to punch the man, but he just walked away. Bernadette was already waiting on another young man, and it seemed to Tony that although most of the shoppers were women, the male customers were particularly seeking out his wife to wait on them.

During the long train ride, Major Devereux wondered why he didn't walk right up to her and, taking her by the hand, lead her outside to take her into his arms, just like he used to do. Then he remembered. *Tomorrow I could be dead, or next week, or next month, so perhaps it is all for the best.* He closed his eyes and fell into an uneasy sleep on his way back to the carnage that awaited him in France.

It was Sunday and the best friends' day off, and Bernadette and Margaret boarded the train to Winchester in Hampshire, with a local connection to Willow Grove, the nearest station to Devereux House.

The stationmaster, of course, remembered Bernadette and said, "Good afternoon, your ladyship," as he doffed his cap to her. "The townsfolk have very much missed you and his lordship and are so gratefully anticipating his safe return."

Bernadette didn't want to ask the man if he knew when that would be but had a distinct impression that he did.

He continued, "The town plans a big welcome for him with a brass band and food and entertainment. Of course, the dowager viscountess has instructed us to at least give him a week to rest and recuperate."

He practically sneered when he mentioned the dowager, and Bernadette was not surprised. She was a hateful woman to everyone who she considered to be beneath her, as indeed she considered Bernadette to be, despite her family's money and, more importantly, despite her being her son's wife.

The stationmaster made a phone call to the post office in town. Soon, the owner of the local hardware shop appeared with a cart to carry the two women up to Devereux House, which was once Bernadette's happy home with the man she loved so much, before the terrible war tore her life apart.

Margaret said, "It feels strange to hear you called your ladyship, Bernadette. You are so down to earth like the rest of us and so nice and kind. You certainly don't act like a toff or one of them snobs."

Bernadette answered, "Because I'm not and never could be. Remember, I am the daughter of the Irish bricklayer, and although he could buy and sell the lot of them a dozen times over, that's what I will always be to them. Possibly to Tony now too? I don't know, but I will make him tell me."

Margaret responded, "Well, I think your mother-in-law knows exactly what train he'll be on. Probably the whole town knows."

They arrived at the front door of what was once Bernadette's home, and she quipped, "I'm half expecting to be sent around to the servants' entrance."

Just then, the door was opened by Mr. Higgins, the butler, who greeted her very pleasantly and said, "Your ladyship, you are indeed a sight for sore eyes! Will you be coming back soon? Now with the master coming home?"

Bernadette could hear Arabella calling out to Higgins, so she whispered, "That rather depends on his lordship. Higgins, do you know when he is arriving? What train and what station?"

He answered quickly, "Wednesday on the six p.m. train at Victoria station. Good luck, your ladyship!"

Just then, the dowager viscountess appeared in the great hall and looked horrified at the sight of her daughter-in-law, accompanied by, no doubt, one of her fellow shop girls.

"Why are you here, Bernadette? What do you want? Your marriage to Lord Devereux will soon be annulled, and you have no business in this house."

Bernadette was livid, and how she hated the woman. "Actually, all of that remains to be seen and is up to Tony and of course me. You have no part in it other than the meddling in our lives that you have no doubt already done. But he's coming home, and that is all I care about. I am going upstairs to collect some of my things. I am presuming they are still there?"

"Indeed. I never go in there. I thought I would leave that to Lord Devereux. I am quite certain he will want the room cleared out. You know he was quite disappointed that you didn't visit him after his injury. He was in Sussex for several weeks. Close enough for a Sunday off, I would think."

Bernadette reeled, her stomach turned, and she shouted, "What injury? I didn't know! You didn't let me know—no one did! What happened to him? If you don't tell me, I will go straight to the war office and tell them you were keeping your son's army pay from his wife. Why didn't he write to me?"

Bernadette stopped and finally considered something she should have suspected long ago. "You never passed his letters on to me—nor mine to him. And my Christmas parcels? Did you keep them too? How could you be so rotten, you evil old bitch."

Arabella shouted, "How dare you? Daughter of an Irish bricklayer? How dare you call me that name! How dare you use such language in my home!"

Bernadette, shaking in anger and regret, was already on her way upstairs with Margaret, and shouted back, "But this isn't your home. That would be the dower house, as I recall."

The servants were all listening, of course. They hated the dowager viscountess, and they prayed that their master and his lovely wife would soon be reunited and life could return to the halcyon days before the war. Mrs. O'Leary, the housekeeper, had heard enough Irish slurs to last her a lifetime, coming from Dublin as she did. She had just recently come across her young mistress's letters. They were hidden on top of the dowager's wardrobe. She had been inspecting the room and the work of a maid newly hired, and there they were. There must have been at least twenty, unopened and certainly not posted, and Mrs. O'Leary cried for her forlorn master, who would have so appreciated these to warm his poor heart a little during this terrible war. Instead, his mother allowed him to believe that his wife had abandoned him, while all along, she was working long hours, awaiting letters from her husband that she was never to be given.

Mrs. O'Leary gave the stack of letters to Mr. Higgins, who disgustedly said, "I will see his lordship gets these immediately upon his return. This outrage is worse than I could have imagined, even from the dowager viscountess, and my guess is that he will soon send her packing back to the dower house. How very foolish of her. She should have burned them; however, I thank God she didn't."

Bernadette and Margaret were going through the dresses purchased in Harrods in 1912 when a maidservant appeared with a tray with a silver teapot and china cups. There were daintily cut sandwiches with boiled ham and egg salad and a selection of pastries and cakes, which the kitchen staff must have been baking for their master's return. Bernadette realized that the servants must still be fond of her to be so kind. They no doubt wanted her back with the master; such a loving and happy home it was then.

Margaret looked wistful and said, "You know, Bernadette, either way, I will lose you. I hope with all my heart that you will be reunited with your husband, and then you will be too good for me, but even if you aren't reunited, you will be off to America. These rooms are so beautiful. The maids must have kept them nice for you too. Did you pick the colors?"

"No. Tony did. He hired a designer and told him to make the suite as beautiful as me. Tony always told me how beautiful I was; he was so romantic. We slept in a guest bedroom until the work was completed. I couldn't believe my eyes, all pink and apple green, and my big, canopied bed. The carpets are so sumptuous too, and my own bathroom suite—and he did all of this for me.

Although I really think he was competing with my father and with how he imagined my bedroom must have been in Boston."

At this point, Bernadette began to cry. "I hope he will find me beautiful again. I hope I can make him love me again. Now that I know he will be home in three days, my heart is full to bursting, and I realize how I had to harden it these past years. But, Margaret, I want him back. I still love him and will never love another."

Then she cheered. "I hope this doesn't sound insulting, but I never had a lady's maid, and Tony's valet was killed in action toward the beginning of the war. Your husband was a fine salesman, you have often told me, and he was employed in menswear."

Margaret said, "Oh, Bernadette! That would be like a dream come true, but would I have to call you your ladyship?"

Bernadette laughed. "No, of course not, Margaret. I could never have survived this war so far from home without you. You taught me so many things, not only in Harrods but how to be independent and to keep within my budget. I have saved much of the money my father wired over to me because, either way, I will never sign an annulment since that would allow Tony to remarry. Also, I will never marry Michael O'Connor, which I know is my father's secret plan. I might have to continue in Harrods after the war. My future is so uncertain."

The women looked at a few of the dresses. Bernadette worried that they were old-fashioned. As she told Margaret to take her pick, she said, "They seem so frivolous now—too fussy. What a waste of money. Do you think we can sell them and buy more modern skirts and blouses?"

Margaret said, "They are such fine quality and hardly worn. This one still has tags on it, for goodness sake! Yes, we can do that if you want. I know a place in Chelsea. I could take them there."

Bernadette said, "Okay, it's settled. And then you and I will go to Selfridges and buy a new ensemble each. I need mine for Wednesday! I just received a parcel from my mother containing stockings, satin underwear, and candy bars. I will share everything with you equally, and we are about the same size."

Margaret tried to say that that was too much, but Bernadette shushed her. "The dresses are just sitting here, Margaret, and have been for years. Besides, my father bought them all, and I am furious at him and this annulment business! Also, my mother can easily send more pretty things if I ask her, and I will only ask her if Tony comes back to me. Anyway, there is hardly any rationing in the States, and even if there were, Daddy would get around it."

The women picked out a few of the dresses, and Cook wrapped up the remainder of the cakes and pastries. They were just about to leave when Bernadette thought about the jewelry that Tony had given her and, in particular, her engagement ring, which had belonged to his paternal grandmother and was never given to Arabella. It was a substantial emerald surrounded by brilliant diamonds. It was gorgeous and fit Bernadette perfectly. She had left all of her jewelry behind since it wouldn't suit her new life as a working woman, and she was scared the expensive items would get lost or stolen. She only took a simple gold chain and a locket that contained a tiny photograph of her husband, which had gotten destroyed one day at the public baths because she had forgotten to take it off.

"My jewelry, Margaret. She must have taken it—even my engagement ring. Horrid, evil woman. But I won't ask her for them. Let Tony find out what she did."

The coachman took them all the way to Winchester, where they would catch the train to London. There was much to do after all, and they left without saying goodbye to Arabella, although they did so to Higgins and Mrs. O'Leary, who gave them another food parcel Cook had made up for each of them and a bottle of the master's sherry.

"I hope the butcher at Mealey's can make me a steak and kidney pie. I can serve it up with mashed potatoes and peas. That's another thing I am so grateful to you for, Margaret. I can cook—well, badly but a little bit anyway—and clean and tidy up. Remember how clueless I used to be? I hope I don't have to do so, but if worse comes to worst, I can manage fine on my own." And she laughed. "Well, it would be nice if Daddy keeps on paying the upkeep for my nice flat in Knightsbridge, of course!"

Margaret was laughing too. "I had never met a girl who was so clueless! You couldn't even boil the kettle or make the bed. You have come a long way, Bernadette. I suppose we all have, and this bloody war has made us all have to grow up."

CHAPTER 4

It was Wednesday morning, December 18, and Bernadette and Margaret were given the day off. There was a lot to get done before they could head for the station and be there by 6:00 p.m.

Margaret had stayed the night, and both women were busily tidying the flat and changing the bed linen. Margaret had gone off earlier to Chelsea to sell the dresses while Bernadette ran to the butchers to collect the steak and kidney pie awaiting her. She was peeling potatoes when Margaret returned with enough money to deck out both ladies with a new outfit, winter coat, felt hat, and a pair of leather shoes. They headed off to Selfridges and finished off their shopping spree in ladies' lingerie, where they spent the rest of their cash—Margaret on a modest nightdress and dressing gown, and Bernadette on a scandalous silk negligée ensemble. It cost considerably more than Margaret's night attire, but Margaret insisted that was as it should be, since the money had come from the sale of Bernadette's very fine dresses.

The plan was that Margaret would wait at the back of the station, just in case there was any bother, since they were worried that Tony's mother would show up. Bernadette was wearing her brand-new outfit, but Margaret had gotten word that her husband wouldn't be home until January. Consequently, she had put all of her new clothes away in the meantime.

Margaret was worried about Major Devereux's reaction when he saw Bernadette. She was apprehensive because Bernadette seemed to have forgotten that he had been estranged from her for over two years, without so much as a letter. He must have been home on leave during that time since officers received more leave than the infantrymen, but never a word. Bernadette had also said nothing further about his injury. She was so very excited, and Margaret worried that she would be let down.

Margaret had heard about the large country estates in England and the toffs who lived in them. Still, when she went to Devereux House, she found it hard to take in—her best friend being addressed as your ladyship and the casual manner she accepted becoming the mistress of such a fine home—if only for an hour or so. Her bedroom suite was more spacious than Margaret's whole two-bedroom flat and certainly very much grander. Margaret wondered how it would turn out and what sort of gentleman and member of the English elite would propose marriage to an Irish American girl upon one day's acquaintance. She hoped he wasn't regretting it. However, Bernadette was lovely and charmed every man who came to her counter. And she was funny, and could be quite cheeky too, and Margaret would often have to stop herself from laughing out loud at her antics, so as not to get in trouble with the floor walker.

To Margaret, it would be a dream come true to become Bernadette's lady's maid. She was practically that now, taming her friend's mass of unruly chestnut brown curls and darning her stockings and sewing on a button or two since Bernadette was hopeless at these tasks. The red socks took Bernadette more than a month to knit, working each night on them after a long day at the perfume counter. There was constant unraveling to fix a dropped stitch, and Margaret found the whole enterprise highly amusing. It broke Bernadette's heart not to receive a thank you for them. She worked so hard at making them nice, although they were really quite comical since one sock was much longer than the other.

However, what about Tommy? Could he genuinely become Lord Devereux's valet? Of course, it was all just a dream, but she asked, "Bernadette, if everything works out for you and Lord Devereux, and Tommy and I can indeed come to work for you—"

Bernadette interrupted her. "There will be a cottage, and you can take almost everything in my flat as furniture. Oh, Margaret, I feel so nervous."

"Well," said Margaret, looking at her wristwatch that Bernadette had given her the previous Christmas, "it's time to go, and, Bernadette, you look so beautiful—like royalty. I hope that old bitch decided to stay at home."

Bernadette responded, "Oh, so do I, Margaret, since she will be determined to spoil everything."

The friends arrived at Victoria Station with half an hour to spare and sat in the station café with a nice cup of tea and a slice of apple crumble pie with custard. Some ladies at the table next to them were talking about the Spanish flu killing thousands in Great Britain and how the returning servicemen brought it home. Bernadette couldn't help herself from turning to them and saying, "You might mean to say the returning heroes who have gone through hell to save our skins."

Margaret shushed her and mouthed, "It's her nerves," to the seated ladies, who smiled at her in understanding. Margaret led Bernadette over to the platform. They could hear the train approaching the station, and Margaret told her friend that she would be watching her from a safe distance.

The servicemen began to descend, and Bernadette felt sick to her stomach with nerves. And then finally she saw him. He looked gaunt and battle weary but still so handsome that Bernadette felt her heart stop. She stepped forward, and he stood and stared at her for a moment. He wasn't smiling, and Bernadette wasn't sure what to do, but just as she was about to run to him, he turned. He turned, and there was his mother awaiting him. They embraced and then walked out of the station together, and Bernadette stood and watched them as she thought her whole world had just ended. No matter what she quipped to Margaret, no matter what the servants at Devereux House believed to be true, it was clear enough; her marriage was over. She thought that surely her heart would shrivel up and die.

Margaret ran to her, and it seemed Bernadette needed assistance to even walk. She took her friend home, made her some warm milk and honey, and left her to her grief. "I can see you want to be alone, but I will come by after work. I will tell them you had a shock and won't be in."

But Bernadette sat up and said, "No, I will be at work at my usual time. It is the busiest time of the year, and just because I have been let down, it is no excuse to let down others."

When Margaret left, Bernadette replaced the warm milk with a glass of the sherry that Cook had placed in her care basket. As she sipped it down, she thought, *That's not the end of it and not even close to the end. I am still his wife, and I will confront him. If he no longer loves me—*. She didn't finish the thought since it was too unbearable to consider.

Bernadette Devereux, known mostly to others as Bernadette Barrymore, tidied away the food and candles and wrapped her new negligee set in tissue paper before climbing into the bed she had excitedly been anticipating sharing with her husband after three long years. It was still early, but in her grief, she fell instantly asleep without kissing the two photographs under her pillow—the photographs she had kissed every night before.

Tony Devereux was livid to see his mother standing at the station. He had told her not to come. He planned to quietly go home and figure out what to do after a long sleep in a real bed. "I will take you back to the dower house, Mother. I am in no mood for talking tonight."

Arabella was forced to explain that she was actually residing in the main house. "Well, when that girl left, it seemed the sensible thing to do. Of course, if you prefer, I can have the servants return my things to the dower house tomorrow—but surely not tonight, Tony."

"That girl? Oh, you mean my wife? The one I just left standing at the station. What is her address? I know you know it. If you don't tell me, I will follow her home to find out."

Arabella saw the change in her son, once so easygoing and cheerful; he was such that it almost scared her. "All right, all right. I just thought to spare you some grief. Nine forty-one Wisteria Park Crescent."

He answered calmly, "Expensive. Overlooking a private park. Sounds very nice."

Arabella scoffed, "Well, of course, he is paying for it. The Irish bricklayer—he is coming here in February to take her back. He wrote to me. And you will be glad to know he is bringing the annulment papers all taken care of and just in need of both of your signatures."

Tony was incredulous. "All sorted out, is it? Well, I won't be signing them. I am bringing her back here to her rightful place.

Whatever has been going on—she was all dressed up with a new ridiculous hat to meet me tonight, and since I haven't heard one word from her since 1916, I intend to find out why."

They had reached Devereux House, and Tony told his mother she could stay the night but to make sure to return to the dower house the next day.

He told the chauffeur that he would take it from here and drove back off in his distinctive Silver Ghost, which had been kept immaculately clean, awaiting his return.

Arabella Devereux was certain he was returning to her—despite everything—and worried that Mr. Barrymore's planned trip would be too late. She thought she should send a telegram that her son was home, and perhaps he should bring his trip forward—in the possible event of reconciliation.

Of course, she couldn't have known that James Barrymore was concerned about the very same thing and had booked passage to England immediately upon the announcement that the Allies finally triumphed over Germany.

Higgins and his staff were ready to greet their master, but he drove right off after dropping off his mother. Higgins especially wanted to give him the letters, but there was no opportunity to do so before Lord Devereux left.

❧

Tony Devereux's stomach was churning when he rang the doorbell. He looked at his watch; it had gone 11:00 p.m., but he didn't care. The need within him was overtaking reason. The sight of her standing at the train station, looking so magnificent and looking at him in a way he didn't understand, given her choice of abandoning him while he was fighting in the trenches for king and country.

He heard her distinctive Boston accent. "Who is it?"

And he responded, "Tony. Remember me? Your husband?"

Confused by his comment and the fact that he was even standing there at eleven o'clock, after ignoring her at the station, Bernadette opened the door gingerly, but when she saw his poor, tired face and empty eyes, she opened it wide. She wanted him to take her into his arms, but he just walked past her and around the flat.

"Nice," he said. "Nothing but the best for James Barrymore's daughter."

He sounded so bitter that Bernadette now knew without a doubt that his mother never posted her letters. He knew nothing of her heartbreak of losing his child and the nastiness and cruelty of his mother when she was at her very lowest, brokenhearted about losing her baby and not being able to lean on her husband for comfort.

She said, remembering the steak and kidney pie, "You must be hungry. Let me make you something to eat."

Tony responded, "It seems my wife has learned to cook. I wonder what else she has learned."

This man was not the Tony that Bernadette knew. The man she knew was romantic and kind. This man was bitter and cruel. She knew she had to make allowances for what he had gone through, and obviously, his mother had been telling lies about her too, but she was determined to bring him back from whatever dark place he was in—no matter how long that took. Clearly, he was here because he still loved her. Whether he knew it or not. Her task was to make him remember how much.

She made to speak to him, since he had gone quiet, to ask him if he would like a glass of sherry, which was all she had that was fortified, but when she turned, he was gone. She surmised her bedroom since, thank God, she didn't hear the door, which had a bell attached to it in case of intruders.

She walked into her bedroom, and there he was, fast asleep,

exhausted, lying on top of the bed. He had removed his coat and boots but was otherwise fully dressed in his uniform. At first, Bernadette was just going to cover him up, but she made a brazen decision. He was her husband, and she loved him with all of her sad heart.

After going to the kitchen to turn off the oven and lights, she returned to her bedroom, where she gingerly unfastened his belt and unbuttoned his shirt. That was the easy part. But she carried on, undoing his trousers and pulling off his socks. She remembered his glorious manly scent—she remembered his legs and his feet—and Bernadette was euphoric. She puzzled over removing his shirt, but he seemed in such a deep sleep that she tried without awakening him, but he stirred and mumbled, "What are you doing, my love?"

My love. She was ecstatic. "I'm trying to put you into the bed. It is all fresh with clean sheets, and you will be much more comfortable without your clothes." She continued to undress him, and he allowed her to do so. Soon, he was completely naked, and Bernadette felt such desire for this man—her man—that she felt quite giddy.

She then pulled the covers over him. He was clearly in a deep, exhausted sleep, and she removed her nightdress and crept in behind him. She embraced him with her whole body until she was asleep, beside the man she loved with all her heart.

Tony awakened a couple of hours later. He had gotten used to no more than two or three hours of sleep. He thought he had dreamed it, but here she was, naked beside him, ready and willing, or so it seemed, for him to make love to her. It came back to him, her undressing him although he was barely awake, and he had felt her body behind him. It had made him feel safe and content. However, as he pulled the blankets back and gazed at his wife's naked body that he hadn't seen in three long years, his body returned to life. She was truly magnificent, and he luxuriated in her wonderful hair before kissing her face, neck, and breasts. As he made his way down, she awakened and pulled him into her arms, saying, "Tony, make love to me."

He said, "Dimples first," and she smiled at him. How he loved her dimples. Then, of course, he obliged, tenderly and joyously, until again he was asleep. The next time he awoke, it was not yet five in the morning. He gazed at his Bernadette for a little while, sleeping contentedly beside him, and thought, *Is that a smile on her lips?* He then grabbed his clothes and quickly dressed. He found and ate most of the steak and kidney pie, smiling at the uncooked potatoes in a pot next to an unopened tin of peas. He was trying to get a sense of who she now was. There was bread and butter in the larder but little else other than some American sweets that her mother must have sent her and a bottle of sherry that he recognized from his cellars. He realized that she had put together the dinner just for him, and the steak and kidney pie must have cost a fair number of her ration coupons. He felt like crying at the sweetness of her preparing such a feast for him, since it otherwise seemed she ate little, other than bread and butter—and of course American candy bars. She must have been so disappointed in him for leaving her standing at the station. He had seen his mother and felt such anger at her being there—even as he walked up to her embrace. Every nerve in his body wanted him to walk in the opposite direction—toward Bernadette.

He found some paper, took out his pen, and wrote a note that read, *There will be no annulment.* He then took one last look at the beautiful woman who was actually his wife. He wanted to stay, but his mind was in turmoil. He was then startled when she said sleepily, "Did you like your red socks? I almost knitted them all by myself."

Bernadette turned over and went back to sleep, but Tony's head was in a quandary. *My mother told me a maid; she lied to me. The parcels weren't from her. They were from Bernadette, and I gave the socks away for two cigarettes. Had I known Bernadette knitted them, I would have treasured them.*

Lord Anthony Devereux wasn't sure if he was angry or sad, exalted by the love he just shared or worried that Bernadette acted out of pity for him. She undressed him and climbed into bed naked with him. She didn't mention the scars on his back and shoulder. She didn't mention why she hadn't written to him. Then the thought occurred to him, *If my mother sabotaged my Christmas parcel, could she have also kept Bernadette's letters? But then why didn't she post her letters in London?* He was still so tired and so bewildered. He decided to take a few days away on his own to clear his head, but first he had to stop at home. He needed to get out of his uniform and take a bath and put on some civvies. He also needed to make sure that his mother was moving back to the dower house, especially since he could hardly bear to look at her.

CHAPTER 5

Harrods was very busy with Christmas shoppers—the folks with money, due to the high prices of the merchandise. Bernadette marveled how she used to be one of these people and how she now got by on two pounds five and sixpence per week. Still, that was good wages, especially since she paid no rent, and her lunches were so filling that she needed to purchase very little food for her flat. Bernadette saved the money her father wired to her bank account in the Bank of England, since she was so unsure about her future. Her fellow sales associates knew none of her secrets, except for Margaret. When she was first working at the store, Margaret had taken her on a couple of girls' nights out, but she didn't enjoy herself. For one thing, she didn't like strong liquor, and for another—if she told the truth—these women were so very different from her girlfriends in Boston, and she felt like a fish out of water. Although soon she was very different from those girlfriends too. She was caught in the middle of the Atlantic Ocean, in neither one country nor the other.

She never felt out of place with Tony—only happy and in love—but when he left her to go to war, she was lost. She had no friends, and her family was so far away. Her mother-in-law and sister-in-law showed her no kindness, and she was so terribly sad and lonely.

By the end of the war and with her new life in London, she had grown up considerably. She had gotten used to the city, the people, and how they spoke, and she tried to copy it. She doubted that she could ever settle again in Boston, beside her old girlfriends who by now were all wealthy wives and mothers, with absolutely no clue about the death and destruction going on in Europe.

Bernadette told Margaret about Tony coming to her flat that first night and how she expected him to return the following day. However, she had not seen him since and wondered what was happening in his head. Margaret suggested that Bernadette go to Devereux House and ask him straight out, but Bernadette decided to give him time. She would go after Christmas if he didn't come to her by then.

"You should turn up on Christmas Day!" Margaret exclaimed. "Join them for their roast goose with all the trimmings. He has no right to come and go as he pleases."

But Bernadette had his note, and she carried it in her pocket. *There will be no annulment.* And that was good enough for her at present.

Major Devereux returned to his family home and his role as the master, Lord Anthony Devereux.

He turned up the long driveway to see the much reduced household staff lined up in the distance. His butler and housekeeper must have alerted the whole household when they saw his Silver Ghost approaching the house, and they were all there to welcome him home. He thought, *No wife or family to greet me, but then again, I am more fortunate than many men returning from hell.*

He greeted them patiently and was undoubtedly in better humor than the previous night. Bernadette still loved him. That much was evident to him, the more he thought about it. It wasn't pity that caused her to undress him and wrap her nakedness around him. It was love. However, he still needed to know what had transpired during the years he was fighting in France. What had happened to cause her to leave him and to cease in her correspondence to him? Didn't she realize how important these letters were to men at the front? His men continued to receive letters from their girlfriends and wives, but he did not, only his mother and the terrible letter she wrote to him to explain why Bernadette's correspondence had stopped. What was the truth?

Mrs. O'Leary informed him that the dowager viscountess was still abed having breakfast, and her master told her that his mother would be leaving that morning for the dower house.

"Have one of the maids assist her, Mrs. O'Leary. You have enough to do."

His housekeeper ventured, "Will Lady Devereux be returning soon? The servants will be so happy to see you both settled."

Tony said, "We shall see." And when Mrs. O'Leary looked crestfallen, he added, "I think I need to get rid of my mother first. I should have a new valet starting in January. Walker is his name. Thomas Walker. He was my batman in the army. An excellent sort of chap."

He then noticed Mr. Higgins hovering a little nervously, carrying what appeared to be a small package. "Higgins, perhaps you could assist me until Walker arrives. Or have one of the footmen—if there are any left, of course."

Mr. Higgins responded, "Certainly, your lordship. I will see to it myself. The staff is rather light at the moment, but perhaps when his lordship has rested? In the meantime, may I talk to you in private? I have a matter of some delicacy."

Tony said, "Of course, Higgins. Perhaps you could run me a bath. I am desperate for it, and we can talk in my room. No, make that her ladyship's room. I will be staying there in the meantime."

Once inside Bernadette's suite, which he once so lovingly had redecorated just for her, he turned to his butler, who was still standing awkwardly, holding his small package.

"What are you holding, Mr. Higgins? Is that for me?"

"It is a little awkward, your lordship. Mrs. O'Leary was checking on a new maid's work in the dowager viscountess's chamber and ..."

Tony put his hand out to take the package being proffered to him. He unwrapped the brown paper and stood astounded. He leafed through what must have been more than twenty unopened envelopes addressed to him and written in his wife's hand. He sat down on the bed. "Where did she find these? What the hell is going on, Higgins? These are all letters written and addressed to me. Why weren't they posted?"

Mr. Higgins was not about to have Mrs. O'Leary or him be accused of some wrongdoing. Emboldened, he answered plainly, "These were just discovered two weeks ago by Mrs. O'Leary on top of the wardrobe in your mother's chamber. She immediately gave them to me, and I have kept them safe awaiting your return, since by then the war was already over. Neither of us has mentioned this matter to the dowager viscountess. However, we have no idea whether she has discovered they are missing."

Tony was shocked yet elated, although very confused. "Why did my mother have them? Why didn't Lady Devereux post them herself? Or perhaps I should ask my wife and mother that question."

Higgins responded, "Her ladyship used to come by"—he paused and cleared his throat—"on her day off and give the letters personally to the dowager viscountess. There seemed to be an agreement between them not to inform you that her ladyship was living in London."

Tony began undressing, although still holding the letters. "Thank you, Higgins. And I appreciate your discretion in keeping this business to yourself. I will take it up from here."

Higgins then silently ran his master's bath and made to leave the room. His master was leafing through the envelopes again and hadn't yet opened any. He addressed his butler. "Have Mrs. O' Leary tell the dowager viscountess that there will be a carriage awaiting her at ten a.m. to take her back to the dower house. Have one of the footmen assist her with her luggage. How long has my mother been living in the main house?"

Higgins responded, "Since before your wife left. Actually, more or less right after your leave at Christmas 1915. September that same year, the young Lady Devereux left for London."

Tony's heart was thumping. "Thank you, Higgins."

Lady Arabella Devereux knew immediately that her treachery had been discovered when Mrs. O'Leary informed her of the carriage. It had gone nine o'clock, and she told the housekeeper that she couldn't possibly be ready by then since she wasn't yet dressed and had many of her possessions to be packed up.

Mrs. O'Leary had long awaited this very day and responded, "I will send two of the maids up to assist you, your ladyship. Lord Devereux was most insistent."

Arabella was livid and easily detected the smirk on this awful Irishwoman's face. She would send a note to her daughter to come to her immediately at the dower house. They needed to devise a plan and concoct a story to explain the bricklayer's daughter's departure from Devereux House in 1916.

CHAPTER 6

Lord Devereux sank gratefully into Bernadette's bath and wondered about the contents of the letters that were still lying on Bernadette's bed. What was he about to discover? The fact that his mother would do such a thing to her only son, fighting in an endless war, was so shocking that he could hardly take it in—the years he longed to hear from his wife and thought she no longer cared. The red socks she knitted for him—so very sweet. He thought, *Better my mother hadn't sent the parcel off to me at all, rather than pass it off as her own kindness and that of a servant girl.*

He dried off and rang for a huge lunch to be brought up to him, along with a bottle of his best cognac. He had no wish to face anyone, but he was hungry and looking forward to some real food.

Tony opened all of the letters and placed them in date order—all twenty-two of them.

Early 1916, the letters were full of love and possibly even excitement. He couldn't fully comprehend why, although he had just been home the previous month. Soon the letters changed and became almost downcast—not the upbeat, cheeky Bernadette he knew, and they didn't contain any news as such, almost as if Bernadette wasn't sure what to write. That much he understood now since she would have been living and working in London—a fact that was meant to remain a secret. She never mentioned his mother, nor even the servants. She didn't write about anything other than the weather and how much she loved and missed him. A couple of the letters contained photographs taken in a studio in London. That would have been a clue had he been searching for one. He would have so loved to receive those new photographs. He had only one with him that he had wept over so many times. It was creased and torn, and he recalled how he had asked her repeatedly for a new photograph. She didn't tell him that his mother was withholding his wages. There were a couple of mentions of her family in the States but little else of note.

Then the letters began to beg him to write to her and to ask him if he no longer loved her. He felt his throat constrict when he read these, since he was begging the same thing from her. He had to control the hatred inside him for the woman who gave him life, the woman who was a mother who allowed her son to be tortured, wondering what had happened to his wife. He finally got to the last letter, which it seemed was enclosed in a Christmas parcel, another "gift" from his mother. It was late afternoon, and he was lightheaded from drinking so early in the day. His cheeks were wet with tears, and he braced himself to read the contents— most especially since there was a gap of two months between this and the other letters. His Bernadette clearly wrote this cruel letter through so much pain and confusion. It was so much more bitter than he could ever have imagined.

December 16, 1917

Major Devereux,

I wasn't sure whether to send this parcel to you, as it has been over one year now since you have written to me. However, I understand that your mother still receives occasional letters. I am sure you must have been home on leave since 1915. Did you notice I wasn't there? At Devereux House? Did you wonder what had happened to me? Did you even care?

Still, you are living in the very worst of circumstances, such that I can't even imagine, so I hope these socks and thermal underclothing keep you warm at least. I bought them in London, where I have been living now for some time.

I have written to you many times and wonder how you couldn't see or care about the heartbreak and confusion contained in those letters. This will be my last letter to you. I am unsure if you ever read the others and doubt you will read this one. So that allows me to express some home truths.

Possibly you regret our short union—the whirlwind romance. Perhaps you are of one mind now with your family—the bricklayer's daughter, not good enough after all for such a fine English blue blood. Tony, is your blood blue? I wonder. I know you are still alive. I know you are still in one piece, and although you have broken my heart, I pray for your safe return, although I realize that it will be to your mother and not to me.

My father and your mother are concocting an annulment between them—probably for the best. You can marry a fine English lady who can trace her lineage back to the Tudors or some other lot of blue bloods—just like you. That will be much more fitting for any future offspring. After all, had we a son together, he would have hated your father and grandfather, who voted to take away food from the starving mouths of his ancestors in Ireland. I know all about it. My father taught me, and I have read about it since. It wasn't the failure of the potato crop that killed so many and caused so much suffering; it was the English troops taking away wheat, oats, barley, beef, mutton, pork, eggs, milk, fruit, and vegetables. All done at gunpoint and under instructions from Parliament. It was a deliberate act of murder, and the House of Lords (of which you are such a proud member) bears much of the responsibility for over a million deaths of Irish men, women, and children.

You see, Tony, I might not be an Oxford graduate, but neither am I stupid, and neither am I a murderer, and you come from a family of stupid murderers.

I know this letter will not reach you. It will no doubt be confiscated, and the Metropolitan police will come for me and put me on a boat back to America. So be it. Such an irony since I am planning to go back anyway. Did you know my brother Jimmy died in the fields of Flanders, two months in active service and leaving behind a wife and three daughters? My father and mother are heartbroken, and his body still lies in France. As you can imagine, my father is full of hate—for your mother and most especially for you.

You both dared to look down your nose at a man who earned everything he owns and could buy and sell you many times over. He didn't tell me how much he sold me to you for. Was that what our marriage was all about? I hope you don't find it all gone upon your return, all used up on wigs for your ugly mother.

I have so enjoyed writing this letter to you. If I ever thought you would read it, I might have been a little kinder, but what kindness does a man deserve who married a stupid, naïve girl when she was eighteen and he was twenty-eight? A man who basically dumped her two years later when he should have instead seen her home to safety and to her family who loves her, before going off to lead young boys into the killing fields of France.

The more I think about it, you will survive. I am sure of it. I have read and heard tales with great sadness about the fields of Flanders running red with the blood of fallen, brave soldiers. However, none of these reports mentioned any blue blood— so you should be safe enough.

Well, I suppose that is enough pain and sorrow and bitter regret for one letter, and no need for you to worry. I will never write to you again.

FAITHFULLY,
Bernadette
(The wife you tossed away)

Tony dropped the letter on the bed. *December 16*, he thought, *I was in Harrods a day later watching her serve the RAF flyer, her smile and dimples masking the bitterness she must have felt so intensely after being abandoned by me. A hatred that she further fueled by reading the history of my country's shameful treatment of the Irish less than a century earlier. She must have been seeking out further reasons to hate me, since clearly her heart was broken.*

If only he had walked up to her counter that day. They would have discovered that neither had ceased to write to the other, and neither had stopped loving the other—that they were both in pain.

The anger inside Lord Devereux was such that he knew he had to get out of that house. The stables. He almost dreaded going there since so many of his horses had been requisitioned by the army. He had been paid for them, meagerly, and he kept a few of his finest. When he reached the stables, his chauffeur and groomsman, John Mackie, was there cleaning up, and his stallion Perseus was saddled and awaiting him. The sight of his magnificent horse cheered him. He was a five-year-old when he left and was now ten but still in excellent condition.

He checked on Genevieve and her foal, who was now a stallion, and Mackie told him he would be a fine sire. He would need to build them up again. His stables and breeding horses were his second love, next only to Bernadette. And Bernadette was a fine horsewoman. She had been riding since she was only three years old. Money was short, but there was the dowry. He hadn't touched it thus far, and it was a considerable amount. Perhaps he and Bernadette could work together on this renewed endeavor; however, all that was up to her.

Tony rode off on his horse and felt his head begin to clear. The war was over, other than a parade the village had planned for him in the new year, but that would only happen if his Bernadette was sitting by his side. He would go through his study and safe and talk to his lawyer, Samuel Gold, and get a clear picture of his financial situation. He would also need to go into London to purchase new clothes, a suit, riding apparel, a winter coat, and a new white tie ensemble. His old one must be careworn and old-fashioned.

All this before he could return to Bernadette, and his plan was Christmas Eve. All this and a robust conversation with his mother.

Tony knew he needed to calm down before he could handle that, but in the meantime, he had Higgins send a footman over to let her know he would call on her in a few days and would be dining alone before that time.

Lord Devereux's finances were in even worse shape than he imagined. He sat down with his lawyer, who told him that the way of life would change drastically for many of his class. "The war has significantly impacted your way of life. Living off the fat of the land is no longer an option to keep these large estates like yours going. You have an advantage, of course. You love horses and know how to breed the best. However, to get back into stride with that—well, it will take a significant investment, and, Tony, four years of army wages will hardly cover it."

Tony expected bad news but not this terrible. Where was his money?

Samuel Gold continued, "Your mother has mismanaged your estate—overspending despite my sound advice. I suppose I don't understand why you gave your mother full control, and if you don't mind me asking, where is your wife? Back in America? Her dowry—time for you to break into it, Tony. You are very fortunate. At least I kept that away from the dowager viscountess. Easily done with all of your father-in-law's stipulations for its use."

Major Devereux left his lawyer's office angry and confused. He had given his mother no such authority. She lied to Sam—even about Bernadette having returned to Boston. She spent lavishly or stole from him—and he believed the latter. It seemed she was driven by her hatred of his wife and had done everything in her power to destroy his marriage. To what end? She was killing her son, who was still trying to get beyond the nightmares of men screaming and dying. As he sat in the Regent Street café, where he once took a very young Bernadette Barrymore, Tony reflected upon that wonderful day. Somehow, it was so innocent, as was the world at that time, and he was falling so deeply in love with the young and spirited American girl with such unruly curls, wide eyes, and dimples—and lips that he was longing to kiss. She was trying to act so sophisticatedly and was no doubt spouting forth her father's politics—unconvincingly so—because he couldn't help but smile at her nonsense, and she blushed every time he smiled at her. Those dimples—they got him every time, and he could feel an invisible force drawing them together. They were two completely different individuals, both from other worlds, and for all she criticized his world, he somehow knew she would remain in it just to be with him. *And now,* he thought, *it seems that I am indeed the impoverished member of the nobility that her father— daddy—thought me to be.*

Tony knew that in order to get the estate running smoothly again, and to find and buy the quality horses that would allow him to become the breeder of such high-quality equestrian specimens, for which he once had a fine reputation, he needed his wife's dowry—or a good portion of it.

Would she understand? Would she decide that "daddy" was right about him and his kind all along? He had left her in a strange country. He knew he should have sent her back when it seemed that a war in Europe was inevitable; he knew it at the time but was afraid to lose her—back in her world—and instead, thanks to his mother and his own stupidity, she ended up working in a shop, living off her father's benevolence since her husband was clueless. He may have lost her anyway.

He paid his bill and left the café. He had to purchase his new clothes and get a shave and a haircut—smarten himself up in order to sweep the lovely Bernadette off her feet again. He knew with her support and her at his side, he could become wealthy and successful, as he once had been. There was money to be made while at the same time rebuilding England, possibly not to the country he remembered but to someplace equally as grand. He would most likely never be the millionaire that James Barrymore was, and Tony was confident that a man like Barrymore would have profited enormously from the war. James Barrymore was ruthless, and he hated his daughter's husband. However, despite being ruthless, he was putty in Bernadette's hands, as indeed was Tony—different, of course, for obvious reasons. The way she came to him—the love she gave to him that first night home. It gave him confidence and hope, and so he went on his way to Savile Row to dress himself up as the successful man he planned to be.

CHAPTER 7

December 23 was the inevitable confrontation between Lord Anthony Devereux and his mother—a necessary unpleasantness to be faced before Christmas Eve when his lordship planned to propose again to her ladyship, Viscountess Bernadette Devereux.

The dowager's butler and the housekeeper had an easy few years, with their exacting and unpleasant mistress in the main house, but that was all over now, and a rather unhappy-looking Mr. Dankworth showed his lordship into the parlor, where he awaited his mother, who was also dreading the interview. He hadn't seen her since the night he arrived, and when she came into the room and offered him tea, Tony had to hold himself back from the temper he felt inside.

He started, "I read all of my wife's letters that you kept from me. But tell me, Mother, where are mine to her? I have also been to see Sam Gold, and it seems you have been trying to bankrupt me. It is a shame that Barrymore's specifications were such that Mr. Gold could prevent you from touching those funds. To say I am disgusted, Mother, is putting it mildly. I can hardly look at you. So what do you have to say for yourself? Were you hoping I died on the battlefield? That would have been one way to get rid of Bernadette; however, Uncle Bertie would have soon gotten rid of you too. Oh wait, that's why you stole my money! You had to ensure a comfortable future for yourself in the event of my death. Ah, I get it now."

Arabella calmly rang for tea. "My son, everything you were told I did was done for a reason. I don't know if you saw her, but she didn't come back with you. I wonder why. You don't seem to understand, although I had hoped the war would have brought you to your senses. That girl is not of your social class! The language she used to your mother! The insolence! And there was a miscarriage. That I know, although I know no more than that. Ah, she didn't tell you, did she? I am sure she didn't mention that in her letters!"

Tony sat down. "No, she didn't mention any miscarriage. How would you know about such a thing? I doubt you were in each other's confidence. Are you trying to tell me that she miscarried another man's child? Are you really trying to say that to your son just home from the front? Dear God, Mother, you disgust me with your lies and innuendos."

"Well, you know she wrote to that father of hers, and voila! Along comes that O'Connor fellow to pick her up and take her to a flat in London. I was glad to be rid of her anyway and her foul mouth. I am quite certain that there is something between those two. He seemed very devoted to her, and she, very grateful to him!"

Arabella was embellishing and making much of this up as she went along. After all, if Bernadette said nothing of the miscarriage, although it happened after her husband's one visit home, that fact alone could cause suspicion or at least uncertainty in her son's mind. Arabella had indeed feared for her son's safety since many men, even officers, were dying at the front. She had to ensure a comfortable future for herself in the terrible event of his death. Bernadette would be well cared for by the Irish bricklayer and no doubt by his henchman, O'Connor, but Bertie wasn't a very kind or generous man.

"I will grant you, Tony, that your wife is very comely, and she seems to get on so well with the servants and lower classes—shop girls and such. She will be just fine after the annulment, and can't you see it will be better for all? She was like a fish out of water with you gone, with no idea how to run a large household, so of course, I had to step in! Tony, no matter what money that man has, her father, money does not buy breeding nor class—a fact I was made well aware of after you left. She was sitting around crying and moping—no fortitude or forbearance."

Tony just stared hard at the woman who gave him life, and Arabella couldn't miss the hatred in his eyes. He was about to speak, but she interrupted him.

"I am assuming that you went to her—the night you returned—and her sort would have welcomed you with open arms. I am sure of it. Foolish man, why can't you see what she is? She is low class, Tony. I don't care how much money her father has. It is in her walk and how she smiles at men and that ridiculous hair—half-wild and in need of a good haircut. Those pouting lips, and I am sure she wears rouge. A painted woman!"

Tony couldn't believe his ears. His sweet girl was being spoken of in such a way by his own mother. There was nothing more to be said except, "I am bringing my wife home on Christmas Day, and I am going to her Christmas Eve. Time for her to leave her life in London and return to her husband, who will always be very much in love with her—his only chosen wife. After the holidays, I will have Sam assist you in finding a flat in London, not Bernadette's, of course. And anyway, I doubt you could afford it since Barrymore won't be paying for it and nor will I. You have stolen enough of your son's money."

Tony stood up to leave. "I suppose you may come for Christmas dinner, unless my wife objects too strongly. After that, we shall be dining alone as we renew our vows and mutual love and affection."

Arabella had one last card up her sleeve. "I will have a

houseguest for a month or so. I am sure you will allow her to use your stables, or what is left of them after the British Army took their pick of the best. Lady Georgiana Villan. Lord Villan perished in this terrible war. However, she is now a rich widow, still under thirty, and you know she always carried a torch for you. At one time, it was her mother's—God rest her soul—and my favorite wish, that you both walked down the aisle together. Perhaps it is not too late after all, Tony?"

Tony was incredulous. "So, Mother, trying to marry me off while still married to another? Isn't that bigamy? Let me make one thing clear. I will never sign an annulment, and no matter what the future holds for me, it will never include Georgiana. If I didn't want her when she was still young and fresh, why would I want her now? Oh and, Mother, I want my letters and my wedding photographs. I am quite certain that you have them. Dankworth can bring them to me at Devereux House—a house you might see for the last time on Christmas Day. And by all means, bring your desperate friend, Lady Villan. I do need to think about her use of my stables, however—possibly ask Bernadette for her opinion."

Tony left without taking tea. His heart was thumping in his chest. The way his mother spoke about his beloved wife, how could he ever forgive her? He said aloud, "Christmas dinner should be a delight," and made his way to the stables to speak to John Mackie and discuss a plan to get back in operation as soon as possible. This done, he went out on horseback to survey his land. He was very proud of it and was anxious to bring his wife back where she belonged—with her husband. "An early start tomorrow, Tony." He was speaking aloud, his head finally clearing in the cold air following the terrible discourse he had with his mother. "I suppose you better buy your wife a Christmas present; you have several years to make up for." He decided on a fur coat and possibly some perfume. The beautiful young woman at the perfume counter in Harrods, the one with the dimples and unruly hair—perhaps she could wait on him.

Tony inspected the huge Christmas tree in the great hall, which his staff hastily set up in hopes of the first happy Christmas in a very long time. He would also need to pick up some silver sovereigns from the bank. Next year, Bernadette would take care of that sort of thing, as she did when they were first married. He was quite confident that very meager gifts were given in his absence to those who served the family so faithfully and so well.

CHAPTER 8

It was Christmas Eve, and Bernadette was tidying up the boxes of scent kept under the counter when Margaret ran back and knelt beside her. "He's here, although I would hardly recognize him—dressed up like a toff in a new suit and overcoat with a fur collar. He looks so different from the soldier standing in the train station, and the girls are swooning over him. He is so handsome! I'll be swooning soon myself!"

"Christ, Margaret! Look at the state of me. Is he looking this way? I need to crawl back to the stockroom and fix my hair. I hate my hair! It is always so untidy!"

Bernadette's heart had leapt in happiness—unquestionably, he had come for her. Nevertheless, she attempted to escape, to tidy her appearance, when she heard a wonderful, posh voice. Someone was looking down behind the counter at her. "Excuse me, miss, but I require some assistance."

Bernadette looked up, and there was the Tony Devereux she remembered, tall and confident and such a snob. He was dressed like a complete toff—Savile Row, she assumed. She could hardly believe that this man was her husband. The floor walker, Mr. Montague, came over to assist him, but Tony motioned him away with his hand. As Bernadette stood up, Mr. Montague said to her,

"Miss Barrymore, kindly assist Lord Devereux with his purchase," and he gave her a hard stare.

Bernadette had to stop herself from laughing out loud, but her huge, dimpled smile said it all. "May I help you, Lord—sorry, I didn't catch your name."

"Devereux, Tony Devereux, but you may call me Lord Devereux. And you are?"

"Miss Barrymore, sir. How may I assist you?"

"I am looking for a perfume for my wife. Perhaps you can suggest something not too expensive. You know us nobility, rather cash poor. Is that an American accent I hear?"

"No, sir. I come from Hampshire, although currently residing in London."

"How very odd," he said, keeping a straight face. "I live in Hampshire but don't recognize your accent. What have you got to show me?"

Bernadette was so happy. She wanted to leap across the counter but said, "What is she like, this wife of yours who deserves cheap perfume? You realize that you are in Harrods, and if you can't afford our prices ... well, anyway ..." She turned and picked up a tester and said, "This one, sir. It is half-empty. I could ask Mr. Montague if I can sell it to you for half price. I like this one very much myself."

Bernadette dabbed some on her wrist, and her customer sniffed it. He looked up at her with a gleam in his eye and said, "I'm more interested in how it will smell behind her ears. That's where she likes to dab her perfume, and she has such pretty ears— pretty dimples too—when she smiles."

Bernadette was enjoying her husband's nonsense; he was coming back, the old Tony—the one who swept her off her feet. "Lucky her," she said, "but you will get me the sack since I am supposed to spray some on a handkerchief, and I doubt if your wife—the one with the dimples—would like you sniffing other women's ears."

He said, "Oh, she won't mind a bit, and if I like it, I will buy your largest size, brand-new, and with one of those crystal atomizers I see over there."

Bernadette wondered how far her husband would carry this on. She reasoned that this would no doubt be her last sale anyway, from how Mr. Montague was looking at her, so she dabbed some behind her ear and lifted her hair, which was coming undone as usual. She tried to fix it, but he stopped her and, sniffing her ear, mumbled, "Delicious," so seductively that her stomach did a somersault.

Then he stepped back. "Okay, wrap up a new bottle and the emerald-green glass atomizer. My wife had a ring that color, but she lost it."

Bernadette knew he was talking about her engagement ring and was shaking with happiness or nerves, she wasn't sure which, as she wrapped up his purchases, aware by now that the other girls were laughing and Mr. Montague looked rather in a state of shock.

Margaret mouthed, "I had to tell them!"

"Okay," he said happily, "you can put them both on my account. I just opened one for my wife. She will be in next week to purchase some new skirts and dresses and whatever else fine ladies wear—and a new hat. Now, if you will carry them to my car for me …"

Bernadette couldn't help her laughter now. "No, sir, I won't be doing that. You can surely carry them yourself!"

He looked thoughtful and then took her hand and led her around the counter, "Very well. I will carry you, and you will carry her gifts."

He lifted her up, and at this point, she no longer cared. Laughing, she kissed him and said, "Tony, my coat. It's in the staff cloakroom. And my purse!"

Margaret shouted, "I will bring them over!"

Tony shouted, "Lady Devereux has just resigned. She needs

to come home and make her husband dinner." And he whispered, "I bought you a fur coat. It's in the car."

Bernadette waved to the girls who had been her colleagues for the past two years and shouted to Margaret, "I'll come and see you, I promise … and what we talked about!"

Margaret was crying, since although delighted for her friend and her well-deserved happiness, she knew that life would never be as good without her. She said a silent prayer about the lady's maid position of which they had spoken.

⚜

Tony put Bernadette down outside and wrapped his warm coat around her. He led her to the Silver Ghost parked in the street and said, "I'm taking you to the Savoy. Remember our night there? It was so wonderful, and I've played it in my head so many times."

Bernadette said, "Tony, I am the happiest woman alive—really I am—but what happened? You were so sad a few days ago. We have so much to tell each other too. I am dressed like a shop girl. They might not let me in the Savoy. Can we go for a coffee first instead? There is a café just across the street."

His face hardened, and for the first time, Bernadette noticed his scar. When he scowled, it was more visible, and he looked a little intimidating. Then his words shocked her, especially since he had been behaving like the old Tony, funny and romantic, just a few moments beforehand. "I thought this was what you wanted, Bernadette. You certainly wanted it the first night I came home and you stripped me bare in my sleep. Do I misunderstand you?"

The remark was cruel, humiliating even, and Bernadette said, "No, I think I misunderstand you—to speak so to your wife! That was love, Tony, deep and enduring love. When I saw you lying there so tired and battle weary, I wanted you to feel my love because I love you so very much." She paused thoughtfully. "I thought you would be taking me home now, a reconciliation and renewal of our love. I have so much to tell you, as you do me. If this is something else, please explain. I have no doubt lost my position at Harrods, and I am now uncertain you are offering me a new position as your wife and mistress of your home. If this is not the case, Tony, please take me to my flat."

He drove off and said no more but turned and pulled into the parking garage at the Savoy, and Bernadette started to cry. "You are scaring me, Tony. I don't know what your mother told you, but I know the true story about all of them, your whole bleeding family—sitting on their big fat behinds, looking down their noses at everyone who knows how to make an honest living. I know you've been through hell, even though I can't imagine it, but I have been working long hours, six days a week—just like the other girls. The only difference is that they receive their husband's wages, and I had to rely on my father since your mother kept yours."

He said sarcastically, "Oh, Daddy, of course. I hear you are planning to remarry after the annulment that you mistakenly think I will sign. Your language is certainly more colorful than I remember. I will grant you that at least."

Bernadette was whimpering, and Tony wondered why he was talking this way to her. It had not been his intention, but what if his family was telling him the truth? The miscarriage, for one thing? She was so young and so lovely, and she was living as a single woman with her own flat. She had been living in London those years he was fighting in France and was even using language that she never did before. If it wasn't for her strong Boston accent—even that was softening—she was talking like one of the shop girls his mother so disgustedly described. However, he read her letters. He didn't understand some—no doubt because she didn't want him to know she was in London, but the last one was clear enough. Why all the secrecy?

He said, "I'm sorry, Bernadette. I didn't intend to be cruel. You have been passing yourself off as a single woman, and you are even more desirable than when I left. You didn't even take my ring. I just need to try to understand. I know my mother's truth is not the real truth—but I need to have yours. I need to ask, have you been faithful to me and honored our vows? Did you have a miscarriage? How, Bernadette? How was that possible?"

Bernadette stopped crying as anger coursed through her veins. Of what was he accusing her? What did his mother say to him?

She thought of getting out of the car—of leaving him sitting there. Then she looked at him, and her heart was breaking. He looked as if he was dreading her answer.

"Okay, the truth. Here it is, and you can believe whatever you want. You came home on leave, Christmas 1915. Do you remember? We shared so much love, and I conceived, although of course, I didn't know until after you left. I was so happy—the thought of having your baby—I was on cloud nine. Your mother moved back into the main house, no doubt to keep an eye on me, and told me to wait until three months to tell you. Then I lost our baby. I was nine weeks, and your mother—the evil old bitch—told me not to tell you about it since you had enough to worry you. She took over the house after that and treated me like dirt. She called me the bricklayer's daughter and much worse."

Tony knew she was telling the truth—even through his horror of what his mother had done not only to his wife but also, through her, to him. He moved to touch her hair, but she pulled it away from him. She continued, "I wrote to Daddy in my misery. I wanted him to take me home to America, but then I didn't because I wanted to be here when you came back. He was afraid of another steamer being hit by a torpedo anyway, like the *Lusitania*, but suggested that I could stay in London. Well, actually, that part isn't true. I begged him to help me because I couldn't stand that woman any longer, or your fat sister—too many cream cakes while others were starving. He found me a flat in Knightsbridge and a job in Harrods to keep me occupied. 'Out of mischief,' he said. Michael O'Connor came over and arranged everything. He even helped me with my furniture and pots and pans. He confronted your mother, and I packed one small suitcase and left to start my new life in London. By then, you had stopped writing, and I carried on writing to you, until in the end I couldn't bear to any longer."

"Your mother told me to bring my letters to Devereux House, and she would post them since you would not be happy to know I was living in London and working as a 'shop girl,' as she also likes to call me. I believed her because, after all, who would do that to their only son fighting in that terrible war—withhold his wife's letters to him? I even sent you two Christmas parcels. My friend Margaret showed me how to knit and helped me with my dropped stitches. I thought you would see the love in your red socks and write to me again. But you didn't. That's about it. So you thought I was seeing other men and got knocked up. Wow, Tony. How do I ever get over that? Please take me home now, and I mean to my flat since that is the only home I have in England."

He felt like a fool, like his stupidity may have lost her again, the girl he fell in love with at first sight—the girl who was now a woman, a woman who had been abandoned by a husband who couldn't see through the lies to find the truth. They sat in silence, and again she began to cry. He said, "My mother told me about that man, O'Connor, and that was the main reason she and your father wanted the annulment. So he is nothing to you? Why did he do all that for you?"

"Because my father was paying him, Tony. And men always do what my father tells them; they wouldn't dare do otherwise."

"I did," he responded. "I married you, Bernadette. Can you forgive me? I don't mean for marrying you." He laughed. "I knew you were true to me. I did know it—when I read your letters, despite my mother's lies. I know they are coming here—your father and this O'Connor fellow. I know you have known him all of your life ..." He trailed off.

Bernadette realized that these caustic comments were coming out of jealousy and insecurity. Her handsome member of the House of Lords, and she, the Irish bricklayer's daughter.

Then, suddenly, the penny dropped. "Letters? What letters? Tony?"

Tony said, "Mrs. McLeary found them. Just a couple weeks ago, or so I am told. All twenty-two of them, unopened, and I read them all. You were begging me to write to you, and at the time, I was begging the same thing from you. Bernadette, my mother never posted your letters, and it also seems that she never gave you mine. However, they are still missing, although I told her to give them to me."

"Tony, I wish I could say I was shocked, but the only thing that shocks me is my own stupidity to trust your wicked mother, a mother who would do such a thing to her son. No wonder then. No wonder you thought I had forsaken you, and now you know better."

"Tony, I was just eighteen when I fell flat on my face for you, and I will still be falling flat on my face until I am eighty." She paused, feigning deep thought. "Well, when I'm eighty-one, I might find a new fellow, but it will never be Michael O'Connor."

She laughed, and so did he, and he finally took her into his arms and kissed her as if he would never stop—her Tony Devereux. And soon, they were both laughing in their sheer happiness.

She said, "Tony, let's go back to my flat. I don't need the Savoy; I only need you—and so very badly. Take that any way you like. If you're hungry, we can pick up some fish and chips. There's a chippy around the corner from my flat and a pub next door. You can grab a pint of ale, while I buy the fish suppers. I have money enough in my pocket. I will even pay for your pint."

Lord Devereux was delightfully amazed; his spoiled American princess was behaving like a London lass, and he loved both of these personas. "Okay, you win," he said. "I want two pickled onions with mine."

They drove off happily, and Bernadette felt him returning to her, although she still expected some moodiness and strange behavior. He had been through hell after all.

Tony took her up on her offer to pay for his pint and laughingly took the sixpence from her. "Maybe give me a couple of extra pennies for the proprietor. I never carry small change. Well, I did during the war, but that is over now—thank God."

Bernadette had donned her fur coat and realized how long it had been since she had worn anything so expensive. When he helped her put it on, she said thoughtfully, "Tony, I love it. It is so soft and warm, but, Tony, there is no need to buy such expensive things for me now—at least until you get back on your feet. I have become quite thrifty, in fact, and have saved up quite a bit. Still, that coat you're wearing must have cost a few bob."

Tony laughed and said, "So my wife has learned the value of money, and I have quite forgotten it. You know it is Christmas Eve, Bernadette. Do you have any food in for Christmas? If not, Mrs. O'Leary is preparing quite a feast."

He walked into the pub, and Bernadette stood in line at the chippy. Even as she thought about her big, canopied bed and sumptuous carpets in her suite at Devereux House, she suddenly felt nostalgic about her tiny flat that she would surely now be leaving. Bernadette also worried and wondered how she could sit down to Christmas dinner with Tony's "people," as she thought of them. Bernadette pushed the thought aside as she paid for her fish suppers and met Tony coming out of the pub.

They started on their chips on the way upstairs to the flat, and both eagerly anticipated a night of unrestrained love after being so long apart. They were laughingly and lovingly feeding each other chips, and as Bernadette lifted the door mat for the key to her door, she suddenly realized it was gone, and the door was unlocked. Tony opened it gingerly, and they both looked at each other as they heard the voices inside that were so easily recognizable.

Bernadette was torn. After more than six years, she was overjoyed to see her father and mother, even Michael O'Connor, another familiar face from back home.

Eugenie Barrymore put her arms out to her daughter, and Bernadette ran into them, and soon she was hugging her father too and crying. She felt, for one reason or another, she had been crying all day. Bernadette turned to her husband, who was standing straight-faced. He finally said, "Mr. and Mrs. Barrymore, what an unexpected pleasure. Mr. O'Conner, is it? I remember you from my wedding. Lord Devereux or Major Devereux, whichever you prefer, at your service."

He seemed to be looking down his nose at her parents and Michael, and she was suddenly aware of her black shop girl skirt and her white shop girl blouse covered up with her new, expensive fur coat, and everyone around her felt like strangers. Her parents were expensively attired, as was Tony, and she felt so different, like she didn't belong with any of them. Her father, with a dangerous glint in his eye, mimicked by Michael, and her husband, looking down his autocratic nose at them.

A strange panic came over her. She dropped her fish and chips, threw down her coat, and ran down the stairs. Tony called after her, as did her father, and they both went to follow her, but amazingly, she encountered Margaret on her way upstairs, carrying her coat and purse. The two women ran as fast as they could and managed to make the bus to Whitechapel, which was just leaving the bus stop. Margaret's flat was on Main Street, Whitechapel. It was the flat above the greengrocers, where the two women often purchased blemished fruit and vegetables at a cheap price.

Tony Devereux and James Barrymore stood and watched the bus drive off. They could see both women laughing as they climbed upstairs, and James asked, "Where the hell is she going? What's going on, Devereux? I am here to take her home!"

Tony was furious; what promised to have been a magical night, Christmas Eve indeed, had just turned into a nightmare. In truth, he had no idea where his Bernadette had gone, presumably to her friend's house. He didn't even know her friend's name, but he was sure Barrymore knew. Didn't she write to them? Didn't they know her better than he?

Despite his anger and worry, he appeared self-assured. It had long been ingrained in him, all the way through his childhood at boarding school—a cold, calm reserve. "My presumption is Whitechapel. That's what the bus said. Thanks to you, your daughter is very well versed in wandering around the streets of London. I am sure you know more than I do about her friend's whereabouts."

James Barrymore wanted to punch this man who was standing, looking down his nose at him. He knew he could buy and sell his whole family—most notably with the considerable profits he had made during the war. He thought it would be much easier than this to get him away from his daughter and to bring her home. "We'll find her then. Or I will find her. That must be this friend of hers. They work together. Margaret Walker, yes—that's her name."

Tony knew London better than his father-in-law and told

him so. "I will wait here. She'll come back. But you have to leave. Tomorrow, you are all invited to my home in Hampshire. I will take you there, and if there is not enough room in the car, your man O'Connor can take the train—if they are running on Christmas Day. By the way, there will be no annulment, whether she wants it or not, especially since she is carrying my child." He added, "Keep O'Connor away from my wife."

Lord Devereux walked back upstairs before James Barrymore had a chance to react to this incredible piece of news, and he thought, *How has he had time? I don't think I believe him.* Nevertheless, James Barrymore's wife was crying, and he was tired, and he knew his daughter had already survived two years on her own in the city, so he gathered his companions up. "We are staying at the Ritz. I'll expect you both there by noon—since you're so confident she'll be back."

And Tony responded, "Just like old times. See you at noon."

They left, and Tony congratulated himself on the perfect strategy. Of course he made up the part about Bernadette carrying his child; but wasn't it possible that she was? After the enthusiastic welcome home she gave him?

He turned on the oven and reheated his fish supper. Major Devereux had also learned many new skills during the war—in addition to killing young German soldiers. He knew about Barrymore's son, Bernadette's brother, killed in action, and that saddened him. So many deaths, and now those who survived were dying from the Spanish flu, as they called it. He needed to get Bernadette out of London.

Tony picked up the expensive fur coat and put his wife's perfume under her sad-looking tabletop Christmas tree. He wondered where she found it and examined the inexpensive little ornaments upon it. Underneath the tree, Tony found two presents, one for him and one for Margaret Walker. He suddenly thought, *Margaret? Wasn't that Tommy Walker's wife's name? And she worked in Harrods.* Tommy was his batman, and he expected him back in January since that was the soonest he could get him out. He had promised Tommy a job if they both survived—his valet— since his last man was killed in action. He promised Tommy a position for his wife too and a cottage.

Major Devereux owed Sergeant Walker his life. He had saved him more than once and looked after him well—no easy job. But surely this wasn't possible? *She's Bernadette's best friend?* He finished his meal and two large glasses of his own sherry from Devereux House. He had the decided feeling that all would be well in the end. They had both been fed a pack of lies—his mother, her father. They had much to answer for. They were both responsible for her life of working long hours so far from home. How could he have known, living in hell as he was? He, too, had much to make up for, and it seemed that he owed as much to Mrs. Walker as he did to her husband. She had looked after Bernadette, who throughout everything was still the girl he remembered. She was laughing when she ran away from him and her father—laughing as she made her way upstairs on the bus to Whitechapel.

He walked into Bernadette's tiny bedroom and began to look through her things. He knew it wasn't quite the thing to do, but he wanted to know who she had become. "American stockings and undergarments—very pretty, all brand-new," he said aloud. And then he found his letters—all very old, none written past 1915 and clearly read over many times. He also found a new negligée and receipt. It was wrapped in tissue paper, and the receipt was dated December 18, 1918. He thought, *She must have bought it to wear for me the night she came to the station, but she decided to come to bed naked instead. I think she understood the need in me that first night.*

Her clothes were all inexpensive, mostly black skirts and white blouses, with a couple of skirts and dresses that she must have worn for her Sunday best. She had one pair of black dress shoes and a pair of boots that had seen better days. Several hats—she liked hats—and an old-fashioned dressing gown. Her nightdresses were very modest and warm, as were her fuzzy, warm slippers. A stack of American ladies' magazines lay on the table beside her bed, many with pictures cut out that displayed expensive lady's wear. She had pinned these pictures onto her bedroom walls, and he felt guilty. His wife could afford to wear these fine silks and satins displayed on her walls, yet she chose to be like the other girls she worked beside, girls who included Sergeant Walker's bride—a realization and coincidence that amazed him.

Tony Devereux removed his fine outer clothes and slipped under the covers. He could smell his wife's delicious scent—so fresh despite working such long hours waiting on women who possessed none of her beauty and grace. Tony reached under his pillow, and there they were. He had wondered why there were no photographs of him, but it seemed she had two, and she kept them safe under her pillow.

Tony put her key back under her mat. It had just gone 7:00 p.m., although the midwinter night was so dark. He waited as he leafed through her magazines and prayed that he had been correct, that she would come back—that she would know he was there waiting for her. He wanted her so badly and needed to tell her so.

Bernadette was laughing, and Margaret said in amazement, "I still can't believe you ran away from them all. Did you see their faces? Your dad looked shocked, but your husband was smiling."

Bernadette responded, "Margaret, Tony is such a snob. I suppose I already knew that, but my daddy was seething, and Tony stood looking down his nose at him. Of course, he is that few inches taller. Michael didn't know what to say or do, and my mother—as always, God bless her—was crying. I just wanted away from them, and I can't believe you were there, bringing me my coat."

"Well," said Margaret, "Mr. Montague didn't actually say you were sacked. He just said, 'Take these things to Lady Devereux and wish her a very happy Christmas.' Anyway, if you don't make it up with your husband, I might be out of a job. I am convinced he is well aware that I always knew exactly who you were."

Bernadette yawned. "Some Christmas Eve this is! Are you going to see your mother-in-law in the morning? I'm going back home. I think Tony is still there, and I am sure my parents are not. Anyway, I'm dying to see what happened, and I'm thinking that either way, I will be going to Hampshire and Devereux House for Christmas dinner."

The best friends parted company, and Bernadette promised to let Margaret know what transpired.

❧

Bernadette was soon back on the bus to Knightsbridge, and as the minutes passed, she became less convinced that it would be Tony she found there but her father instead.

She ran upstairs on the bus, anxious to see Tony again. For all his snobbery and recent accusations, she was still mad about him and desperately hoped he hadn't left and gone back to Hampshire. Then she saw his Silver Ghost. She was elated, and in her hurry to be reunited with him, she tripped on a crack on the pavement and fell flat on her face. The ground beneath her was wet, and she dirtied her new coat and ripped her stockings. She skinned her knee and started to cry both in pain and in embarrassment. She limped upstairs and wondered if the key was back under the mat, but as she was retrieving it, still sniffling, he opened the door.

He was standing in his underwear, and when he saw her, he started laughing and said, "What in God's name happened to you?"

Bernadette began crying in earnest, and he shushed her. "Dr. Tony is going to make it all better." And he did.

"I saved you some chips, although I ate your haddock. Here's a glass of sherry, and I am running you a bath. I need to make you pretty so I can make love to you before midnight. Come on now, let me see those dimples."

Bernadette smiled with a petted lip and said, "I fell in a puddle. I wanted to see you so badly, and ... why before midnight?"

She limped through to the bathroom, and as he undressed her, he said, "Because I have something to place ... actually replace on your finger, and we are renewing our vows at midnight."

Bernadette thought, *Oh no,* and said, "At midnight mass?"

Tony laughed. "No, remember we are Church of England ... in bed."

Tony was singing, as was Bernadette's heart as he soaped her up in her bath. She felt a little shy in her nakedness and at first was covering her breasts. Tony took her hands away and said, "I have imagined your heavenly body for three long years, much of the time thinking that I would never see it again, never hold you, never kiss and make love to you, and yet here we are—and I want to look at you. We were always so free with one another, our bedroom oasis. It is still there awaiting its mistress."

After she was dried off, he helped her into her new negligee, which he had laid out for her on the bed, and she laughingly told him off about snooping through her things. He poured two glasses of sherry from the almost empty bottle and sat down by the fire, pulling Bernadette down onto his lap. Soon he began to kiss her, and as she yielded to him, he carried her into her bedroom. They made love again and again until Bernadette drifted happily off to sleep.

It was midnight when Tony gently awakened her, "It's 12:01 a.m., Christmas morning, Bernadette." He was holding her beautiful engagement ring—the one his mother had taken away. Bernadette happily and sleepily put out her left hand for him to put it back on her finger, but before doing so, he said, "The last time I placed this on your finger, it was to ask you to be my bride. On this occasion, it is to ask you to come back to me, to stand by my side always—to comfort me as I will cherish and comfort you. Please come and return to your role as mistress of Devereux House, just as you have always been mistress of my body and soul."

He placed the ring back on her finger, and again she was crying, this time in happiness and complete and utter joy, and they made love again until they both fell fast asleep in each other's arms.

CHAPTER 9

Bernadette awoke at 6:00 a.m. She sat up and watched Tony sleep and wondered about the last time she had done so. It was so many years ago and felt like a lifetime. She worried about the day ahead, returning to Devereux House, her parents in tow, and Arabella—all sitting down to a lovely Christmas dinner. Who else would be there? Bertie Devereux, she didn't mind him, Charlotte, and daughters who would be teenagers by now? Cecil Fallsington and his mousy wife?

As she watched her husband, she wondered how he got injured. He didn't tell her, and she didn't ask him. Then again, they had only been back together a few hours; most of that time, they were making love. She loved Tony—would never love another—but how could she possibly celebrate Christmas with his people, who were so disrespectful toward her?

At that moment, she decided she would return to Boston with her parents—not forever, or hopefully not forever—but she needed to know. What if she hadn't gone to the station the night he returned to London? What would have happened then? She thought, *It will be hard to leave him, especially since I have just found him again, but I need to know. Will he come for me or just get on with his life in Hampshire? I will ensure my father encourages him to use my dowry to buy his new horses. That way, if he does come, it will be for me and not for any potential profit or access to funds.*

Lord Devereux awoke and was about to pull his wife back into bed when he noticed the expression on her face. "Bernadette, you are very deep in thought. Happy Christmas, by the way, our new wedding day."

He was smiling at her, a bit cautiously, she thought, and she softened toward him and climbed back into bed. "It just occurred to me that I have nothing appropriate to wear to Christmas Day dinner, my triumphant return to Devereux House."

He began to kiss and caress her, and in her love for him, she succumbed. He mumbled, "My love, you would be beautiful in rags."

Bernadette considered in her mind, *Actually, dear husband, had it been left to you and your mother, I might have been in rags instead of my shop girl uniform.* But she had an idea and secretly smiled to herself.

They ate toast and drank tea, which was all that was available in Bernadette's tiny flat, and she packed her suitcase while Tony took a bath. She put in her new American underwear and realized that she had little else to pack. She was wearing the aquamarine skirt and cream silk blouse that she had worn to the train station the night Tony came home. When she put it on, she smiled sadly, remembering the fun she and Margaret had picking out their new clothes that same day. She looked around her bedroom and into her wardrobe and made a decision—a secret smile on her lips— her black skirt and boots and the white shirt she had bought on sale in menswear. It must have been made for a very small man, and no doubt that was why it had been reduced so much. She had also bought a man's black tie that day but had never worn either. Menswear was definitely in vogue, especially for the suffragists, and wouldn't these items make the perfect ensemble for Christmas dinner with the Devereuxes and their ever so fashionable friends?

Bernadette quickly put them in her small valise, and Tony

appeared, wearing the new silk tie she bought him and dressed like a "dish of fish," as her friend Margaret might say. She thought that perhaps she might have some fun that day after all.

Tony locked the door and put the key in his pocket, and Bernadette smiled lovingly at him, thinking, *Ah, but Margaret has the spare key.*

Lord Anthony Devereux thought that his wife was behaving a little strangely and put it down to nerves. Her skirt and blouse were nice enough for a day's shopping, but he regretted not buying her a new dress on Christmas Eve since everywhere was closed on Christmas Day. However, perhaps her mother brought her something nice to wear. He drove to the Ritz and into the parking garage. He remembered those magical occasions in 1912 when they first kissed and realized their love for each other. However, on this occasion, Bernadette opened the car door herself, before he had a chance to do so for her, and said, "Oh, I suppose I am no longer used to such gallantry. I'm hungry, Tony. I wonder if they are still serving breakfast."

It seemed that they were, at least for Mr. James Barrymore's daughter, most especially since the American millionaire was so generous with his gratuities. They were early since it had just gone eleven, and Bernadette wanted to get there early. They both ordered a full English breakfast, and Tony watched his wife eat hungrily, as she had so many years before. Something was different. He pushed the thought aside—nerves of course. That was what it was.

Mr. Barrymore took his seat in the front of the Silver Ghost, and Bernadette was stuck in the middle between her mother and

Michael O'Connor. She was aware of her husband watching her in his rearview mirror—a mild look of concern on his face—but she, like her companions, remained relatively silent for the journey to Hampshire. There was an occasional comment now and again, but no one appeared especially jolly for the occasion—quite the reverse.

When they arrived, the servants were there to greet them and, in the case of Bernadette, very warmly indeed. If the Barrymores were impressed with the welcome at Devereux House, they showed no sign of it; if they were impressed with the great hall and giant Christmas tree, no sign of that either.

Tony told Bernadette that he would check on everything. "Your job, my darling, next year. Why don't you go up and rest and see that your parents are comfortable? I can have some refreshments sent up if you like."

Bernadette could tell he was nervous; the whole situation was strange because this was supposed to be her home after more than six years of marriage. *Well,* she thought, *it isn't my home, not anymore if ever it was. It is his mother's house, or at least that is how I now see it. I would need to change everything, except perhaps my bedroom. Yes, possibly even that. She has spoiled everything, my life, my marriage … and is coming here for Christmas dinner.*

After a while, Bernadette got up. She had fallen asleep, and no wonder—she had been working such long hours. Tony hadn't come back up to see her settled in, and that somewhat surprised her. She walked out to the upstairs hallway and listened. It was already dark outside, and the house was all lit up. She could hear voices, very posh voices intermingled with American accents, and realized that they were all downstairs gathering for dinner. She was standing with her hair a mess and her clothes all crumpled since she hadn't bothered to undress before she drifted off to sleep.

Finally, Tony appeared. "I came up to awaken you, but you were so sound that I left you to sleep."

"Yes," she said, "with all my clothes on and even my shoes. What time is dinner? I hear several voices downstairs."

"In an hour or so. You can take your time getting dressed. Shall I send up a maid? My mother has brought a house guest, Lady Georgiana Villan—known her for years. Her husband was killed at the Somme—sorry business. Charlotte, her husband, Jeremy, Uncle Bertie—oh, and Cecil turned up with Marjorie, you remember, his wife. I am sorry. I didn't notice your shoes. I didn't want to disturb you."

Bernadette thought that her husband seemed exceptionally uneasy and rightfully so. On her first day at Devereux House, all those who hated her were there to welcome her, along with a new arrival, Lady Georgiana Villan, a person she never remembered having been mentioned in the past.

"No need for a maid, Tony. Go join your guests. I will be down in a bit." She turned dismissively and returned to her room, closing the door behind her.

She heard him say, "Bernadette," and she turned the key in the lock.

Bernadette gathered all of her pride and tried to remember who she was. She had spent the last half hour crying in her room, but now, as she gazed at her reflection, dressed as she was in her black-and-white ensemble, black stockings and boots, she said aloud to herself, "You are the daughter of a multimillionaire, his only daughter and the apple of his eye. You will be making a triumphant return to Boston—after replenishing your wardrobe, of course. You will leave behind everything, including your husband, but you are taking his ring this time. He will come for you, or he won't. Walk tall—and to hell with the lot of them."

Bernadette almost lost her resolve when she entered the

drawing room to find her husband in conversation with a beautiful, tall, blonde Englishwoman, presumably Lady Villan, but her determination returned with the look of sheer shock on Arabella's face. And was that anger or embarrassment on her husband's face?

"I'm sorry. Am I late? Ah, I see the gang's all here." She then walked over to her Americans and kissed each one, even Michael O'Connor. She said nothing to the others, nor did she personally greet her husband, who was walking toward her, accompanied by the beautiful newcomer. He didn't look pleased, and Bernadette turned away from them as she retrieved a glass of sherry from Mr. Higgins, who was quite amused by his mistress's appearance, which served the lot of them right.

"My love, may I introduce you to Lady Georgiana Villan. Georgiana, my wife, Lady Bernadette Devereux."

The woman was quite beautiful and so elegantly attired that a stab of jealousy pierced Bernadette's heart. She looked over at Arabella, who was smirking, but Charlotte—was that a bruise on her cheek? Bertie and Jeremy were already half-pickled, but her father and Michael were completely sober, as was her husband.

Lady Villan said, "Very pleased to make your acquaintance, Lady Devereux. Tony has said such wonderful things about you."

Bernadette could feel her husband cringe when she responded, "Hi! Strange, since I have never heard of you. Were you childhood sweethearts?"

Lady Villan laughed nervously and said, "Heavens no. More like brother and sister, and he used to tease me mercilessly and call me names."

Bernadette said, "Such nice, sweet memories, I am sure. You both must have so much about which to reminisce. I daresay I will do the same thing when I return to Boston. I find I miss my family and all of my old friends. The people in Boston are so kind and welcoming. Have you ever been to the States, Lady Villan?

I was sorry to hear about your husband. Of course, I never met him, but the war has ruined so many lives. It has changed so many who did survive too. Excuse me."

Bernadette made to walk away to Join the American contingent, but her husband took her arm and led her outside into the great hall. "What are you doing, Bernadette? And what in God's name are you wearing? I will never allow you to go to Boston. No need to ask who put that idea in your head."

"Tony, you really should get back to your guests. It was you who put the idea in my head. Our first Christmas together in years, and you invite all of your hideous friends and relatives. You didn't even need to invite my family, but at least they are here for moral support, and I will be leaving with them after all. It is time I saw my home and spent time with my own family—what is left of it. This is not my home. If it were, all those dreadful people wouldn't be gathered here for Christmas dinner, and, Tony, this is all I have to wear. Remember—the shop girl who was abandoned by her husband and evicted from her own home by his mother. I have a few outdated dresses left, my wedding gown for one. Should I have worn that? I had to sell the others to buy a new outfit to wear to the train station, where you left me standing, but it is all crumpled since you allowed me to sleep in it. Please go join your guests. I will be back down in a little while."

He realized he should have known his mother would do this. Invite everyone. This was the last thing that he wanted. He and Bernadette needed to rebuild their relationship again after so many years of misunderstanding, deceit actually—created by his mother—so many years apart. He knew Bernadette meant it too. She would go to Boston. She was tired of the disrespect and rightfully so. She wanted to punish him. He knew she loved him, as he loved her. His mother used every opportunity and would stop at nothing to destroy that love and their marriage. He needed to talk to James Barrymore—alone. He currently had nothing to offer Bernadette other than her own dowry, which he planned to use to become the successful breeder of thoroughbreds that he once was. He was certainly up to the challenge, but he needed to reassure his father-in-law that this travesty of a family gathering would not be happening again in the future, never again to his beloved wife. But first—Bernadette.

He told Higgins that dinner would be delayed for half an hour and to keep supplying the assembled guests with drinks. Bernadette had gone back upstairs, and he followed her. She had locked her door, and he knocked, "Please let me in, Bernadette."

She opened the door, and he could tell she had been crying. "I am glad I brought my black tie, especially since I don't own any jewelry except my ring."

Tony answered, "Bernadette, what are you talking about? You make me sound like a miser. I gave you many pretty things when we were first married. Where are they? Did you sell those too?"

"No, Tony. Your mother stole them. Just like she stole my letters, our wedding photographs—my God, Tony, she even stole your red socks, and I put so much effort into them. Anyway, who cares? Is that your mistress downstairs, the one you were having an affair with when I was working as a shop girl?"

Tony finally understood, somewhat at least, what the people downstairs had done to his wife and what he himself had done. She had spent the war years alone in a strange country, and her only friend was a girl she worked beside, who showed her such friendship that she was never given by any one of his guests enjoying his hospitality on Christmas Day.

Bernadette was staring at him—awaiting a denial of her accusation of Georgiana being his mistress. Surely she already knew that such a thing was ridiculous. He suddenly felt tired and wished they had remained in London. He put his arms out, and she ran into them.

"Tell me the truth, Tony." She was crying.

"Okay," he said. "The truth is that I am wondering if they would miss us if I just told Higgins to serve dinner without us."

Bernadette looked up at him, and he dried her eyes. "Bernadette, you are the love of my life, which is why I have left our guests to become inebriated, awaiting their roast goose and plum pudding, and our cook to become exasperated keeping everything from spoiling. What is all of this nonsense about Georgiana?" He led her to her mirror and said, "My love, what do you see?"

Bernadette was quite pleased that her husband had left his guests to comfort her but answered, "A tall, handsome aristocrat with black hair and beautiful blue eyes, very suave and debonair and extremely confident."

He laughed and said, "I'll accept that description. What about the other one in the mirror—the woman?"

"An average-sized woman with an average figure and an average face and way too much hair … on her head, I mean. She doesn't have any facial hair. Well, I suppose that's something at least."

He was laughing, and Bernadette, beginning to feel much better, was trying to hide her smile. "There they are, those dimples. Now the truth, Bernadette, since there is nothing average about the woman in the mirror, and you know it."

"Okay then, you asked for it. I see a truly magnificent woman who is just the right size for a man to put his arms around—not too tall, not too short. Let me see. Oh yes, beautiful chestnut-brown hair that is soft and curly and that some men admire. She also has lovely eyes, the right sort of nose, an ample bosom, dimples—and no nice clothes to wear to her mean but handsome husband's Christmas party, with his ghastly family and obnoxious friends, which includes a too tall, too thin, and too blond, blue-eyed lady in a very fashionable gown."

He burst into laughter. "Now, that is more like it, Bernadette.

Modesty never did suit you very well. Shall I tell you what I see? Other than a suave and debonair man, that is?"

Bernadette smiled with those dimples he loved, awaiting her description by the man she adored.

"The most beautiful girl I have ever seen. Upon first sight, a girl who disturbed my inner soul so that I have never recovered from it. Her complexion is creamy white but with a lovely golden glow. Her almond-shaped brown eyes can easily make the most confident of men tongue-tied. Her hair? A man could lose himself in the softness and fullness of it. What else? Ah, a little button nose that sticks up in the air when she is in a mood, full lips that are so soft to kiss, and a smile that reveals those wonderful dimples and beautiful white teeth."

He stopped, and Bernadette was enjoying this so—especially after her humiliating entrance into the Christmas gathering downstairs. She said, "And …"

Tony laughed again. "Naughty girl. I wonder, what she can mean? Oh, I think I understand. She has the body of a goddess, a temptress with beautiful, expressive hands, perfect arms. Let me see what else. Oh yes, her legs are lovely, her toes adorable."

Bernadette was by now merrily giggling as she said, "And …"

Tony feigned confusion. "Very naughty girl. Again I wonder what she means. Did I forget to mention perfect breasts and a delightfully round bottom, accentuated by a tiny waist? Do I need to go further, your ladyship? Well, I can but say a husband that is so proud to be the only man to know all of these delightful secret attributes, since the rest of the men in the world are denied the privilege she grants him of having an intimate knowledge of all of these details about his adored wife."

Bernadette hugged her husband happily and said, "Okay, I will go back downstairs, and you may come to Boston with me. I think you probably should. I am unsure if I want to leave you with Lady La-dee-dah!"

Tony said, "Possibly I will go ... downstairs, I mean. But first ..." He led her over to the bed.

A short while later, Tony was helping his adored wife into the dress she put on the first morning they awakened together back in 1912. He let down her hair and produced the item he had taken out of the family vault on Christmas Eve. "I was saving this as a surprise for a very special occasion. And my darling, what better occasion than the renewal of our marriage."

Bernadette was entranced. "A diamond tiara with emeralds that match my ring! Tony, help me put it on. Lady La-dee-da can be as jealous as she likes. And my gown isn't so old-fashioned, is it?"

Tony said, "My beloved wife, I have no idea whether it is old-fashioned, but tonight you look like a princess. I think I like this look better than the maître d' impression you did earlier."

They kissed again and then, hand in hand, walked down to join their guests, and Tony thoughtfully asked, "Do you really wear rouge?"

Bernadette, appalled, asked, "Who said that? Don't answer me. I already know. Your mother!"

❧

A grateful Mr. Higgins was about to call the guests into dinner when his lordship and her ladyship finally came downstairs. It was easily noted by him and all of the others—the transformation, not only in Lady Devereux's mode of attire but also in her countenance. She was glowing, and Lord Devereux was smiling and relaxed.

James Barrymore shouted that he was about to go down to the kitchen and fetch dinner himself, and the others laughed good-naturedly; after all, it was Christmas. All except Arabella, who could easily surmise—as could the others—that the couple had settled their differences, indeed to the point of making love. It seemed to her that the bricklayer's daughter suddenly had the advantage, and the unexpected appearance of Georgiana was not having the desired effect on her son that she had planned. However, it was early days yet, and she was never a woman to be so easily outwitted.

Bernadette felt happy, and her confidence was growing. Tony loved her and abandoned his horrid guests to prove that to her. She said, "Mr. Higgins, may I inspect the dining room before you call the guests in to eat? I have to apologize for the delay."

Bernadette praised the beauty of the table setting. "Mr. Higgins, you and the servants have created the most beautiful table that I have ever seen—in England or in Boston. I can't imagine a friendlier welcome home. However, who arranged the seating? Would I be correct in supposing it was the dowager viscountess?"

Higgins confirmed this fact and was quite pleased when Bernadette started switching all the place cards around. "There, that's better," she declared, and Higgins heartily agreed. She placed her father at the other end of the table from Tony, since she always sat beside her husband in the past and desired to continue to do so. She placed her mother across from her and Arabella and Georgiana on either side of her father. Everyone else was somewhere in between.

James Barrymore made the sign of the cross and said the blessing, and Bernadette had to stifle a giggle at Arabella's expression of complete contempt. Dinner was served and eaten. All seven courses, none of which included roast goose, and every course was one of Bernadette's very favorites—from oysters on the half shell and lobster bisque to langoustines and lemon sole. Then onto roast turkey with cranberry sauce and oyster stuffing and brussels sprouts. Finally, there was vanilla ice cream and the strawberry sauce Cook had made the previous summer.

Bernadette exclaimed, "How did you manage to plan all this, Tony? In just one week?"

Tony responded, "The praise belongs to our cook, Mrs. Bobbing, and Daphne, the kitchen maid. All I asked was that they made all your favorites since all who love you know how much you enjoy your food."

James Barrymore stated proudly, "And still keeps her girlish figure. Can't say the same for her father, girlish or otherwise!"

All laughed, except Arabella, of course, and Tony responded, "Indeed, sir, I have no idea where she puts it all. The loveliest girl in the world—from her curly head to her dainty toes."

By now, Bernadette was bright red and told them to please stop it. She knew they were saying this to aggravate Arabella, who had done nothing but insult and belittle her daughter-in-law for the past four years at least.

After dinner, there was to be carol singing, followed by dancing, and Tony had hired a ragtime band to play the latest tunes. The servants joined in, and per tradition, Lord and Lady Devereux danced the first dance with Mrs. O'Leary and Mr. Higgins.

In the end, Bernadette so enjoyed herself that she forgot about her sour-faced mother-in-law. Even her mother was dancing, and Michael and Georgiana danced several times together. Cecil Fallsington and his wife mostly sat out every dance; however, when Tony got Marjorie Fallsington up to dance, Tony mentally noted that Cecil, the best man at his wedding, never bothered to ask Bernadette. He decided to have a word with him about that.

Bernadette didn't care one bit. She was dancing with Bertie, who was visibly drunk, and she was laughing at his antics, especially when he said to her, "You know, Veronica, you're not such a bad egg after all."

Bernadette responded, "It's Bernadette, but I thank you

for saying so, Uncle Bertie. May I call you Uncle? And who is Veronica?"

"Be damned offended if you don't. Pardon my language. I have no idea. Is she a friend of yours?"

Tony found it almost difficult to imagine. A couple of weeks ago, he thought he had lost his beloved Bernadette. He couldn't remember having such a grand time, and Bernadette's devotion to him was evident to all. He had already spoken to James Barrymore, and they were to have a private meeting the following morning.

James Barrymore danced one time with the dowager viscountess, the only man who did so, most notably since her son did not. He deduced that much of what he had been told about Devereux was designed to break his daughter and him apart. He had been fed a pack of lies and told Arabella so, quite threateningly, while they were dancing. Now watching his beloved daughter's happiness, he felt ashamed about the whole thing. His daughter was clearly very much in love, and for all his faults, Devereux seemed just as smitten—even after four years of fighting, almost three of which his mother had worked diligently to demean and dishonor his wife.

The evening finally came to an end, and all were exhausted. The Fallsingtons were to stay overnight due to the distance involved to travel. And Bertie was staying over too, having passed out. He required the assistance of both his nephew and Michael O'Connor to get him upstairs and throw him on top of the bed.

CHAPTER 10

It turned out to be such a wonderful Christmas Day that Bernadette changed her mind about going to Boston when her parents returned there. Tony could never leave so soon, and the ship sailed on the twenty-eighth. How could she be ready by then? How could she bear to leave her husband so soon? And to spend New Year's Eve aboard ship—without him?

She was sure he wouldn't allow her to leave him anyway, and as she finished up her breakfast at ten o'clock, she wondered what Margaret was doing. She had so much to share with her. Had the war not ended when it did, Bernadette would be at work that day, cleaning up her department and getting ready for the after-Christmas sales, which would begin the following day. Instead, here she was, back again as mistress of Devereux House. However, there was no sign of Tony, and she had hoped they would wake up together, just like the old days. He had a restless sleep, tossing and turning. She thought, *I suppose he was dreaming about the trenches. He has only been home a week, and I am loathed to ask him about it, although I suppose I must—especially with regard to his injury.*

Bernadette stretched lazily and finally got out of bed. She looked out the window, hoping it would snow, but couldn't quite believe her eyes. Her husband and Georgiana Villan were riding off together in the distance. Confused that he would do such a thing without inviting her or at the very least coming up to wish her a good morning, Bernadette decided to look out her riding apparel and join them; but although she searched, there was no sign of it. "His mother took my riding outfit and boots, the old witch. I know she did," she said aloud.

Bernadette then began to search through her wardrobe and armoire. Those few dresses were still there, the ones she left behind when she came with Margaret that day, but all of her other things were gone. She already knew about the jewelry, but she hadn't looked any further that day in her hurry to leave. All of her pretty negligées were gone. *My God,* she thought, *my blooming underwear? My wraps, my velvet cape, my shoes and riding boots—oh my God, the books I left behind, my crucifix and rosary beads. How could I not have noticed this yesterday?*

Bernadette rang for Mrs. O'Leary. She was in a temper she was finding difficult to control. She also ran to get her mother and father. Change of plans—she was indeed leaving. Lord Anthony Devereux was undoubtedly very charming and romantic, but he was also either a liar or a fortune hunter—perhaps both.

Her drawers and wardrobe doors were all wide open when Mrs. O'Leary was first to appear.

"Mrs. O'Leary, what happened to my things? My clothes, my personal belongings? What did the old witch do with them?"

By then, Mr. and Mrs. Barrymore had appeared, and Bernadette locked the door behind them. They both stared at the empty armoire and wardrobe.

James Barrymore said, "Where are all of your clothes, Bernadette? Have you been clearing out? Making room for the latest fashions?"

"No, Daddy. It seems Tony's mother took everything I owned away, even my French rosary beads and the crucifix you gave me that was blessed by the pope."

They all looked toward Mrs. O'Leary, who shamefacedly

said, "I cannot tell a lie, although it grieves me to confess it." She seemed very upset, and Bernadette helped her to a chair.

"Do you remember the tallyman, your ladyship? He used to pass by, and we wondered how he could carry so much junk without anything falling off his cart. Well, one day, not long after you left, she told a maidservant to fetch him up to the house. It was Cathy, your ladyship. She has since left to be married. The rest of us stood appalled, but what could we say? What could we do? She sold all your belongings except the gowns you brought with you from London as a bride."

For once in his life, James Barrymore was almost speechless but managed to say, "Well, I hope the evil old witch got a fair price for it all. Perhaps my daughter should send her a bill!"

Mrs. O'Leary began to cry. "Oh, your ladyship, I canna hardly bear to tell you this. The tallyman couldn't believe his luck because she sold it all, everything that is, for a one-pound note."

The Barrymores were horrified, and Bernadette began to softly weep until her tears turned to sobs. How could anyone be so vindictive? To her only son's chosen wife?

James Barrymore had had his meeting early that morning with his son-in-law and approved his plans. Bernadette could go to Boston, and in the meantime, he would get his business back up and running and refurbish the entire living quarters of Devereux House. All for Bernadette, all because he loved her so very much, and the house as it stood held too many bad memories for his beloved wife.

The meeting had impressed Mr. Barrymore to the extent that he released further funds to his son-in-law, to buy the finest thoroughbreds to breed, modernize the stables, hire trainers and jockeys, and purchase a brand-new Rolls Royce. There was also plenty to furnish the whole downstairs and Bernadette's suite too, if she would like that—all brand-new, which was how James Barrymore preferred things to be.

"I don't know what to say," Tony responded. "I didn't expect all of this, and I feel guilty taking it. My mother, well, you know what she is—what she did. Sir, I love Bernadette more than my life, more than I even know how to express to you. She is my life, and I will make this the grandest home just for her, and I will once again become a top-notch and sought-after breeder, all for her. I will hold off on the car, however, until I can purchase it with the money I have earned myself. The old girl still runs like a dream anyway."

They shook hands, and Tony happily went out to inspect the horses. He had much to do and was anxious to get started— inventory, for one thing. He was thoughtfully saddling up for a tour around his estate before he spotted Lady Georgiana Villan coming toward him—the last thing he needed on such a fine morning.

She said, "I was hoping to catch you. I was hoping you would take me riding around the estate. I see Lady Devereux has not joined you. I am sure she is quite exhausted this morning. According to your mother, she has spent long hours working in London while you were in France."

This statement embarrassed him, and he allowed her to mount one of his remaining mares while looking up at the house, hoping that Bernadette was still in bed or, at the very least, not looking out of the window.

It occurred to Bernadette that she had nothing to wear other than the few things she had brought with her. Her new skirt and blouse had been taken away to be laundered, and Mrs. O'Leary went to check on them. She decided she wanted to leave that very day and said, "I suppose I will need to wear my black skirt and white shirt that I purchased in menswear. Thank goodness you brought me some new underclothing, Mommy."

Bernadette had calmed down by now, but her father was livid, especially after his meeting that morning. However, he said, "Wouldn't you like to confront them this evening at dinner? We shall invite the dowager and Lady what's-her-name to dinner, I think, and we will leave for London directly afterward. I will have Michael arrange transportation. The taxi will be waiting for us, and for such a nice fare, it will be easily done. The ship sails on the twenty-eighth, and we can board the day before, tomorrow after you have done some shopping and bought yourself some new clothes to wear on the voyage."

Eugenie was also outraged! She was always the quiet, refined family member, but this was too much even for her to take in. "We will go to Selfridges; no need for you to run into everyone you worked beside in Harrods. We will need to move quickly. I don't want that man to find you until you are safe aboard the ship. Hell mend him! Treating my daughter in such a manner! I prayed for him throughout that terrible war; however, I am removing his name from my daily prayers forthwith!"

This declaration cheered Bernadette ever so slightly, since never before—or at least that she was aware of—had her mother banished anyone from her daily prayers.

James Barrymore was amused by the statement too, although he knew that Devereux would be shattered by his wife taking off for Boston without a word of goodbye, which was her intention. It was now up to him to make a success of his life. He had given him the means to do so, and he expected that one day in the not too distant future, he would arrive at their doorstep to take his lovely Bernadette back.

Mr. Barrymore knew that Lord Devereux would be shocked by the opulence and grandeur of the Barrymore home—the home where Bernadette had spent her youth. "Well," he said to himself, "all this remains to be seen since first we have to get her aboard the ship!"

There was very little for her parents to pack, and Bernadette had nothing at all to take with her—most especially since she decided that she would be leaving behind the fur coat and perfume that her husband gave her for Christmas, and he could also keep his tiara. *New wedding day indeed.* Tomorrow she would go shopping in London, and it now seemed that she would be boarding the ship the very same day. She was no longer going to put up with this family's disrespectful behavior, and again she thought, *What if I had not appeared at the train station that night? Would he have found me?*

Everything was moving so fast, almost all of it beyond her control, and she felt so sad and disappointed. She allowed her father to lead the way and take control, as he had always done when she was a girl. She knew he only wanted what was best for her, and she felt uncertain about what her husband wanted. She kept visualizing Tony and Lady Villan together—how he would tell her about Bernadette's father's money and how they would be laughing at the idea of her being addressed as your ladyship. She further tortured herself by imagining them making love together. An old folly was situated in the direction they had taken that morning. Perhaps that was where they were going. Perhaps his restless sleep the previous night was about Georgiana and not the war after all.

She wondered how well she really knew her husband. The war had irreparably changed lives, even for those whose loved ones had miraculously survived. Tony was romantic and full of fun when they first met and married. She hardly knew him, although she knew she would love him all her life. However, he had changed. He had gone through so much, seen so much, and suffered far too much ever to be the same carefree man she married. In her love for him, she would have endured and hoped that in time the agonizing thoughts and dreams would—if not pass—lessen at least to the extent that they could live out their lives happily together.

These thoughts brought her mind around to children. She had conceived only once and had lost that child. Perhaps that was another matter of great concern to a man who could trace his family back four hundred years. However, even wondering about all of this, she knew she would never sign an annulment. There was enough of James Barrymore inside his daughter for her never to want her husband to find happiness or peace with another woman. As for her, she would never want another man. Of that much, she was certain.

❧

Bernadette was wearing her only skirt and blouse, which by now she was quite sick of, when she watched Tony return, this time with the Fallsingtons as well as Lady Villan in tow. They were laughing, and Bernadette thought that her husband looked quite jolly. She had almost forgotten about the Fallsingtons, whom she very much disliked. Marjorie Fallsington was quite overweight, and they were childless too. Her husband didn't appear to be very loving toward her. Still, Bernadette understood Marjorie's father to be an earl, so that must have made up for her less than appealing appearance—quite a decent catch for Tony's nasty friend. Bernadette had run into her one day, a year ago in Harrods. They literally bumped into each other, and Marjorie Fallsington acted as if she had never seen Bernadette before. The floorwalker reprimanded Bernadette for not apologizing to the countess, and she had to hold back her tears. Absolute humiliation and not one of Bernadette's finest hours. She had cried in Margaret's arms that evening in her wretchedness.

Thoughts of Margaret decided Bernadette, and her parents were in complete agreement. She could be dropped off at Margaret's flat that night, especially since—should her husband come after her—he would never find her there.

Tony went immediately upstairs to get changed and to check on his wife, whom no one had seen that day. "My darling, the Fallsingtons are leaving tomorrow. I know you dislike them, but I can hardly throw them out today. Given that, I thought we might as well have my mother and Georgiana for dinner as well—even things out a bit."

Tony was afraid of his wife's reaction, but he was cornered into the invitation and was pleased albeit somewhat surprised when Bernadette agreed that there was little else to be done. She told him she had a dreadful headache but would rest a while before dinner and see him downstairs.

Somewhat confused, Tony left her to rest. He felt she was smiling a little too sweetly at him for someone with a "dreadful headache" who had just been informed that people she so disliked were staying to dinner. Then he thought, tomorrow they would all be gone, and he would tactfully deal with Georgiana, who was most certainly attempting to seduce him. Never had he been so happy to come upon the Fallsingtons—so much so that he asked them to join him and Georgiana on the tour of the estate.

Cecil had suggested a glass of ale at the local pub, and it felt like the whole town was there to welcome the squire home and thank him for his service. Major Devereux didn't enjoy the honor he was given that day. He felt disloyal and ashamed for even being there without his lovely wife.

Bernadette, although smiling sweetly at her husband, really wanted to slap his face. All of his loving and romantic behavior on Christmas Eve and Christmas Day—what was that really all about? Bernadette could tell that Georgiana Villan was making up to her husband, a lonely widow with nothing to lose. *Well,* she thought, *if he wants her, he can have her; I am done with all of it and all of them.*

Bernadette was dressed for dinner, wearing the same skirt and blouse that she had worn all day—not at all the done thing, really quite shocking! Eugenie Barrymore brushed her daughter's beautiful, waist-length hair and tied it back with a ribbon that matched her aquamarine skirt. Eugenie was such a gentle soul who was well aware that Bernadette was more like her father than her. Eugenie's heart was breaking for her daughter, who was wearing such a brave face. Bernadette was always very energetic and athletic in school sports. She excelled in every activity she set her mind upon, and Eugenie thought that possibly that was the reason that she remained so youthful and vibrant. Her daughter was still just twenty-four, and Eugenie's prayers now included a fervent desire for her Bernadette to find true happiness. The young girl's life had been turned upside down, as many lives had been during that dreadful war, but Bernadette should have spent those years at home with her family and those who loved, rather than hated her.

The Barrymores, Bernadette, and Michael O'Connor were

last to enter the drawing room for cocktails that were being served before dinner.

Bernadette was sure she heard one of the women snicker, no doubt at her appearance, but she ignored it. She would get all of them very nicely at dinner.

Tony immediately approached her. He had been talking to Georgiana Villan, and Bernadette was livid—or was it just heartbroken? He said, "I hope you are feeling better, my love." And then quietly, "Why didn't you change for dinner?" He, of course, was standing there in his white tie and cutaway. All the men were dressed like that; even her father and the ladies were wearing their best gowns.

Bernadette was well aware that she was done up as if she was about to pop off down the shops to pick up the evening's dinner but said, "I know. Oh dear, I will explain to you later." And then aloud, for all the room to hear, she said, "I am so sorry, Lady Villan, for disturbing your conversation with my husband. He is quite the lady's man. Please think nothing of his attentions toward you. Next week, it will be some other lucky woman."

The room went quiet, and even Tony was speechless until Georgiana said indignantly, "I beg your pardon?"

And just as Mr. Higgins was announcing a perfectly timed invitation to dinner, Bernadette took her father's proffered arm and said, "Oh, think nothing of it. Just a bit of friendly advice."

Bernadette had again switched around the seating. Her father was still sitting opposite Tony, but she and her mother were both at his side. Bernadette placed Georgiana and Arabella on either side of her husband.

Tony was seething. He knew his wife was up to something, and she was behaving very badly. She had worn her hair down that night with a pretty blue ribbon to match her skirt. She looked like a little girl seated at the adult table—a little girl with a vicious mouth. He asked, "My love, you have no wish to sit beside your husband this evening?"

Bernadette smiled at him with those dimples he loved and responded, "Well, dear, I thought your mother and her widow friend might enjoy your company this evening. Lady Villan, have you been enjoying my husband today? Reminiscing? He is so very handsome, and some would say most enjoyable too. For obvious reasons, I couldn't join you, although I am sure you were pleased about that anyway." She smiled sweetly, aware that Georgiana Villan was glaring at her. However, Bernadette had learned enough during her years in London to know that this woman was after her husband. She owed her no respect.

Tony fell into the trap she set for him, "What obvious reasons, my dear? Kindly enlighten us since I know you are an excellent horsewoman."

"Oh dear," she responded, looking straight at her arch-enemy, Arabella. "Didn't you know, beloved? Allow me to enlighten you. Actually to enlighten all of you extremely unpleasant people seated at my husband's table—except, of course, for the American contingent and Uncle Bertie." She stopped, and Uncle Bertie and her father burst into laughter, although her husband certainly didn't. She looked around at the faces, all of those faces that hated her for no other reason than she, the Irish bricklayer's daughter, dared to make Lord Anthony Devereux—a most eligible bachelor indeed—fall in love with her and marry her before they had time to sabotage the wedding; certainly as they had continued to sabotage their marriage.

"Well, my darling, you might want to ask your mother, but since we are all gathered together—"

Arabella interrupted her. "Bernadette, this behavior is outlandish and unacceptable at the dinner table. Tony, please put a stop to this."

Tony said, "Bernadette, I think that is quite enough. Can we talk about this later? Also, I think you owe Georgiana an apology as a guest in our home."

This was all Bernadette needed to hear, and she decided to put every one of them in their place before she left forever. "Apology? Really, Tony? To some old has-been trying to get my husband into bed with her? Oh, and to return to your question, your mother sold everything I owned to the tallyman for a one-pound note. These things included my riding apparel, my clothes, my rosary beads, and my crucifix that was blessed by the pope and which my father gave to me to keep me safe. She also sold all of my intimate apparel—you know what I mean, underwear, corsets, stockings, and my wedding night peignoir—all for a pound note!"

The table sat in shocked silence; no matter what they had felt about Lord Devereux's chosen wife, this was beyond comprehension.

Arabella shouted that she was lying, but Tony knew she wasn't. The ultimate humiliation for this sweet, young girl he had left behind to go to war. But what could he say?

"Bernadette, please calm down, and if this is true, my mother will be held accountable, I promise you." He stood up to go to his wife, and by now, everyone was standing, dinner having been ruined for them all.

But Bernadette put her hand up and shouted, "Stop! I have watched you all this day and long ago, and you dare to judge me, or my father who can buy and sell each of you, many times over? Charlotte, you're very quiet. Has your husband beaten you again? Such a shame to have to put up with that, especially since you have no gumption to do anything about it. Also, you, Marjorie, you do know your gawky husband married you for your money." She stopped and said in mock shock, "Oh dear, who am I to talk? My husband was so desperate for money that he married the Irish bricklayer's daughter!"

She started to cry as the enormity of what she had just done hit her. She had just burned her bridges, if indeed she had any, with her husband and his snotty family and friends. She said, "Daddy, can we please leave now?"

Tony wasn't sure whether to go to her or to let her leave, and his hesitation was his undoing. The taxi had been waiting for them, and Michael O'Connor and the driver loaded the luggage, none of which belonged to Bernadette. She kept her ring and thought, *If he wants it back, he can come to Boston to get it.*

The taxi drove off, and Tony, who had finally come to his senses, shouted after it, after Bernadette—the wife who was treated so badly, so disrespectfully by everyone, including her ungrateful husband.

Tony returned to where his guests were standing in the great hall, dinner having been thoroughly abandoned. Cecil poured him a large scotch and said, "Tony, it was bound to happen sooner or later. The girl might be a stunner but not the type of girl one marries. She showed her true colors tonight."

Tony Devereux was astounded. He had just lost his wife, and his idiot friend would dare to say such a thing to him. His instinct was to swing for him, but he had his own home truths to say before he did. "Really, Cecil, not the type one marries? Do you mean one should marry someone boring and rather plain who has money enough that a man can have his fun elsewhere? And, Mother, I will never call you that again. I knew you certainly weren't the nicest of women, but to give away Bernadette's every possession, even her most intimate apparel, to the rag and bone man. What type of evil is that? I could say more, but I am so disgusted at the lot of you who just cheerfully ruined my life. I want you all out of here now. I don't care if you have to walk. Uncle Bertie, you can stay. You are the only one who showed my wife any kindness."

To his amazement, Georgiana made to go to him with

words of comfort, but Tony Devereux disgustedly said to her, "Georgiana, I didn't want you when you were young and pretty. Why in God's name would I want you now? I am married to the loveliest girl in the world, who just left me, but I will win her back. In the meantime, none of you will ever be welcome in my home again."

He then grabbed a bottle of scotch, slammed out the front door, got into his car, and drove off, but not to follow the Barrymores; he knew he had much to do before he could ever face them again. He stopped the car eventually, took a swig from his bottle, and broke down in tears. He had only been home a week. How does one lose a wife within a few days of returning from a war in which one had spent four long years fighting? Watching young men get blown to pieces, watching others go mad and desert, only to be brought back and shot as cowards. And then there were those who survived disfigured to the extent that they could never lead a normal life, or who were limbless. So much sorrow, so much meaningless suffering, and for what? He had been blessed. He returned to a beautiful wife who still loved him and was not afraid to show it. He thought back to that first night he was home, when she silently undressed him and wrapped her naked body around him—so beautiful, so pure; Bernadette's love for him. Tony then thought of his mother. What type of woman would intercept her son's letters, letters of love that would have warmed him in the cold and desolate trenches where instead he felt abandoned and heartsick, crushed and forsaken?

He drank a considerable amount of the whisky and eventually, in his misery, fell into an uneasy sleep. When he awoke the following day, he realized it had been snowing. Possibly it had been snowing all night since the Silver Ghost was completely covered and was stuck in the snow. He was still wearing his cutaway and had no coat or boots. He attempted to start the engine, if for no other reason than to get some warmth, but the battery was completely dead. He had no blanket and no food—not even a pair of gloves—just a half-full bottle of scotch, which he took with him as he attempted to find his way back to the house in the falling snow.

Such heavy snow was unusual for Hampshire, and a search party was put together, which included Cecil Fallsington, Mr. Higgins, and an assortment of groomsmen and servants who were able and willing to help. They found the car first and cursed him for leaving it. However, it wasn't terribly long until Cecil called out, "I've found him!" Tony was clearly dazed and confused, a combination of the cold and the whisky, and Cecil helped his best friend to walk to the horse-driven sleigh they had unearthed for the enterprise.

Tony slurred his speech, but he managed to say, "You are supposed to be my best friend, yet you insulted my wife, and now she has left me. She has returned to Boston, and I cannot go on without her."

Cecil finally realized the folly of how he had treated and spoken about his best friend's wife. "I'm so sorry, Tony. Really I am. It is just that, well, wives don't normally look like that. Bernadette is a temptress. The type of woman men want but can't have, and well, look at Marjorie. I suppose I was jealous that you were the man that made Bernadette Barrymore blush that night so long ago, long before the war changed everything. You smiled at her, and I thought she bewitched you. I still think that she has, but that is no excuse. She'll come back, and when she does, I will …" He stopped speaking as he noticed that his friend, Lord Devereux, had passed out.

At first, everyone thought it was the whisky that did it, and it certainly played a part, but he had succumbed to the Spanish flu and was kept in bed for the next ten days. For the first few days, he was delirious and shouting for Bernadette. Arabella and Georgiana had stayed to care for him, and for a while, he thought

Georgiana was Bernadette, but eventually, he fully awakened, and his mind began to clear. He looked around him and saw his mother sitting with Georgiana, who was holding his hand. He pulled it away from her and asked, "Where is Bernadette?"

His mother responded, "I imagine she's in Boston by now. You must rest, Tony. We need to care for you and help you to regain your strength and get well. You came down with that dreadful flu, but Dr. Morris says you're over the worst. He will be here to see you shortly."

Tony's mind was clearing, and as he recalled those wonderful few nights of intimacy, he asked his mother, "Bernadette. Is she well? She didn't get this thing from me, did she? We were … well, for a little while."

Arabella was frustrated but not terribly surprised. She and Georgiana had just nursed her son for almost two weeks, and all he cared about was that wretched girl. "Tony darling, I have absolutely no idea. No one has heard from her. I imagine she is settling back into her life in Boston, where she belongs."

Tony tried to get out of bed but was still very weak. He said, "No, Mother. She belongs with me, but I have much to do first. Now, will you ladies please—"

Suddenly his door was opened, and there stood the one person he could talk to and trust. "Sergeant Walker? I don't believe it! When did you arrive?" He spoke while waving his hand at the women, a gesture for them to leave.

Sergeant Walker said, "Just plain Walker now, your lordship. I see you still do that thing with your hand."

Tony was grinning ear to ear. "Walker, as I live and breathe. All dressed up in a new suit. What thing?"

Walker responded, "You wave people away when you are through speaking with them. Well, at least I see you behave that way with the upper echelons as well, your lordship."

Tony laughed. "It's an upper-class thing, I suppose. We do it to make ourselves feel important. How the hell are you? Are all the men on their way home?"

Walker sat down beside his new master, and they chatted companionably until Walker suggested that he help his lordship to get washed, shaved, and dressed. "I've seen you look cleaner in the trenches!" The friendship between the two men was unmistakable, and Tony laughed and did exactly as suggested by his old friend and new valet.

Lady Devereux stood to take her leave and to allow the men to get on with it. Her son was ignoring her anyway, and as she closed the door behind them, she said to Lady Villan, "I'm afraid Lord Devereux has developed somewhat of a penchant for the lower orders, my dear. I am sorry to say it but feel it my duty to warn you that you are wasting your time."

A freshened-up Lord Devereux suddenly remembered, "Walker, your wife, Margaret—quite remarkable, and I never had a chance to tell Bernadette before she left me. They were best friends, working together throughout the war—well, the last two years of it. Where is your wife? We need to get you properly housed. Bernadette may have left me, but I will be bringing her back. It's a long story—but goodness, she will be shocked and absolutely delighted to know this!"

Walker answered dryly, "Your lordship, I have no doubt that she is delighted, but I doubt if she is shocked. I haven't actually seen my wife. I arrived home, after four years fighting in the trenches, to a hastily written note stating that she was on her way to Boston with her ladyship. After working such long hours while I was in France, she felt she deserved a break away. Let me see. Oh yes. She has accepted a position as Lady Devereux's lady's maid, compensation yet to be decided upon. The actual employment will not commence until that—and I am quoting— nasty snob comes to fetch his beautiful wife—not that he deserves her, mind you!"

Tony was laughing happily. "Well, Margaret is right. I don't deserve Bernadette. I have been a dreadful husband—all to be rectified. Much to do, Walker. I am fetching her back to England in May, before her birthday in June. Our birthdays are just a day apart. I will take you with me to fetch Margaret. Meanwhile, you will need to get your own house in order. There is a cottage you might like—very rustic and that sort of thing. Of course, I'll need to have it painted and spruced up a bit."

Lord Devereux was happy, even though it would be at least four months until he saw his beloved wife again. He decided he would give her no choice in the matter. He was bringing her home—in handcuffs if necessary. In the meantime, he wouldn't write—as she hadn't written to him. He knew through Walker that she had not contracted the flu, that she was fit and healthy, and that would be how he would get news of her in the months to come, through his valet's letters to and from his wife.

CHAPTER 11

"I think he was glad to see me gone, Margaret. And that ghastly Lady Georgiana Villan; she made no secret of it. She was after him. Perhaps he prefers tall, blonde, posh women past their prime."

Margaret was laughing as she read out Tommy's letter. "Oh nasty ... nasty. Then why did he marry a not-so-tall, brown-haired, Irish American beauty, Bernadette?"

"For my daddy's money!"

"Oh yes, I forgot about that part. Well, be that as it may, Lady Villan has left empty-handed—and the house has been turned upside down. His lordship has been buying horses, and the stables will be spectacular. Oh dear. He had Spanish flu but has recovered and is building up his muscles every day, with the laborers building the new stables and with the groomsmen looking after the horses. He is ready to breed in the spring—horses, that is, before you start again. Why not write him, Bernadette?"

"Because I refuse to write. Ask Tommy if his lordship gets many visitors, such as women and the like."

Margaret was exasperated. "Bernadette, you honestly think Tommy won't see through that question? And the like? The likes of what?"

Bernadette said, "Okay. Just ask who has visited his lordship."

Margaret responded, "Now, Bernadette, why would I ask *who*. I will say, 'Does his lordship get many visitors?' How's that?"

Bernadette jumped up. "Fine. Now let's get ready for the party. Make sure you mention we go to lots of parties, and there are too many handsome men there to count."

Margaret mumbled, "Sure thing, Bernadette, but where have they all been hiding themselves then?"

❧⁓◗€⌒↻

Bernadette had appeared at a very surprised Margaret Walker's flat at 10:00 p.m. on Boxing Day. She was crying and telling Margaret that she had made a fool of herself and burned her bridges, and now she had to return to Boston the very next day.

"Oh, Margaret, I wish you could come with me. I suppose you are looking forward to Tommy coming home now."

She spoke hesitantly, hoping that in reality, Margaret would regard the chance to go to America as too good to pass up—even for a husband who had been gone so many years.

Margaret had been bursting to tell her friend the amazing news she had just received in a letter from her husband.

Bernadette stopped crying and said in amazement, "Tommy was Tony's batman? That means Tommy is going to be his valet, and that was what we dreamed of, Margaret! I can't quite take it in! But I have spoiled everything now, and he hates me—Tony that is, not Tommy, unless Tony has told him terrible things about me!"

Margaret laughed and said, "I doubt that, Bernadette, with regard to either man. How could any man hate you? And the way Tony came into Harrods on Christmas Eve—so romantic. This is a bump in the road, and I am not going to Devereux House without you, especially with that mother of his. I'm coming to Boston! Yes! Why not? I will need to write Tommy a note, and

I'll leave it on the bed. I can wear my new outfit we bought in Selfridges. Where is your suitcase, Bernadette?"

"Oh, the old witch gave all my things to the tallyman for a pound note. We are going shopping tomorrow and then to board the ship before Tony comes after me. I doubt if he will, but if he does, I will ignore him. We must buy lots of clothes—which Daddy will pay for. He will also pick up our wages, and then we will take the train to Southampton."

All of this was well accomplished, and Mr. Barrymore went to fetch the girls' wages. He was not surprised how little his daughter earned during her two years of employment, but he was surprised she stuck it out, for she had no need to do so. It showed a strength of character that Bernadette rarely displayed to others. He was somewhat concerned that Devereux didn't come after his wife and hoped he was finally getting his head in gear and putting his plans into motion. The war had played havoc in young men's lives—the ones who survived—and there was no doubting that his son-in-law was a hero, although he didn't expect he would ever say that to his face, not until he made things right for his daughter at any rate.

Bernadette had strained her eyes, looking out from the ship for the one face she loved with all of her sad heart. Perhaps he was there and she couldn't see him. No—she knew he wasn't there. After waving merrily along with the other passengers, many of whom were soldiers returning to their families in the States, she ran into the stateroom she was sharing with Margaret and cried her eyes out. Margaret said, "If I had a pound note for every time you have cried over that man or his family, I would be a wealthy woman. Bernadette, he loves you. I promise you. You will be together again. After all, where else am I going to find a job as a lady's maid?"

Margaret often cheered Bernadette with her stoic observations. And Bernadette cheered Margaret with her cheeky remarks and dramatic nonsense. The Barrymores were thrilled that Margaret came with them—such a charming Irish girl, and she had taken such good care of their daughter during her two years in London.

Bernadette hadn't been home in over six years. She was as much a part of life in London as in her past life in Boston, but they weren't sure about her life in Hampshire since they had only witnessed it as their daughter's life appeared to fall apart. However, regardless, Eugenie Barrymore allowed Lord Devereux back into her prayers—for the sake of her daughter, because she loved the man so very much.

The Barrymore residence was immense and magnificent, located on the outskirts of Boston and surrounded by a vast park with a stream and a small man-made lake. It was a beautiful, snowy landscape, like a Christmas card, and it was still snowing since it was just early January. Bernadette told Margaret that it always snowed in Boston, and she had missed that very much in London. Meanwhile, Margaret was more looking forward to the spring and said a silent prayer to Our Lady that she would be there to see the spring and even the summer, since she had never seen such a beautiful house and grounds and was in no hurry to return to England.

Margaret was wide-eyed when they went in the front door. They were greeted by a kindly housekeeper, who gave Bernadette a big hug and Margaret a wary eye, but no butler. And the housekeeper, Mrs. O'Hare, seemed to be the one in charge of the household staff. Margaret heard so many Irish accents that she couldn't help but exclaim, "Everyone is Irish! I heard it to be true but could never have dreamt it!"

Mrs. O'Hare softened. "Ah, Bernadette! Your wee friend is Irish. I expected her to be English like your husband. Welcome! Margaret, is it?" She didn't expect an answer and gave Margaret a welcoming embrace.

Bernadette took Margaret by the hand, and they ran upstairs together. And then Bernadette opened the door of her old bedroom, which looked freshly painted, and it was just so beautiful that both young women threw themselves on the four-poster bed. They were girls again. They felt it and said it—but not shop girls, just girls on a brand-new adventure. Margaret said, "My God, Bernadette, your home makes Devereux House look downright dowdy, just like the dowager. Wait till our husbands see this place!"

Bernadette said, "Do you really think they will come?"

Margaret responded, "Yes, but hopefully not till summer. I don't think I ever want to leave!"

Bernadette realized what she once took for granted was outrageously rich and resplendent and beautiful beyond belief. Yet she remembered the magazines she used to cut up to pin pictures on the walls of her tiny bedroom in Knightsbridge, and she became quite nostalgic. Still, it would be fun to spoil Margaret, who never had much. Her father got crushed by falling boulders on a building site in Liverpool, and her mother had died young, having had to make her way after that, taking in laundry and cleaning houses. She had three brothers, but they were all in California. At one time, Margaret thought she would follow them there, but her destiny took a different twist of fate. It seemed she was meant to look after her magical friend and that it would be a job for life—a job she would gladly do for food and board alone if it was ever asked of her.

Eugenie finally appeared with Mrs. O'Hare, who was carrying

a tray laden with sandwiches and cakes, and as both girls tucked into it, Eugenie said, "You must be tired, girls. Margaret, I have had a room prepared for you. Would you like to come and see it? You may bring your sandwich. This is not Devereux House. We are much more relaxed."

Bernadette led Margaret a little bit down the hallway and opened the door of the guest room that Margaret was to occupy. Both girls were still eating their sandwiches, and Bernadette wanted to cry because she knew this was the family's very best guest room. The kindness of her parents to want to make her friend feel special was so very lovely. Margaret started to cry and then dropped a crumb and bent to pick it up, apologizing. "It is much too beautiful for me, Mrs. Barrymore! Really, it is. I'm no one special."

That remark softened the hearts of the other women standing there, and Mrs. Barrymore said, "Margaret, next to my daughter, you are the most special girl in the world to me, and you looked after her when others were so cruel. You are indeed a most important guest in my home."

Margaret was crying, Bernadette started crying too, and they knelt and embraced each other as Mrs. O'Hare relieved them of their unfinished sandwiches.

"Well," said Eugenie, "that's that. I will leave you two to freshen up before dinner. Tomorrow you can go skating at the pond. It is still quite frozen, and you'll be safe enough. Bernadette will teach you, Margaret. She is an excellent skater. Then, when you are ready, we will go shopping. Mr. Barrymore is planning a welcome-home party for Bernadette and a welcome party for you, Margaret. I need to see what you girls bought in such a hurry, but if it was what you wore aboard ship—well, new dresses are a necessity!"

125

And so the girls' lives began in Boston. In many ways, Bernadette felt that her marriage and life in England were all just a dream. Some of it was beautiful in those innocent days before the war, but most of it sad and lonely. But for Margaret, she could never have lasted there. Torpedoes or not, she would have had to come home. But Margaret had shown her another life, and it certainly had its funny moments. They stuck together like glue—both alone in England.

Bernadette knew that in order for her marriage to work, indeed, if that was Tony's true intention, there would need to be change, and she would need to change too. However, she would never entertain those who were rude and disrespectful to her. Tony could see them in London, or he could visit his mother in the dowager house. She felt it was good that he was coming to Boston to fetch her—if indeed that was his plan. She needed him to see where and what she came from and get off his high horse. Just a little bit, since Bernadette fell in love with his snooty, upper-class ways, but just enough to realize that she was every bit as good as him and his people. She thought about all of this but feared that when she saw him again, she might fall back into her old ways in her adoration of the man.

However, she put all that to the back of her mind. She was teaching Margaret to skate, and Margaret was slowly but surely getting there. Bernadette was athletic and skated so well, despite her years away, that others often stopped and watched her.

Bernadette was also teaching Margaret to dance in time for the party being held in their honor. Eugenie Devereux had treated the girls to beautiful new wardrobes, including gorgeous silk and satin negligees, which she said could be put away for later.

Margaret had been worried. "Bernadette, your mother, she is so very kind, but when our men come for us, won't I have to wear a black-and-white uniform again? As a lady's maid?"

Bernadette had thought about this too. "Margaret, you are

too much of a friend to me to wear any black-and-white uniform. Perhaps you can be more of a companion?"

Margaret answered, "Bernadette, old ladies have companions, not lovely young women."

"Okay, lady's maid it is but no uniforms. You have had enough years wearing uniforms, and when we are alone, I am still Bernadette, and since I have no friends over there, I will often be alone, except when I am with Tony, and you can call me Bernadette then too. Actually, just always call me Bernadette. To hell with them all."

Margaret was thoughtful. "I wish I could stay here forever. I don't think I love Tommy the way you love Tony. I would never have given this up for him. That much I know."

Bernadette chirped, "Well, perhaps they won't come!" But inside, she was worried. Margaret had married Tommy right before he went off to France. She only spent a few days with him. Perhaps it was selfish of her to show her friend this whole other world.

⁂

The days passed quickly. Nancy, James Jr's widow, was staying at the house with her three daughters, and everyone sat together for dinner. The oldest, Emma, was fifteen. Then there was Wendy at twelve and Nanette, just nine years old. The girls were a lot of fun, and Nancy was lovely, even if she did talk too much. She was still young since she was just eighteen, like Bernadette, when she married. Bernadette's brother Sean was still unmarried, and at thirty-four, Eugenie was skeptical that he would ever choose a bride. Bernadette quipped, "You should come to England, Sean. I can introduce you to a desperate widow, Lady Georgiana Villan, a tall, blue-eyed, blonde—the snob who was making up to my husband the last time I saw her."

Sean, who never took much to do with the family business, asked Bernadette, "So what's the story, sis? Are you separated or on some sabbatical? Mom told me your husband is very handsome and full of himself. Are you sure it was a good idea to leave him alone with all those English widows? I understand there is a significant number of them since the war."

James Barrymore told his son to hold his tongue, but by now, it was April 15, three and a half months had passed, and Bernadette had indeed started to worry about that same thing. Consequently, she ran off from the table crying, and Margaret went to follow her. However, Mr. Barrymore said to leave it to him.

He found her in the conservatory—one of her favorite haunts. He sat beside her and took her in his arms. "Oh, Daddy, I don't think he will come for me after all. I behaved too badly on Boxing Day. He believes me to be impolite and unrefined, just like his mother does, and that I am just a silly shop girl."

James Barrymore lifted his daughter's chin, looked into her beautiful eyes, and said, "You know, Bernadette, I often wonder how on earth I could have created such a beautiful child. And your husband thinks you are the most beautiful girl in the world. Possibly you are, since I have never seen a prettier lass. Here is the thing. I told him that what we encountered at his home was unacceptable, and, Bernadette, even you know that is true. I also told him to put his life in order, get back to work breeding those thoroughbreds he was once known for, and make that mausoleum he lives in worthy of my daughter as its mistress. He'll come, or he will call himself a failure."

"Oh, Daddy, I don't care if he's a failure. Anyway, he isn't a failure. He is a war hero. He served his country for four whole years."

"Then why did you leave, Bernadette? Since when have you ever listened to my advice? I gave up on the whole annulment nonsense, since I had only decided upon it due to the pack of lies his witch of a mother told me. I know he loves you. It was obvious to me. So why did you leave?"

Bernadette stopped crying as she remembered. "Because I deserve to be treated with respect, and I will no longer put up with the rudeness and cruelty of his family and friends. I told him so. I told all of them so. You are right. If he doesn't come—well, in the end, he decided I wasn't worth it."

"Oh, you're worth it all right, bonnie lass. Why don't you write to each other? You haven't done so, have you?"

"Because I refuse to do so, and anyway, Margaret always puts in a question or two from me, and so I find out things. But valets are very loyal and secretive, so what if it is all lies and Sean is right?"

James Barrymore stood up. "Sean? What the hell does he know about anything? What woman would put up with him and his drinking? Speaking of drinking, why don't you make your daddy and all of us one of your Bernadette gin specials? That man will come for you, or my name isn't James Barrymore."

Bernadette felt immensely better; after all, didn't her father know everything? Besides, Tommy Walker said in his last letter that his master was busy working all the time, and the only visitor was Cecil Fallsington, without his wife.

Margaret said, "Tommy wrote that his lordship has worked wonders with the house—not that Tommy knows what 'wonders' might mean. What taste does Tommy have in home furnishings?"

Bernadette said to Margaret, "Precisely. What if I don't like it?"

And Margaret responded, "Well, I am all for coming back to Boston if that is the case! More importantly, what if I don't fancy Tommy anymore? I have no recent photographs, and he won't be in uniform when they come."

Springtime brought parties galore, and neither woman was ever without dance partners. Bernadette's high school sweetheart, Brenden Connelly, was hanging around her too much, and Bernadette had to tell him to get lost, not that he listened. She secretly wished that Tony was there to see how popular she was.

There was to be a barn dance on June 7, Bernadette's birthday, in the old barn, and the gardeners and maids were preparing everything for the occasion. There were to be Irish fiddlers and Irish dancing and beer by the barrel. Bernadette and Margaret were to wear Kelly green dresses, which neither of them ever expected to wear again.

It was May 15, and Bernadette said her prayers that Tony would come in time. The idea of him at a barn dance was just too funny. It had been long enough now. She couldn't stand it any longer. He needed to come—and come soon.

Margaret seemed in no such hurry, and Bernadette was praying that Margaret would be happy once she saw Tommy again.

Of course, she couldn't possibly know that Margaret was quite relaxed about the matter because the men were already aboard ship and on their way to America. She had been sworn to secrecy, and who was she to spoil the surprise?

CHAPTER 12

"So what do you think of the old place, Mother? Do you think my wife will like it?"

"Isn't it rather modern? And all those beautiful pieces languishing in Walker's cottage? I swear you haven't got the brains you were born with."

"Well, Mother, I gave you your pick of the furniture and the dusty old draperies, and you are still residing in the dower house. Also, I left all of our ancestors on the walls. Now, remember you have promised to behave yourself when she comes. I don't intend to spend the rest of my life as a referee."

Lady Arabella Devereux had finally accepted the inevitable. She had no desire to reside in London, and for some unknown reason, her son was besotted with the girl. She had hoped the months apart would change his opinion of Bernadette, especially after her behavior the night she left. But then again, four years at war without correspondence didn't lessen his affection for her, nor did her insolence and Irish temper. She felt slightly sorry about selling the girl's belongings to the tallyman. That was so vindictive. Her son was correct about that. The letters were also a mistake. The Irish bricklayer's daughter would soon be back in residence as mistress of Devereux House, and Lady Arabella Devereux had made a spontaneous decision. She knew the address through her correspondence with her abhorrent father during the war. She hadn't sold the rosary beads or the crucifix. She had feared she might be cursed upon such an act. However, it seemed she was cursed anyway, so she packaged up her son's letters—there were a dozen or so, still unopened—the rosary beads and crucifix, and the missing wedding photographs and posted them off to Boston. She thought about including a note of some sort, but in the end, what could she say? She wasn't sorry, so why lie? She simply didn't want to lose the affection of her son, most especially since, remarkably, she hadn't as yet done so.

Arabella decided to tell her son what she had done. "I posted a package with your letters, the crucifix, and her rosary beads. There! I have met her halfway, and you should be pleased about that at least. I suppose she'll bring that other Irish girl—Walker's wife. He seems a decent enough chap—well-spoken at least—but I am quite certain his wife is entirely a different kettle of fish. Bernadette brought her here once, and the language—I can't even repeat it."

Tony responded, "Well, I know she referred to me as 'a nasty snob,' so I will take that into consideration when I decide upon her wages."

Then he grew somber. "Seriously, Mother, she looked after Bernadette when no one else did—not her mother-in-law, not even her husband. I owe her a debt of gratitude. We all do."

Arabella huffed and turned to leave, saying, "Fishwives!" on her way out the door.

Lord Devereux had been spending more time than usual

in London. At first, he stayed at his club in Pall Mall but had more recently been staying at Bernadette's flat. It turned out that Barrymore owned it—of course, he did—and the first time Tony went there, he had to clean the place and throw out old food and moldy bread. The bed was unmade from their last night together, actually only the second night he slept with her, and he reflected that since he returned from France, he had only slept with his wife three times. He counted how many times they made love and got to nine. Or was it ten? He smiled, thinking that soon he would hopefully lose count. He tidied her things, her simple black skirts and white blouses, and wondered what she was wearing now. Even her stockings were darned. She didn't have to live that way, and he wondered if he would ever truly understand his beautiful wife. That night, he slept holding her dressing gown in his arms. It still carried her scent, although ever so faintly, but in the morning, he changed and freshened the bed. Bernadette had one other set of clean white sheets and a blue candlewick bedspread. He was laughing at himself, utilizing the skills he learned in the army. "Chambermaid Devereux," he said aloud and then rang the bell at the flat next door.

An elderly woman answered the door. A man was standing behind her, presumably her husband. "Excuse me," he said. "I am sorry to disturb you. Do you know if there is a laundry service hereabouts? Perhaps, better yet, a charwoman? I can pay good wages for the service. By the way, I am Bernadette's husband, Lord Anthony Devereux."

They invited him in and introduced themselves as Mr. and Mrs. Parsley. They were a comical pair who talked simultaneously, and their tiny flat was crammed full of Victorian knickknacks. There wasn't a space on the walls, and Tony endeavored not to keep looking all around him while he spoke.

Mrs. Parsley offered him tea, and although he very much wanted to get out of the tiny flat that smelled of boiled cabbage, he knew that would be rude and unkind. So he braced himself and sat down to a "nice cup of tea."

Mr. Parsley said, "We didn't know she was married—introduced herself at first as Miss Barrymore. Then later, it was Bernadette, although she always gave us our proper due as Mr. and Mrs. Parsley. Do you say, Lord Devereux? Well, I never! Although the missus said, she had a touch of class about her."

Mr. Parsley asked, "Is Bernadette all right? She hasn't been here since Christmas. Is she back in Boston? Her family is there, you know. That explains why she never had a young man— her being so pretty. Were you here on Christmas Eve? Quite a commotion we heard. Still, as long as she is doing well. We will miss her chat and her fresh cream cakes. How we laughed. Both the butcher and the baker were after her. She charmed them with those dimples of hers and once or twice bought the pair of us a nice, juicy roast. Of course, we shared it with her and her little Irish friend, Margaret."

Tony enjoyed hearing about his wife in so charming a manner. Indeed she was lovely, inside and out, and it seemed that only his family and friends failed to see that—Uncle Bertie excepted.

The old woman took the soiled bedclothes from him and said she would have their cleaning lady give the flat a good going over. He paid the going rate, plus a little extra for their service and for saying such lovely things about his wife, and went on his way to the Houses of Parliament to take up his seat in the House of Lords.

Ireland had always been a continuing problem for the British government, and Prime Minister David Lloyd George had enough on his plate coming out of a war that caused so many deaths and so much misery. However, there was an uprising in January 1919 after Sinn Fein won a landslide victory and formed a breakaway government, declaring Irish independence. On the same day, they murdered two royal Irish constables, the RIC, in an ambush, and the violence was again escalating as it had so many times before. The Irish Question was on the parliamentary agenda almost every day, and it was necessary to send troops, the Black and Tans, to help bolster the RIC. However, this had very mixed results, with tales coming to the House of Commons of civil disobedience and reprisals from the Black and Tans, who were becoming infamous for their lack of discipline and attacks on civilians.

The whole thing was a disaster for Britain so soon after the war. Lord Devereux was well aware on what side of the fence James Barrymore would be seated and fervently hoped he was keeping his opinions and the news of the uprising away from Bernadette and her Irish friend.

After all, Bernadette was married to a member of the House of Lords, whether Barrymore liked it or not. As such, she couldn't be seen expressing opinions or support concerning the situation in Ireland.

At any rate, it was almost time to set sail, and he was taking two months off, away from his responsibilities. He had sufficient staff to look after everything from the horses to the newly refurbished house. The tradesmen he hired did a grand job. There wasn't much money about, most especially since not many could lay claim to having a multimillionaire as a father-in-law. Therefore, they were grateful for the work, as were the folks they hired to carry it out. None of this came cheap, and now and then, he had a twinge of conscience about how much money he was spending, but it was all for Bernadette, and he had just successfully mated his stallions with several of his newly acquired mares. The first of his foals would be born in eleven to twelve months. Bernadette would be here to assist him, and she was very good with horses, having known them all her life. Her father made her care for her horse and not just ride it, and from that first experience of doing so, she told Tony that she was often to be found mucking out in the stables.

It was finally time to set sail, and Lord Devereux and his valet, Walker, were equally excited by the prospect of seeing their wives. In addition, Tony was excited to see America and, in particular, Boston, where his Bernadette had grown up. He wanted to experience a little of what her life was like before the fateful cruise her parents took her on for her eighteenth birthday. She had just arrived at the Ritz. He remembered it so well. She turned toward him, and they locked eyes. He smiled at her, and she blushed. She smiled at him with those dimples that seemed to drive an arrow straight through his heart. He had long since given up trying to understand it. Moments like those can often be just a passing fancy, but this was no passing fancy, and he was desperate to hold her in his arms again and never let her go.

CHAPTER 13

James Barrymore called his daughter down to his study. A package from the dowager viscountess had just arrived, and he wanted to be with his daughter when she opened it, since he could trust that woman not one bit.

Bernadette was wide-eyed and asked her father to open it instead. "I very much doubt it is a birthday present," she said nervously.

Soon the contents were revealed, and Bernadette could feel her whole body shake and her teeth chatter. "Tony's letters," she said almost reverently as she touched them gently and held them to her face. "My wedding photographs, my rosary, and crucifix. She may have sold everything else for a pound, but she kept these. But, Daddy, I am almost afraid to read these letters and the agony they contain, yet I must."

She started to cry, and her father said, "Go you to your room. I'll have a maid bring you up a glass of brandy, and other than that, I will see you are not disturbed, not until you want or need any one of us. They will be difficult to read, but now you will know the truth."

It was Margaret who brought up the brandy. She said, "I heard. I will be in my room. Just call me when you are ready. I am avoiding your mother and Mrs. O'Hare; they are making pies for the barn dance, and somehow I got roped into it. I am going into hiding."

Bernadette smiled weakly, and Margaret left her to it. By now, she almost wished she had never received them, although was grateful that she did, and all unopened.

Without realizing that she was doing precisely the same thing as her husband several months ago, she put the letters in date order. They ranged from early 1916, and the last one was dated March 1918. She took a sip of her brandy and, before reading them, laid out her wedding photographs—the happiest day of her life. Everyone looked so young. It was not quite seven years ago, and she supposed a lot could change in seven years.

She kissed the photographs of Tony and then braced herself to begin reading his letters.

Early 2016, he had just been home on leave, and there was a sad joy to those first few letters. Bernadette couldn't think of another way to describe it. They were very intimate, and she was thankful that at least Arabella hadn't read them. He wrote that he was "so very grateful" for the love they shared, and she thought that was a strange thing to say since she always enjoyed his lovemaking and wasn't afraid to let him know this in no uncertain terms. She put that part down to the desolation and fear he must have felt on a daily basis in the squalor of the trenches.

Then the letters became so sad that she cried as she read each one. Tony was practically begging her to write to him and to send him a photograph. Really, that was all that was in those letters, and he was asking her if she stopped loving him. In one letter, he pleaded that she could at least pretend to love him a little and write him a few lines. Then he got angry at her. He accused her of finding another man, and Michael O'Connor's name came up. He told her there would be no annulment and that he would never sign it. He told her he knew she was in London, living, no doubt, the high life, awaiting her return to Boston.

Bernadette wondered how he could have ever forgiven his mother for keeping her letters from him. If anything, Tony needed hers even more than she needed his. He was living in hell, and he was hopeless.

She finished her glass of brandy and felt a little lightheaded. She had one more letter to read—the last one he wrote to her. She braced herself. She remembered her last letter to him, not exactly word for word but a lot of nonsense about blue blood and nastiness about what the English troops did in Ireland. Bernadette could recall that she wanted to find every reason she could to hate him, and yet she never could do so.

March 6, 1918

My lovely wife,

Bernadette, you are still that. There will be no annulment. I've thought about this. Not much else to do in the trenches—when you're not being shot at—thinking that is.

I don't know why you are working in Harrods. I saw you there, chatting with an RAF officer buying perfume for his wife. It was right before Christmas. You looked so lovely. You stood out from the rest of the girls. I wanted to approach you—remind you that you are still mine. I think I was afraid to do so. Fearful of what I'd see in your eyes. I'd been injured. It was nothing terrible, a few scars from shrapnel that I couldn't run away from fast enough. I wonder if you knew. My mother said she told you—but I wonder if she did.

You were smiling with those dimples I love so much, but your eyes were empty. Or perhaps

I've just imagined that because I wanted them to be empty—empty because you weren't smiling at me.

They say the war will soon be over. I won't write to you again. You probably don't read my letters anyway, or else how could you be so cruel? So heartless? You used to be so loving, so responsive when I made love to you. You said such beautiful things. What happened, Bernadette?

Anyway, I intend to survive. I have made that decision, and I know where you work. One night, I will follow you home to Daddy's flat, and then we shall see, because I will make you explain how my sweet girl became such a heartless woman.

Your obedient servant,
Tony Devereux (Lord and Major)

Tears were rolling down Bernadette's cheeks. The letter was short. It didn't say much, but it said enough, and finally, she knew. *He was coming for me.* Bernadette finally knew that from the last letter. She had questioned that so many times in her head. *What if I hadn't shown up at the train station? It was most likely shock I saw on his face as he stood there. The surprise that I was there. And he was so weary. I am happy he came to me that night and so grateful that Mr. Higgins gave him my letters. Now I have his. He needs to come for me now. It has been far too long already.*

Bernadette ran downstairs and encountered her father. "Daddy, you need to send Tony a telegram. He needs to leave tomorrow, today even. I wish he already had the telephone installed! Oh, I doubt it would work so far away anyway!"

James Barrymore knew that the men had just landed in New York. Tony had called him from the hotel they were staying in overnight. They were boarding the train at 5:00 a.m., and he expected them in Boston by noon. Margaret knew this. She also knew they would be wearing their uniforms because Tommy promised her, and she too was getting quite excited to be reunited with her husband finally. However, all had agreed that it was to be a surprise for Bernadette. The timing of the letters couldn't have been any better—whatever they said—and Mr. Barrymore couldn't help but laugh at the state his daughter was in.

"Okay, I will send him one in the morning. What shall I say?"

Bernadette said impatiently, "Oh! I don't know! Just tell him he must come!"

The family sat down to dinner, and Bernadette sat playing with her food. "Even if he leaves tomorrow—which he won't—he won't be here in time for our birthdays. I wish we lived in New York; that would be closer! Margaret, do you think Tony can play tennis? I wish I had asked you to mention that we had a tennis court. Do you think he can play? Maybe I should buy him tennis whites. I should have asked you to ask Tommy what size. I wonder if he will be shocked by my riding jodhpurs."

James Barrymore finished his dinner and announced his intention of finishing his wine on the terrace. "Daughter, I daresay you can solve these pressing issues when he finally gets here."

Bernadette was giving her nieces and Margaret riding lessons and suggested it for the next day. However, Margaret rolled her eyes and said they needed to finish the pies, so Bernadette told the girls she would teach them to do cartwheels in the morning. "And then after we go riding, we can have a game of tennis. I feel so restless!"

Margaret was enjoying her friend's prattle and mentioned, "Oh wait. I did tell Tommy about the tennis court. I also told him no one likes to play with you because you hit the ball too hard."

Bernadette was up very early the following day. She bathed in her newly installed shower, and although she still preferred a bath, the shower made it easier to wash her hair. She wondered if showers were yet available in England but doubted it.

She sat down after breakfast and started a letter to Tony, but her nieces soon appeared and reminded her about the cartwheels, so she changed into her jodhpurs for decency's sake and ran out to the front lawn with the girls. Emma and Nanette were the best, but poor Wendy was hopeless, and of course, Margaret was still getting stuck making pies with Eugenie and Nancy. Bernadette told Margaret that her mother would have preferred her for a daughter because she always reprimanded Bernadette for being too cheeky and disobedient. Margaret was delighted to be told such a thing since she was very fond of Eugenie. Mr. Barrymore scared her a little, but he doted on his daughter. Margaret looked up at the clock and thought, *They will be here within the hour.* She was excited too and had given a noncommittal answer when Bernadette had asked her earlier why she was wearing one of her very best dresses.

Bernadette and her nieces were running around doing cartwheels when suddenly Nanette stopped and shouted, "Look, Auntie Bernadette! Soldiers!"

Bernadette was almost afraid to turn around, in case she got disappointed, but then, didn't she think everyone had been acting strange the past few days?

And there he was, standing with Tommy in their uniforms—but Bernadette only saw Tony. He smiled broadly, and she realized that he must have been watching her doing stupid cartwheels, and as she ran to him, he just stood and watched her.

Her hair was, as usual, undone and flying behind her. She was wearing jodhpurs, and her blouse was half hanging out of them. She had rolled up her sleeves, and if Tony was concerned about how pleased she would be to see him, he had no need to be, as she ran into his arms and practically knocked him over in her exuberance.

Bernadette greeted Tommy briefly and told him that Margaret was in the kitchen with her mother. "They are baking pies for my birthday barn dance. Oh, Tony, your birthday barn dance too!"

Tommy ran off to find his wife, and Bernadette said, "I thought I would die if you didn't come soon. Tony, kiss me!"

He was laughing happily. "What—here? And what on earth were you doing?"

"Cartwheels!" She laughed and proceeded to do one just for him. "Do you want to try it?"

"No," he said, "I don't think so. I'd rather just kiss you."

And he did, and soon the girls were shouting, "Bernadette's kissing a soldier."

"My nieces," she said. "Come on. Follow me!"

She made to grab his suitcase, but he laughed and told her he could manage, and the girls shyly came to check him out. Bernadette said, "Curtsey to Lord Devereux, ladies," and they did, and he laughed again. She then took his hand and led him through the front door and upstairs to her bedroom, shouting, "Tony's very tired! We'll be down later!"

Tony was laughing at his wife's usual outlandish behavior.

She was once again the girl he married, and it seemed she had shaken off the war. *No wonder,* he thought. *This house is beyond belief.* He said, "Bernadette, I expected splendor, but your home is beyond comprehension to this Englishman. The grounds are magnificent too."

He seemed a bit bemused, and Bernadette said, "What about me, Tony? Am I magnificent and beyond comprehension to this Englishman?"

And he said, "First dimples, and I will tell you."

She pulled him over to her four-poster bed and threw herself down. "Tony, you look so handsome in your uniform. You may wear it to dinner. Are you hungry? Of course you are. I will shout downstairs. We don't use bells in Boston, or at least the Barrymores don't." And she ran to the top of the stairs and shouted, "His lordship is hungry. We will have lunch in my bedroom in one hour."

Tony heard a woman shout, "Yes, your ladyship. Is that what we are calling you now? What does his lordship require to drink? We just made fresh lemonade."

"Mrs. O'Hare, he will take that now. Just have one of the maids put it outside the door and knock."

Bernadette turned. "We don't have a butler either. Mrs. O'Hare is in charge, and all the maids are Irish. Daddy brought them over for a better life."

"Tony, do you remember the last time I saw you in your uniform?"

Bernadette was looking at him with her make-believe shy face, smiling with those dimples, and Tony was getting quite excited, knowing where this was heading. Then he noticed his letters. "I see you got them. Poor sad blighter, wasn't I?"

"No, Tony, they were sad, that's for sure. But they proved one thing I always worried about—at least the last one did."

He looked confused.

"Tony, I wondered if you would have looked for me if I wasn't at the station the night you returned. You looked at me and turned away. Now I know it was because you thought I had stopped loving you, but, Tony, I will never stop loving you, and you love me too, right?"

It was said as a question, and Tony responded, "Well, I did just sail across the Atlantic to get to you."

Bernadette said, "I wonder how Margaret and Tommy are getting along."

Tony said, "Who cares? Now, what about this uniform?"

Bernadette undressed her husband and then playfully undressed herself. It had been too long and not long enough that they were together. Tony was enjoying the show and said, "I hope this is something you didn't pick up during the war. Cooking is one thing. By the way, I met Mr. and Mrs. Parsley. I'm keeping the flat. I even cleaned up when I first went there, you untidy girl. We can go there together sometimes, just the two of us, to get away from everyone for a day or two. Eat fish and chips. That sort of thing."

Tony was nervous, and Bernadette could tell. "Lord Devereux, your wife is standing here almost naked, and you are drooling about fish suppers?"

She walked over to the bed, and he pulled her down, and other than the door being opened for lunch to be brought in, no one saw the Devereuxes until dinnertime.

❧

Tommy Walker felt a bit strange at first, sitting with the family, but he soon found that he fit in very nicely. There was a casual friendliness about the Barrymores that, even with all their wealth, they just behaved like ordinary folks. Margaret had filled him in on everything, and he could see why his lordship fell so hard for his lovely wife. Margaret was undoubtedly pretty, and he loved her so very much, but Bernadette positively lit up the table.

Dinner was good home cooking and delicious, and every time Tony opened his mouth to speak, Bernadette's nieces started giggling. Bernadette said, "Stop giggling at my husband, who will report you to the king of England, and then none of you can ever visit me there."

Nanette was the precocious nine-year-old, and she kept asking questions, such as "Do you wear a crown in England? Does Auntie Bernadette have to curtsey to you? Do you ride horses? Auntie Bernadette beats everyone at tennis. Did you bring tennis whites?"

Tony said, "So many questions, Nanette. I think you must take after your auntie. Yes, I always wear my crown, and your aunt curtsies every time I pass her in the hallway. As for riding, I am rather good at that, and I doubt your lovely auntie will ever beat me at tennis."

And so that first day and evening, the fun continued, and when James Barrymore asked Tony to speak with him over a glass of cognac, his manner was not at all unpleasant.

Bernadette was seated on the porch swing when Tony came out to join her, and she offered him a cool glass of lemonade, surprising him by including a dash of gin.

"Ah," he said. "More like it. Bernadette, your home is lovely, and so is your family. It makes me ashamed of how my lot treated you. Even my nieces are bland compared to yours. I have a lot to make up for, don't I? And I intend to, with you as the mistress of Devereux House, even if that involves cartwheels! Let's see. If you even come close to beating me at tennis, I might consider building you a tennis court. Don't you want to know what Daddy and I spoke about?"

Bernadette said, "Not really. Was he at least nice?"

Tony said proudly, "He thanked me for my service in the war and praised me for my courage and bravery. Oh, and he also thanked me for loving his Bernadette so much. He said I was the perfect man for you, and he didn't know why he didn't see that for so long. Then he laughed and said only his girl could have snagged a member of the English nobility before she was in the country for five minutes."

"I can't believe he said that!"

He laughed and continued, "Other than that, the usual stuff— business, the horses, and of course my mother. I reassured him on that point, and, Bernadette, I meant it. By the way …" He took the gin bottle and freshened both of their drinks. "Cecil made a surprising confession when I told him he was no longer welcome upon your return. Jealousy. I made you blush and not he—that very first evening at the Ritz. Well, of course, he is still a bona fide snob, like me, but I thought you might like that he said that, a little bit anyway."

Bernadette found she really didn't care about any of his family and friends, although she did ask about Uncle Bertie. All she knew was that Tony was here, and he would be here for two whole months, during which time she could show him how much fun life could be.

Bernadette's memories of London and of working in Harrods and even of her little flat were fading in her mind, and Tony tried not to notice it. She was happy here; of course, she was. He began to worry if, even after all he did, he and Devereux House were going to be enough for her.

Bernadette was awake early, and Tony awoke to her lovingly stroking the scars on his shoulder and face caused by the shrapnel.

"You never asked me about my battle scars, and I wondered why. Are they ugly?"

Bernadette responded, "Oh no. I find I love them very much, your battle wounds of survival, and the scar on your face makes you look like a handsome pirate—a very posh pirate but also a very handsome one. I think you are the most handsome man in the world, with the best body. Your chest has just the right amount of hair to make it manly, and you are not thin or fat. You have the best legs for riding britches and are especially admirable in riding boots. I like your hair too and your eyes—oh, I love your blue eyes. I'm also quite fond of your feet—most especially since I am the only woman, or at least I better be, who gets to see them. Well, unless we take a trip to the seashore."

Tony was enjoying all the compliments but said, "Why do I feel you are up to something, my love? All this praise might go to my head and make me even more arrogant than you say I am now."

"Impossible," she said, climbing on top of him. "You already are an absolute snob. However, you are my absolute snob, and, Tony, I love you so very much. I am the happiest girl alive to be married to you."

He said, "I'm glad you feel that way, my sweet Bernadette. I was a little afraid you wouldn't want to leave all of this for your boring old Englishman and his ramshackle house. But I have fixed it all up, just for you. Bernadette, I have to ask. I am so looking forward to my two months with you in Boston. We can restart our marriage like before the war, and we are so lucky to be still so much in love. However, how do you honestly feel about returning to England with your dull old husband? You are positively glowing, my love. You are so free, and I am so lucky to have the loveliest girl in the world sitting naked on top of me without any blushes."

Bernadette did indeed blush when he said this as she pulled the sheet up to cover her, but he pulled it away and pushed aside her mass of long curls. "No, my love, don't do that ... never do that. I love that you are so free—with me."

Bernadette saw the haunted look that still came once in a while into her beloved husband's eyes, and she so wanted to chase that away forever. He was right, she did love Boston and the freedom she felt being here, but it could never be anything without Tony. Life could never be anything without Tony.

"Tony, I have spent the last five months longing for you, yearning for you. And before that, four years doing the same thing! Yes, it is fun and relaxed here; of course, it is. And I wanted you to see that so that when we restart our life together again in England, we can recall these days and weeks. Every time I feel I hate your mother, I will remember that she doesn't understand what it truly is to be happy, and I will do my best to be kind. The same thing with your sister, Charlotte; I believe her husband is abusive. I am sure of it, and I will do something about that. I think your sister is wretched, which is why your nieces are so shy. My nieces lost their father just two years ago, but there is love all around them, so they flourish. I want to give you everything in my power to give because that is how much you mean to me."

Then she stopped and assumed a worried frown. "Tony, I worry too. What if I can't give you children, an heir? Your mother is convinced about that—that I can't. How will that be, Tony? If I can't? Will you then want an annulment? Give me a year or two, and then if nothing happens ..." And she started to cry.

Tony pulled her down into his arms. He had sometimes wondered about the same thing, so the answer was easy to say because he had thoroughly thought it out, and it was the truth. "I don't care, Bernadette—about heirs, I mean. I care about my life with you. I would like us to have a baby—of course, I would— as a gift that came from our love. But it won't bother me if we don't, as long as you love me as you do now. Perhaps the Lord has decided that four hundred years of Devereux is enough. Bertie will never marry, and that ends the family name. So be it, my love. So be it. But please, Bernadette, never any more mention of annulments. Never let that word be used with regard to us. Never again."

His words reassured Bernadette, at least for the present time, and they made love and got dressed for breakfast to meet the brand-new day.

They were trying to escape the others to enjoy each other's company. And they were fortunate the girls' mother, Nancy, stopped her daughters from following them to give them some time alone. As the couple rode happily away, they laughed out loud when Nanette shouted, "But you had Lord Devereux all night, Auntie Bernadette!"

Tony said, "Somehow, I imagine you just like Nanette as a child."

Bernadette responded, "My mother used to say I was incorrigible, and I had no idea what that meant. I thought it meant courageous, and I told everyone that Mommy said I was courageous."

Tony smiled. "Well, that too, I think. You ran off with an Englishman you only just met."

Bernadette responded, "Well, I knew I would marry you—provided Daddy didn't scare you away, and I warned him not to dare do so. He thought you only wanted to marry me for the money. Was that the truth, Tony? I don't mind if it is because I think you loved me too."

Tony said, "I never touched his money until after the war, and I intend to make a huge success of our new breed, the Devereux's, our family legacy."

Bernadette rode on ahead and shouted back, "Instead of children!"

They came to the private lake in the vast Barrymore estate,

and Bernadette tethered her horse and began to strip off her clothes. "Come on, Tony. No one is allowed here. Get undressed."

Not for the first time, he wondered about his wild-child wife and said, "Bernadette, I can't allow this. It is okay for a man but not a lady."

She laughed, and he said straight-faced, "I'm serious, Bernadette. No."

She was a little confused and thought he must be teasing her. "I keep on my underwear, but I always come here—well, not always but a lot."

"Not anymore, Bernadette. It is not becoming to a lady, let alone a viscountess. Stripping off in public."

"Tony, hardly in public since you're the only one here—other than the horses. I don't care what you say. You can just go on your way. I'm going in for a swim."

Tony was putting on his superior face. He fancied a swim, but he had noticed that his wife never—or rarely—obeyed her father. Could he make her listen to him?

"Bernadette, I think I have already made myself clear. Now please fasten up your blouse and get back on your horse. You are not going swimming in the lake. Those days are over!"

He expected her to rant at him, but she didn't. She started to cry and fastened up her blouse. "Okay, if it is that important to you. I'm going home."

Tony started laughing, and Bernadette realized he was teasing her, quite wickedly too! "Were you trying to prove something, Lord Devereux? I hate you now."

"Yes," he said as he walked over to her, standing there glaring at him with a petted lip. "Respect, Bernadette, because sometimes you can be quite foolhardy, and I needed to know if you would respect my judgment, even if you might not agree with it."

"Tony, does this mean I passed the test, and we are going swimming after all?"

Tony was already stripping off. He jumped in the water and then shouted about how cold it was, and Bernadette jumped in, laughingly telling him that this was Boston and not Miami.

Tony grabbed hold of his wife and said, "I always wanted to do this."

And when she realized what he meant, she shouted, "Not a chance! You are crazy!"

And as they both lay on a blanket drying off in the sun, Tony reflected that was possibly true because he was crazily in love with his willful wife. He said, "Years ago, I remember thinking that you must have been a complete handful for your parents, and now it seems you are my complete handful instead. Your father told me you rarely listened to him and never to your mother, and he laughed and told me you were his revenge on the English aristocracy. I was the poor sod who got caught in your web."

Bernadette wasn't sure whether to laugh or be offended. "He seriously said all that? I will make him pay. We will go shopping tomorrow, and I want to buy you something nice for your birthday—very nice. Did you buy me a present?"

Tony laughed and said he might have forgotten. He was rewarded with his beloved dimples when Bernadette declared that she didn't believe him.

CHAPTER 14

Mr. James Barrymore was called away to New York one Monday morning and would be gone until the day before Bernadette's birthday barn dance on Saturday night. He was taking the two Englishmen with him. Of course, James Barrymore would never admit to it, but he was exceedingly proud to have a viscount for a son-in-law. He wanted to show him off.

Bernadette was livid, most especially since her father didn't invite her. "Daddy, Tony probably doesn't want to go, and also, we have our tennis tournament on Sunday. He might want to practice this week so he can try to beat me. Tony, do you want to go with Daddy? You can say no."

Tony was thinking, *Spoiled, willful child indeed*, and said, "Actually, Mr. Barrymore, I would love to come. Quite excited about it."

James Barrymore said, "Tony, it's James and Eugenie. Do you think you can manage that?"

Tony smiled because, in truth, he thought it was about time he was told to address them in such a manner. He also noticed the expression on the lovely Bernadette's face.

"Well, Mr. Devereux—or sorry, is it Lord Devereux? You better hope you are up for the tournament. I am practically unbeatable!" She then developed a smug little smile, and Tony couldn't resist. He thought he might go easy on her, but she didn't deserve mercy.

"Well, Mrs. Devereux—or is it Lady Devereux? I think it is time to come clean. I was going to go easy on you, but you see, I was undefeated at Oxford, actually never beaten. Of course, I hadn't played for years, but I had a tennis court built just for you this spring since you have always told me how good you are at it. One never really loses the knack—once an ace, always an ace. Therefore, if I were you, I would expect a sound thrashing. You only have a few days to practice, and isn't there a birthday barn dance on Saturday night? You might have a bit of a sore head too."

Tony carried on eating his steak and potatoes, and everyone laughed as Bernadette sat there open-mouthed. "You little liar! Or rather, big liar! Okay, the tournament is canceled until Sunday next. Tony will be too drunk Saturday night to be on top form Sunday. This Sunday is his birthday anyway, so not fair to beat him on his birthday, especially since he is such an ace."

Tony said, "James, I believe your daughter intends to practice all week. Won't that give her an unfair advantage?"

James said, "I wouldn't worry too much about that, Tony. No one ever wants to take her on or play with her."

The gentlemen left early Monday morning, and Bernadette was, of course, sulking as she waved goodbye. Tony put on a playful, cheerful smiling face as he waved goodbye. However, he had grown accustomed to them being together every day, and he knew he would miss her, as she would him—their daily rides, frequently to their private lake, as he now thought of it. Even the evenings on the porch swing, drinking gin-spiked lemonade.

They talked about so many things, and he began to open up about the war, making Bernadette feel very tender toward him. She would tell him funny stories about her time at Harrods and the odd assortment of customers she encountered. He felt happier than he had ever been, even at the beginning of their marriage, because at the time, he worried that Bernadette was so young that she would eventually find him boring and cease to be in love with him. However, she showed that love almost every night and sometimes at the lake. He could never doubt it and sometimes felt undeserving of it, but he intended to spend a lifetime earning the love that she had so freely given to him.

The week dragged on for Bernadette, although she finally got Margaret to open up about Tommy.

"Oh, he is a very sweet man and certainly does his best to please me, Bernadette."

"Margaret, what exactly does that mean? Do you love him?"

"Yes, I suppose so. But, Bernadette, do you genuinely want to go back to England?"

Bernadette was slightly concerned. "Margaret, I would follow Tony to Siberia, so England is not so terrible. You will come back again, Margaret, with me. What is wrong? Here—let me make you a cup of tea. Speak to me!"

"I think I'm pregnant."

Relieved, Bernadette said, "Well, surely that's good news? Although, how can you tell so quickly? I mean, aren't you happy? My problem is the opposite. I worry that I can't have children, and no matter what Tony says, he has to be disappointed in me."

Margaret said, "Yes, but, Bernadette, for once, this isn't about you, is it?"

It was unlike Margaret to be cruel. She was Bernadette's best friend in the world—and only true friend. The penny dropped. "Whose is it, Margaret? Is that what this is about?"

"Bernadette, I'm so sorry. You will hate me."

For a brief moment, Bernadette thought she meant Tony, in which case she was correct because she would hate her. She would hate him too. She was almost relieved, therefore, when Margaret said, "Sean."

A million accusations came into Bernadette's head, such as *How could you be so stupid? How could you be so cruel? How could anyone fall for Sean?*

"Who else knows, and do you love Sean? Does he know?"

"No, because it was one time, and he was drunk, and he ..."

"Forced himself upon you?"

"Sort of. I just thought it was a kiss and a cuddle, but he got a bit carried away."

Bernadette thought, *Two brothers who didn't have the brains they were born with, but at least James could marry Nancy, and he did right by her, God rest his soul.*

Bernadette needed Tony; she needed his advice. But then Sean was her brother. Tommy was his valet but was also very special to him. What if he exposed Margaret?

"Margaret, none of this is your fault. Sean is rubbish! Although I shouldn't say that about my brother. He must never know. I could kill him. No one can know. When did it happen?"

"About a month ago?"

"God, Margaret, that's easy, and you cannot be sure it is his, and you have made love with Tommy, right?"

"Sort of. He's having difficulty. And I felt a bit funny, unworthy, sort of."

Bernadette was thinking fast. "Enough with *sort of.* You will need to seduce him. Tomorrow, as soon as they come back. If you can manage that, then it's easy. Lots of babies are born early, and how do you even know? I mean, after just one month? Maybe you will lose it as I did."

Margaret was shocked. "Bernadette, that's an awful thing to say! How do you seduce a man anyway?"

Bernadette grabbed Margaret's hand and took her to her room, where she produced a bottle of gin that she kept hidden for her and Tony's late-night glass of lemonade. There was a pitcher of lemonade there too, although it had gone warm. She poured them both a drink.

"Right, enough with your granny nightgowns. Here ..." She searched through her endless supply of inappropriate night apparel and found one. "Voila! This should do the trick. You will first seductively undress him and then imagine you are a burlesque queen and very slowly and provocatively undress. Put on the negligee and go to him with a nice cool glass of lemonade, spiked with the gin I'm giving you, but not too much. Just enough to loosen his inhibitions. You might need to triple spike yours! Christ, Margaret. Don't you even know how to seduce a man?"

The gin was going to Margaret's head. It was just the middle of the afternoon, and both girls were a little tipsy and were soon in peals of laughter as Margaret, dressed in the negligee, was attempting to seduce Bernadette, who was dressed in her husband's suit, playing the role of Tommy. Bernadette was making it into something that wasn't as terrifying or as terrible as it was. She had dressed up and was trying to talk like an Englishman. Bernadette loved Margaret, and no matter how this went, she would stick by her. She was also making fun of Margaret's "old lady" underwear and was digging some of hers out too. "They're all clean," she said at Margaret's look of shock.

Margaret said, "How did you learn all of this, Bernadette? Did you and Tony ever—you know, before you got married?"

Bernadette laughed. "Of course not, silly. First of all, I was only eighteen, and more importantly, he was a viscount. There was only one way he could have his evil way with me, and that was to marry me!"

They didn't notice the door open. "Evil way was it, my love? Dare I ask why you are wearing my suit and why Margaret is wearing … well, whatever that is she is wearing … and why you are both drunk at three o'clock in the afternoon?"

The women both burst into peals of laughter, and then Bernadette asked, "Where's Tommy?"

"Bringing up the bags." Tony was wearing his upper-class, looking-down-his-nose expression that Bernadette loved so well.

She ignored his previous question and helped Margaret into her room with her newly acquired lingerie. "Why not go for it now? Tell him you were watching him and wanted to give him a special treat. Here—take the gin. I'll carry the lemonade."

This done, she returned to her bedroom, acting as if there was nothing peculiar going on. "Well," he said, "I'm all ears, Bernadette."

She said, "I thought you were coming home tomorrow."

"Evidently" was his only response, but whatever had been going on, he was having to hold in his laughter.

"Well, you see, Margaret asked for lessons on how to seduce a man … for her husband, of course. She wanted to be more alluring, so I thought I would help her out a bit."

"Ah," he said, "my wife, the expert in male seduction. Would you like to teach me too?"

"Tony, I seduce you all the time. Stop being silly."

He couldn't help but laugh by now. "I come home a day early, having missed my wife so much, and I find her drunk, dressed up like me, wearing my best suit, and her lady's maid friend dressed up like my wife, in some very provocative lingerie. Therefore, your punishment for such bizarre and unladylike behavior is—let me see—oh, I've got it. Why not try to have your evil way with me? I can tell you if you are any good at it. Seduction, that is."

He took off his shoes and jacket and lay down on the bed. "Go on," he said.

Bernadette stood, still wearing the suit, with her hands on her hips. "You already know how good I am, but here goes."

Bernadette disappeared into her bathroom and reappeared wearing only her husband's suit jacket and white shirt, both wide open. She then imitated his posh accent and said, "Bernadette, why not be a dear and pour me a drink."

No sooner were the words out when Tony leapt up from the bed and took his jacket and shirt off her. She stood there naked and saw the desire in his eyes as he said, "Bernadette, it's not something that can be taught to another. You are either born with it or you are not."

Bernadette asked, feigning innocence, "So was I born with it, your lordship?"

"Most definitely," he said as he led her over to the bed at a little after three o'clock in the afternoon.

CHAPTER 15

The big day had arrived, the birthday barn dance—and the house was at sixes and sevens with the preparations for it.

Bernadette, of course, being the birthday girl, was not participating and was still abed when Tony presented her with a brand-new gold locket. It was more substantial than the one she had worn for years, and she loved it, even though she told Tony that she felt a little sad taking off her old locket. She had never taken it off in six years.

"Oh, and you already placed a photo of yourself inside! I love it!"

She kissed him, and he said, "Well, I couldn't have you wearing a photograph of a sea monster around your neck any longer."

Bernadette responded, "I explained that to you. It got all ruined at the public baths, but your mother wouldn't give me another, and I didn't want to cut up the only two photographs I did have. She also admonished me for shameful behavior—the public baths, that is—but where else could I go swimming? Can I give you your present today? It is only a day early, and you will have a sore head in the morning. These barn dances can be brutal. There might even be a fight or two. Not that you have to get involved, of course."

"That's exactly how I imagine it, Bernadette. Men getting drunk, women dancing themselves into a frenzy. Not sure I want you to go actually."

"Tony, it's my party—remember?"

"Well, you must take hold of my hand and behave yourself. We can go for an hour or two. Now let me see this birthday present you got me."

Bernadette was flabbergasted. "An hour or two? I don't think so, Lord Devereux. You are not in England now. I will stay as long as I like! You are such a snob!"

Bernadette got up to fetch the porcelain miniature she had painted by a renowned miniaturist in Boston. She had wrapped it up in several boxes, ranging from very large to very small, and tied each with a blue ribbon to match her husband's eyes.

She watched excitedly as he opened each box. He adored her when she was this way, almost childlike, and he scolded her that he didn't think anything was inside the package.

When he finally opened the last box, he exclaimed, "It is beautiful, Bernadette, just like you."

Bernadette was very excited about her gift. "The frame is real gold too."

Tony looked around at the opulent bedroom of such a spoiled girl. He loved her childish innocence and often wondered how she managed to toil for two years, working long hours, feeling that her husband had abandoned her. She was a woman with many sides to her. She was wearing a pretty dressing gown and bare feet, and he loved her toes. At a loss for words, he said, "Bernadette, this must have been very expensive."

She said, "I expect so, but Daddy paid for it. Well, I contributed my last pay from Harrods, or most of it, two pounds."

Tony was charmed. "I will treasure it always, Bernadette. A family heirloom …"

No sooner were the words out when he regretted them, and

Bernadette seemed to crumble as she shouted, "What family, Tony? Remember! I'm the wife that can't give you babies."

She ran out the room, downstairs, and outside, still in her dressing gown, and Tony followed.

He met her father in the downstairs hallway, who looked down at the miniature in Tony's hand and said, "Try the swing. That's where she goes to cry it out. What happened anyway—or none of my business, I suppose. She was very excited about that thing. I paid way too much for it too."

Tony said, "I mentioned that it would be a family heirloom, and then …"

James Barrymore responded, "When she lost the baby in early 1916, your mother made her life hell. That's why I moved her out. I would have brought her back to the States if it wasn't for the German U-boats. Bernadette can be rather emotional; well, you already know that. I know I've spoiled her, but she's my only girl. I'm sure she'll have her baby one day, but the thing is, she isn't sure about that, and your mother is such an evil woman."

Tony responded, "I told her that I don't care. I have Bernadette, and that's all I need. I meant it too."

The older man patted him on the back and said, "Best go tell her again. After all, today's her birthday. We can't have tears."

And there she was, swinging on the swing tied to the giant chestnut tree. Bare feet and legs, hair flying in the breeze. Tony stood and watched her as she pretended to ignore him. He wished he could capture the sheer sight of her in a photograph—a moment in time. She was enchanting.

"Go away," she eventually shouted. "I need to think. It was a stupid gift."

"No," he shouted, "I will never go away." Then he added playfully, "After all, look what happens when I do for a few days. You dress up in my suit and get tipsy—in the middle of the day!"

Ah, he thought, *at last dimples,* as she slowed down the swing and sat with a petted lip.

"Too late for that," he said. "I already saw your dimples."

And she smiled again but said, "What if you change your mind? I mean, what if I really can't?"

"Then I will buy you a puppy. I was going to do so for your birthday, but I thought it best to wait until we are back home in England. Our home, Bernadette. Come what may. Now it's your birthday and almost mine. I can't have you running around in bare feet in the garden. Come on. Let's get a shower together. I love that contraption. You have dirty feet, and I smell like horses."

Bernadette got down from the swing and ran to her husband. He lifted her easily and carried her inside. It was the type of home where no one took any notice of such strange goings-on, except perhaps Mrs. O'Hare, who shouted, "You'll do your back in, your lordship!"

❧

Bernadette was standing in her Kelly green dress with her hair in pigtails, tied with green ribbon. Tony burst into laughter. "Okay, have you a Kelly green suit for me too?"

"No, you can wear your riding pants and boots and just your shirt, no tie or jacket—very lord of the manor sort of thing. The whole neighborhood is dying to meet you, and they already know you are such a snob. However, what they don't know is how good you look in those tight-fitting pants."

Tony exclaimed, "I'm shocked, you naughty girl. What type of talk is that from a lady?"

Bernadette smiled and said, "The type of talk from a lady who fancies her husband, I expect."

And the dimples got him every time.

When they arrived at the barn dance, it seemed that many

men were already inebriated. It was the Barrymores' way to allow their workers and less affluent friends and neighbors to have some fun before they joined the party. *King of the castle,* mused Tony as he watched James Barrymore graciously greet and accept compliments from his guests. Many wished Bernadette a happy birthday, and Tony held her hand tightly. He was wearing his upper-class snob expression, and those who might have embraced and pecked Bernadette on the cheek refrained from doing so.

The Irish fiddlers were stirring up a frenzy, and Tony found that in view of the recent uprising in Dublin and the goings on between the IRA and the RIC, he felt decidedly uncomfortable and out of place. One look at Tommy Walker told him that he felt the same way, yet at least Tommy had no say in the running of the country or the situation in Ireland. Tony was quite confident that all there knew he was a member of the House of Lords, and even though he introduced himself as "Tony," they all knew he was Lord Anthony Devereux.

The night wore on, and he stood with Tommy watching Bernadette and Margaret reeling with the rest of them. He also noted one man in particular who had been introduced to him as Brendon Connelly. He kept taking Bernadette's hand as she danced and laughed to the rhythm of the music. At one point, the man lifted Bernadette up in the air, and Tony decided he had had enough. He walked onto the dance floor, straight-faced, to lead Bernadette off of it. The man seemed to take exception to this and shouted, "English murderer!" The barn went completely quiet, and even the fiddlers stopped. Tony had his back to the man when he shouted, but he turned. The man was clearly drunk and probably close to passing out. Tony decided to help him on his way and landed one punch square on his chin, and the man fell to the floor.

Tony and Tommy were on their guard and wanted to get

the women out of there when suddenly it seemed the mood changed, and all were congratulating Tony on his left hook. James Barrymore was laughing and approached him. "Well, Lord Devereux, you have won their respect now, since many were claiming you would be nothing more than an English snob. Well, you are that, too, but one that packs a fair punch! Another beer? Then for God's sake, get your wife up to dance. Tommy too! You're both standing there like a pair of outsiders. Tony, you are not an outsider. Not anymore. You are a member of the British nobility and, more importantly, a member of the wealthiest family in the whole of Boston and its environs."

So Tony swigged back a couple of tankards of ale and took to the floor. The music eventually slowed down, and he thankfully took Bernadette into his arms. She said, "Look up there, the hay loft. Nobody uses the barn anymore except for these get-togethers. I might take you up there this week, sort of a belated birthday present. I wonder why Margaret is dancing with Sean. Oh, never mind."

Tony said, "Strange question. Why wouldn't she be? Tommy is still standing around. He doesn't look very happy. I wonder why."

Bernadette felt Tony was looking at her strangely, and she sometimes thought that he could see right into her soul. "How would I know, Tony? Maybe he's a bore! So, I suppose, forget about the hayloft. You might get your nice clean clothes dirty."

Tony could feel there was some sort of secret between his wife and Margaret. He had thought that since the afternoon he came home from New York. He wasn't enjoying himself, and his hand was sore from the punch. *English murderer.* Was that the general opinion of him? Everything had been wonderful until this barn dance fiasco. Most everyone was either intoxicated or well on their way to becoming so. Michael O'Connor was standing around watching Bernadette—or was it him he was watching? He could tell that Bernadette must have been very popular as a girl, and a strange jealousy overcame him. She and Margaret were keeping secrets, but about what?

It was growing late when a young blonde woman appeared, seemingly on her own, and Bernadette was drawing her daggers. "She wasn't invited," she said. "Why is she here?"

Tony asked, "Who is she, Bernadette? It looks like she is searching for someone."

"Yes, and I wonder why. Anyway, what's it to do with you? I guess you think she's pretty. Well, I suppose she might be, if you like that type of girl."

Tony was concerned; clearly, this young woman had a past that somehow involved Bernadette. "What type, Bernadette?"

However, before he was to receive an answer, Bernadette's birthday cake was announced and brought in, and Tony thought it more resembled a royal wedding cake by the sheer size of it. Bernadette blew out the candles but seemed distracted as the dancing began again after a chorus of "Happy Birthday."

Bernadette took her husband's hand and said, "Please don't look at her, Tony. That's what she wants. Her whole family is trash, especially her—complete and utter trash. She hates me, and I hate her, and she shouldn't be here."

Tony asked Bernadette what was going on, since she was visibly shaken, but she wasn't listening to him and said, "Excuse me, Tony. I have to go talk to my daddy." Tony was left standing there, quite bemused. Clearly, barn dances were something he would prefer to avoid in the future.

Bernadette had no sooner walked away when the young woman approached him. She was very pretty, although shabbily dressed, and looked like she was about to cry.

"Excuse me, sir, I know I probably shouldn't have come, but I so wanted to join in the dancing. Bernadette hates me, and whatever Bernadette wants, Bernadette gets. The whole town was invited—all except for me. She thinks because my family ain't rich like hers, we are dirt. Sir, will you dance with me? Just one dance, and then I will leave. Everyone has been talking so much about you, and I just wanted to meet you."

Soon the tears started, and Tony looked around for Bernadette, who had disappeared outside with her father. He thought, *Well, what harm can it do? She looks no older than Bernadette, and everyone is shunning her*—so he led the young woman onto the dance floor, still looking for Bernadette to rescue him, when suddenly she was upon them.

"You can just get your filthy little body out of my daddy's barn and away from my husband—unless, of course, you want me to tell everyone what you did, and everybody already knows what you are!"

The girl started crying in earnest and threw her arms around Tony's shoulders. Bernadette was livid and sneered, "Oh, poor little Shona, crying on big, bad Bernadette's husband's shoulder."

She then called for Michael, who appeared out of nowhere, grabbed the girl roughly by the arm, and led her away. "You have to leave, Shona. You weren't invited, and Bernadette doesn't want you here at her party. You know exactly why."

Tony, shocked, angrily spoke up. "Wait a minute. What is going on here? She is just a young girl, for God's sake! And, Bernadette, after what you yourself have gone through? I am utterly disgusted—behaving like a spoiled child. Birthday girl or not, I expect much better behavior from my wife." And he turned and walked out of the party—with the birthday girl still standing there, shocked at his words and at what had just occurred.

Of course, he returned moments later to find her. He had jumped to conclusions without knowing what was really going on and had spoken cruelly to Bernadette. He knew his little speech was way out of line. It was just that he felt so silly dancing with the wretched girl in the first place.

It turned out that Bernadette had already left her birthday party with her mother.

Tony approached James Barrymore. "What the hell just happened here, James? I know I was harsh on Bernadette, but she was so cruel to that young girl, so shabbily dressed, and more to be pitied surely than scorned?"

James said, "You tell me, Tony. You seem to be the one sitting in judgment. Just as I accepted and loved you as a son too. Your wife, my daughter, has left with her mother. She is reliving a very terrible thing. Perhaps she will tell you about it or perhaps not." And he walked away, leaving Tony standing there alone.

Tony left the party after that and walked back to the house. He and Bernadette were supposed to be going on a romantic, early-morning hayride, but clearly, that wasn't going to happen now. He was confused and worried that he had done something terrible, unforgivable even, simply by showing some sympathy for the young girl who was so poorly clad.

It was past midnight, and Tony thought, *My birthday. What the hell have I done now? All at once, there are secrets all around, and everyone is in on them but me.*

He ran upstairs, but Bernadette wasn't in her room. He assumed her mother's room and went back downstairs to sit in the parlor awaiting her father. Bernadette certainly deserved an apology, but he also deserved a full explanation of what had just occurred that night in the barn. He truly couldn't get his head around that whole unpleasant scene.

He must have fallen asleep and was awakened by James, who said, "Away up to your bed, son. It's a shame that yin had to show up. Ask Bernadette about it tomorrow. She's with her mother. There was a terrible incident, and thank the Lord that Michael was watching and saved my daughter. Bernadette slept with her mother for many months after it. She was just fifteen, and that trollop set her up. It was dealt with very severely."

Tony sat up. "What incident? Was she attacked? Oh God, please, no. I had no idea. She never told me about this! I am desperately sorry about the way I spoke to my dearest girl."

Just then, Bernadette appeared and said, "Daddy, I'm okay. Away you to bed."

James stood up, kissed his daughter, and squeezed his son-in-law's shoulder.

Bernadette took Tony's hand and said, "Come on. Let's go to bed."

He said, "Is that it? What's going on, Bernadette? I'm feeling a bit lost and sick inside."

She responded, "Tomorrow morning. We will go to the lake together. I will have Mrs. O'Hare pack up breakfast and lots of coffee. I will tell you my secrets then, but you can rest easy tonight since none of them involve anything I have done wrong or otherwise. But a wife shouldn't keep secrets from her husband. Most especially if she loves him as much as I love you."

Tony took her into his arms and kissed her. "I should never have spoken to you like that! The beer was too intoxicating, but that is no excuse. So everything is okay now?"

He looked almost afraid, and Bernadette just said, "Well, for you and me, it is."

Tony decided this was good enough, and it took no time at all for each of them to fall fast asleep.

❧

Bernadette laid out the blanket and food while Tony poured the coffee. He felt much better because Bernadette had told him that all was well between them, and he realized that was all he cared about.

"Two secrets, Tony. One because you deserve to know and the other because I can't let it stand between us. Which one first?"

He said easily, "The girl. What did she do to you?"

Bernadette thought for a moment and then began. "When we were young children in grade school, we were friends. My daddy and mommy disapproved of her because her family was poor, and her father and brothers were drinkers. Anyway, I stayed friends with her, even though they told me not to do so, because I felt sorry for her. Now and then, I would give her some of my clothes that didn't fit me. She was much smaller than me. I don't think she got fed much. I also used to pack a huge lunch for school. As you know, I have a big appetite anyway, so no one thought too much about it."

Tony smiled and took Bernadette's hand. He was dreading where this was going, but he also needed to know.

"Eventually, we went to high school, and we grew apart because, well, this is hard to say, but she wasn't very clean, and she went with boys behind the school gymnasium. I saw her once, and she saw me, and I told her I would tell on her."

Bernadette stopped. "Actually, I missed a bit. When we were still friends, I took her once to my lake, but she couldn't swim and her underclothes were dirty and ragged. I laughed at her. I know that was mean, but I was only twelve, and soon after, we stopped being friendly."

Bernadette paused and took a drink of coffee. It was as if she was bracing herself. "Shona tried to spread untrue rumors about me, and my father went to the school, and she was punished. My father contributes a lot to the high school and even built the library—not that that matters, because what she said was malicious, and she deserved to be punished. She was expelled from school, as my father would accept no lesser punishment than that. She was fifteen anyway, and she wasn't very smart; she was probably ready to drop out anyway."

So far, Tony was thinking that there had to be more to the story than this to have caused the girl to be ostracized from the whole town, and then Bernadette told him the final part of her story.

"One summer day, I went to my lake to swim. I always wore my bathing suit except when I came with you, Tony, in case you wondered about that. Anyway, I knew that Daddy secretly had Michael or James keep an eye on me. So I swam for a while, and then I heard laughter. It was Shona, and she was with her three brothers. I was scared, and I was crying, afraid to come out of the water, and she was shouting, 'Cry baby,' at me. Then one of the boys came in and grabbed my arm. I was so terrified, and I was screaming and screaming, and right then Michael appeared, then James, then Sean, and two other men, and finally my daddy."

Another pause, and Tony was now holding her in his arms, his heart thumping. "Sean was told to take me home, and that's all I know for sure. I heard the boys were beaten very badly, and my father held on to Shona and made her watch. He then sent her on her way. Two of her brothers are now in prison for something unrelated, and one of them is a bit simple. Her father is an abusive alcoholic, and she has the life of a dog. It is well known that she goes with men for money. She is stupid really because she should have left town and maybe started a new life. She is pretty enough. You thought so."

Tony bowed his head at that remark, embarrassed by his own stupidity.

Bernadette finished her story. "I don't feel sorry for her. I hate her. She brought her brothers with her to the lake that day for one reason, and, Tony, you know what that reason was without me saying it."

Tony was holding back tears. "I wish I were there! I would have killed them. My poor, sweet girl, and to think I danced with that …" He cut off what he was about to say or call her.

Bernadette said, "I believe the men near did kill them actually."

Tony said, "That's why Michael is special to you. Of course he is, but you never loved him."

Bernadette was candid. "No. It would have pleased everyone if I did, but I've got a one-track mind. I've only ever loved one man, only ever kissed one man, and I think you know the rest."

Tony said, "Weren't you afraid to come here after that?"

"Only for a while. I knew I was always well guarded. Also, I believe those boys were threatened with death if they ever so much as looked at me again. And they never did. They would avert their eyes if I saw them on the street."

"So why do you think she came to your party? Surely she knew what would happen?"

"Well, Tony, everybody has been talking about Bernadette Barrymore's viscount, and perhaps she thought she could have her way with you and spoil everything for me."

"That could never happen," he responded. "Come on. I've exhausted you. Let's go for a ride."

Bernadette said, "What about the other secret?"

Tony said, "Has it something to do with Tommy and Margaret?" And when Bernadette didn't answer him, he said it could wait.

CHAPTER 16

The tennis tournament was again delayed a further week, and the Barrymores invited a few more affluent friends to meet Tony. This was a conscious decision following the disastrous barn dance. It seemed their son-in-law and his man were not entirely up to drunken rabbles, and of course, the appearance of Shona McPhee did nothing to help matters.

There were tables with dainty sandwiches and petit fours, tea, coffee, and most importantly, gin-spiked lemonade.

Tony never inquired further about the situation of Tommy and Margaret. He didn't really want to know, and Bernadette never volunteered the information. Margaret had eventually managed to seduce Tommy, but by Bernadette's reckoning, the baby would now have to be around six weeks early. Bernadette reassured her friend that they would get through that part together, but what more worried her was the fact that Margaret had confessed that Sean did not force himself upon her. Margaret fancied herself in love with Sean. Bernadette never really believed that he had done so, not with the way Margaret blushed when he spoke to her, and she seemed to seek him out deliberately.

Bernadette first became suspicious the night of the barn dance. *That blessed barn dance,* she thought. *All the trouble it caused.*

Bernadette noticed Margaret disappear for a while, and there had been no sign of Sean either. And, of course, she was dancing with Sean, and what woman on earth would dance with a man who forced himself upon her? Sean was very handsome with his dark hair and eyes, and at thirty-five, he was still single and a bit of a lady killer. There were many local girls after him, and his mother used to say, "They'd be made up with him!"

The trouble was that Sean was taken with Margaret too, or at least for a little while, because he paid her too much attention, especially with her being a married woman. They were complete opposites in nature, he so wild and Margaret so sensible, although Bernadette pondered, *Not as sensible as I once thought.*

Still, the big day had arrived. The previous week, she and Tony went on long rides together and talked about the future, his horses, and Devereux House. Bernadette seemed to be looking forward to returning there, and for this, Tony was much relieved.

She said, "Tony, I was only twenty years of age when you left me there and, at the time, no match for your mother. The woman I have become would have tossed her back to the dower house for sure and held my own with your stuck-up friends. I am quite looking forward to doing so actually."

Tony responded, "I am much relieved. I must confess that I was apprehensive that you wouldn't want to leave Boston. Your father's estate and mansion are beautiful. Our estate in Hampshire is beautiful too, but not much swimming in the lake to be had, and the house is a mismatch of updates since 1550. I hope I have done a good job though—fixing the old place up for you."

Bernadette responded, "Oh, I intend to leave my mark on it too, and I am afraid it might well involve placing some of your ancestors up in the attics! But I am excited. For the first time, I will be mistress of my own home, my husband's home. At eighteen, I didn't understand what that meant. But now I am an old woman of twenty-five."

She grew serious. "I hope to be wrong, Tony, but if I can't give you children, I will make it up to you in every way I can."

Tony kept it light. "Now that part sounds very promising! So shall I book passage then, in another week or two? Are you ready to come home, my love?"

"Yes, ready and willing, Tony. That is, if you still want me after your embarrassing defeat today."

Bernadette was happy, and that truly gladdened Tony's heart. He had worried about her willingness to return to England, and he was becoming anxious to get back and get on with their brand-new life together.

Bernadette had been practicing her tennis technique every chance she got, and she and Tony had played a few practice matches together, but he always won—every time. However, Tony had a plan. His wife had an excellent underhand serve and drop shot, and for such a petite person, she packed a lot of power behind her stroke. Tony planned to make her work for her victory. It seemed to mean so much to her. He so loved her serious expression when she ran to hit a deep shot and her little dance when she won a game or even an advantage. He knew it would be much less fun if he held back a little during their practice games. However, today he intended that she would be the triumphant champion.

Bernadette appeared on the court to a rousing cheer, adorned in her brand-new tennis whites. She had kept the outfit a secret from Tony since he would probably say it showed far too much leg. She had her hair in pigtails again and was wearing a very serious demeanor. Tony walked out to a chorus of boos from Sean and James Barrymore, causing Bernadette to giggle, although the others politely clapped their hands.

Tony won the first set. That was his plan. Then Bernadette won the second. He watched Bernadette's demeanor develop a worried look. The final set and winner would take it all. He played with her a bit in the first two games by soundly and quickly beating her. He thought she looked as if she might cry, but as she came back, hitting the ball with everything she had, he lunged but couldn't quite hit it. The last game came down to advantage Tony, then he lost it, and Bernadette got back the advantage and beat him! She was dancing and crying, and Tony thought if there was ever a time to get beaten, this was it. He walked over to shake her hand and then kissed her for the world to see, or at the very least, those who were watching the match. She suddenly said, "Tony, I don't feel very well, and she threw up all over her brand-new tennis whites. She had started feeling that way during the match, but she so wanted to beat her husband. He offered her a drink, but she ran off to throw up again.

Everyone was looking at him, and he said, "Possibly too much exertion. I best find her and get her changed."

Eugenie followed him. "She's been a bit peaky these past few days. I wonder—still too soon to jump to conclusions. Overexertion, I agree. She has always been so competitive in sports. Not so much in her schoolwork, however!"

Tony looked stunned. "Surely not. I mean … I don't think she can, and she shouldn't have been running around and playing so hard …"

He looked worried, and Eugenie said, "She is made of stronger stuff than that. Let me see to her."

Eugenie found Bernadette getting changed in her bedroom, "Oh, Mommy, I feel so foolish, but I really don't feel very well. I was sick this morning too and thought it was nerves. Mommy, is it nerves? Anyway, I beat Tony fair and square! Or at least I think I did."

Tony appeared. "Are you all right, my love? I swear you play like a man. Thank God you don't look like one, however."

Bernadette said, "Mommy, will you tell Tony to go drown his sorrows somewhere else, please?"

Eugenie ushered him out of the room just as Margaret appeared. "Mrs. Barrymore, go see to your guests. I will stay with Bernadette."

Once both friends were alone, Margaret confessed, "I've made a proper fool of myself, Bernadette. I should just run away and hide myself forever."

Bernadette understood. "Sean? He can be very charming, but he's an idiot. It is my fault, and I should have warned you. Did you tell him?"

"No. I was about to do so, and he said that I best go see to my husband, that he looked a bit down in the mouth. And now what do I do?"

Bernadette thought about it. "Two choices. You either confess all to Tommy and hope he understands."

Margaret looked wary of that choice.

"Or we carry on as we were. Tony wants to leave in a week or two. You will have your baby early, and if I truly am with child, I will probably lose it anyway."

Margaret was thoughtful. "Bernadette, you told me you were never sick the first time. My mammy used to say that wasn't a good sign. So if you continue being as squeamish as you look right now, it will be a good, strong boy."

Bernadette said, "Margaret, I am too scared to hope, so I won't just yet—and not a word to Tony. Do you still want to be my lady's maid? The job is still on offer, no matter what happens with Tommy, but I think, either way, he will be a good, loving husband. He seems a bit lost, like he feels he isn't good enough for you, and maybe he isn't, but you married him."

Margaret said, "I was afraid you would change your mind—after my behavior, I mean."

"Margaret, you are so very dear to me and always will be.

Just stay away from Mr. Higgins when we get back to Devereux House."

Both women laughed at the very idea of a dalliance with Mr. Higgins just as Tony reappeared. "I was checking you're all right, Bernadette."

Margaret left them to it, and Bernadette said, "Tony, don't get your hopes up. It's just overexertion. I'm much better now."

However, Tony did get his hopes up, especially when he awoke the following day to the sound of his wife throwing up in the bathroom. He sat up and was smiling when she reappeared, but she told him to shut up before he spoke a word, which had him thoroughly convinced.

Bernadette said, "It's a stomach bug is all, Tony. Don't get any ideas. I mean it!"

The stomach bug continued for several days, and Dr. Finnegan was brought in to see both ladies and confirmed that both were with child and around seven weeks. Margaret knew she was further along than that but was overjoyed that the doctor said that, and most especially when he agreed, in her case, it could be a bit less. Of course, he knew better but had sensed the importance of timing in the case of Margaret.

Tony booked passage for four, and Bernadette grew tearful about leaving her parents behind. She told Tony she had gotten used to them taking care of her as they did when she was a girl, and he tried not to be offended, especially given her condition.

"Bernadette, it is my duty to care for you, especially now, and you will see them in December. They will be at Devereux House to see you through ..."

"Tony, don't mention it to me yet. I should be glowing, but I look squeamish and sallow. I hate food and am tired of getting told I must eat up. Also, as far as duty goes, we've been married for seven years, out of which I have seen you for less than three. Where was your duty then? I really don't think I like you at all!"

Bernadette was miserable and felt sick much of the time. They were leaving in a week, and she kept saying she wasn't going, even as she packed up her not inconsiderable collection of clothes, shoes, boots, tennis rackets, her western saddle, several of her dolls, her dollhouse, and all the furniture.

She spent her last week in Boston shopping for everything from underclothing to bed linens, and Tony reassured her that there were shops in England, and didn't she actually work in the world-famous Harrods for two years?

She did not purchase any baby items, saying it was bad luck, and then said one night at dinner, two days before they left, "Mommy, if all goes well, I will send you a list, and I will also need to have nursery furniture shipped over. God alone knows what the nursery is like in Devereux House. Something out of Bleak House, I imagine, and I don't know whether Tony is generous or not. I might be quite poor."

Tony was getting used to being picked on by his wife. It seemed Bernadette was indeed the very opposite of glowing in her confinement, thus far anyway. "My love, I opened an account just for you on Christmas Eve when I went to Harrods to collect you. And tell me what you need, and I shall see you have it. Didn't you check out the nursery before? You know, when ..." He trailed off, realizing too late that he shouldn't have brought that up.

"No, because your mother locked the door, and she had all the keys. Also, I don't think you will be generous. Daddy, can't you give me an allowance? What if Tony is mean? I might need to spend a great deal to make Devereux House inhabitable, and also, I need to change all the locks to keep out Tony's mother."

James Barrymore had been enjoying his son-in-law's put-downs since Bernadette discovered she was with child. He and Eugenie knew it was all just fear. In so many ways, Bernadette was their little girl again after so many years apart—years she spent working and living on so little, although she had no need to do so. "Daughter dear, I am quite certain now that your husband will do his best to make you happy, and of course, we will be in correspondence to ensure that he does."

Bernadette was glaring at Tony, and when they finished dinner, he said, "All right, Bernadette. Porch swing. We need to talk in private. Lemonade—but no gin for you."

She just said, "Do they even have lemons in England?" as he led her by the hand outside.

He sat down and pulled her onto his lap. "All right, Bernadette. What's all this about? Have you decided you hate England, or is it just me you hate?"

She started to cry, and Tony wasn't particularly surprised; he too knew his wife was terrified—too terrified to hope and plan for her baby. "Everything will be wonderful, I promise you, and isn't part of the fun planning and shopping for our new baby? My love, you can't be this miserable for nothing. I know that in a matter of months, you will be a happy mama."

Bernadette said, "Mommy, not mama."

Tony knew he was making progress and said, "Good Lord, does that mean I will have to be daddy?" She smiled, although she was looking down and not at him, and he lifted her chin and said, "I knew it! The dimples are still there. I've missed them this past couple of weeks."

Bernadette said, "I'm scared to let you down, Tony. I mean …"

He said, "Bernadette, you could never let me down, not unless you stop loving me, and I don't think you've stopped doing that, for all your frowns and nasty little remarks."

"Tony, did you let me win that day?"

Tony smiled. "God, no! And I need to ask you to keep it a secret in England. My perfect record broken—by a girl!"

Bernadette laughed and said, "Come on. Let's take a walk.

It's a lovely night, and I want you to make love to me outside on the grass."

He said, "What about the hay loft?"

Bernadette seemed to suddenly brighten. "Okay, let me fetch a couple blankets."

CHAPTER 17

As they drove up to Devereux House, Bernadette could feel her stomach lurch, which had nothing to do with the baby. Tony was holding her hand and trying to be positive. "Of course, the outside still looks the same. Could use some work and possibly a rose garden or kitchen garden, something like your mother's."

Bernadette's sickness had lessened on the voyage back to England, and now she could feel a new illness take its place—or was it just dread?

The servants were standing to greet them. Mr. Higgins was in the middle with Mrs. O'Leary, and that helped a great deal. Margaret and Tommy walked around to the back of the house, and Bernadette tried to stop her, but she told her, "We're back in England, your ladyship."

Ever since she had known Margaret, they had been on equal terms, and this was the first part of her homecoming that felt strange and somehow wrong.

They walked inside the great hall, and Tony seemed so nervous that Bernadette tried to keep things happy and light, but she felt as if she had a frozen smile on her face. Still, this was now her home, and she was mistress of it. Her things would be brought by a hired truck the next day, and one look at the paintings confirmed that she would be taking them all down. Well, maybe leave one or two of the less menacing-looking persons.

Tony had done much to brighten up the parlor and drawing room, and really he made a decent job of it, but Bernadette decided there and then that she would be putting her own personality into these rooms if she was indeed to be the mistress.

Tony said, "You must be exhausted, my love," and he motioned to a maid to see her mistress to her bedroom suite. Bernadette pondered that Tony never seemed to motion with his hand to anyone in Boston. At any rate, he went to check on everything, and Bernadette dutifully followed the maid. The bedroom was a little brightened up but not enough, and Bernadette thought that between her bedroom, the parlor, and the nursery, she would have much to occupy herself. She was also having most of the ghastly paintings taken down. She dismissed the maid and asked her to fetch Margaret when she had settled. Bernadette was not about to start calling her best friend Walker, and that was her husband's name anyway. Tony had his own room, although he barely slept in it all those years ago, and Bernadette checked that out too. A photograph of his mother was on his bureau, and Bernadette placed it inside a drawer. *She's been here,* she thought, *all those months I was away.* She said aloud, "Many changes about to occur in your life, Arabella. Sending me my husband's letters and wedding photographs years later fixed a little something, I suppose, but not much."

Margaret appeared with tea and sandwiches, "Bernadette, you are not going to be staying in your room, are you?"

"No. Honestly, how's your cottage?"

Margaret said, "Adequate," and both women started laughing.

A short while later, Tony appeared. Margaret curtsied, and Bernadette awaited the hand-waving thing, but he didn't do that. He said, "Margaret, when we don't have guests, we are friends.

A bit awkward, but I'm sure we'll get used to it. Do you like the cottage?"

When Margaret merely smiled, he said, "Well, I am confident that you and my wife will get your heads together and make it much nicer. Bernadette, my mother and my sister are dining with us tonight. Margaret, do you have something special unpacked yet for my wife? Well, I will leave you to it."

The women stared at each other, and Margaret told Bernadette to stand firm.

Margaret was trying new ways to fix Bernadette's masses of unruly curls and came up with a unique style piled so high that she grew several inches in height. Some tendrils surrounded the back of her neck and a few on her forehead. It was so very different and gave Bernadette the lift she needed to go face the monsters downstairs. Her pale green dress was form-fitting and quite sheer, and the silk lining was skin toned. The look was modern and cut a few inches above her ankle. The final touch was a feather in her hair and costume pearls that reached down to her navel. None of these purchases were shown to Tony before they left Boston, but she was reassured by the salesgirls at Jordan Marsh that these were the very latest thing from Paris.

Bernadette told Tony to go down and greet his guests, emphasizing the word *his*. And when she heard Cecil Fallsington's irritating, highly affected voice, she said to Margaret, "Is this some kind of joke? My first night home—*again*! By the way, my tiara is gone and my fur coat. I'm putting an end to this tonight, and if he doesn't like it, I will be right back on that steamer."

Margaret just said, "Aye and me and all!"

Bernadette's entrance was flawless and so different from that terrible Boxing Day dinner when she left, for many months actually, since it would almost be September.

She walked over to Tony, who kissed her hand and looked up at her questioningly, and then greeted the others by saying, "My, my, here we all are again. None of you have changed a bit. You look exactly the same as when I left last year."

Higgins offered his mistress a drink, and she said, "Just a tiny sherry, I think. So what's the news in Hampshire?"

It felt to her that they had all been struck dumb, including her husband, and she continued, "Ah, I see. I'm assuming that the lack of response means nothing. We have had such a wonderful time in Boston, exploring my father's extensive estate, and gee whiz, Tony even got involved in a barn dance brawl. What fun we all had together."

Tony motioned to Higgins for a refill, and Bernadette thought, *Two different men contained in one body.* But he surprised her when he boasted, "Hardly a barn dance brawl, my love. I knocked the fellow out with one punch!"

This remark pleased Bernadette enormously, as did the effort he made to be *normal.* Then he almost choked on his drink when she said, "Arabella, have you been taking things again? I seem to recall that I had a brand-new fur coat and diamond and emerald tiara that I was given by my husband last Christmas. I can't seem to find these things."

Tony said, "Bernadette, perhaps we can look into the matter later."

Cecil actually spoke up. "What do you think of the old place, Lady Devereux? Tony spruced it up very nicely."

Bernadette thought, *Oh, my title is being used,* and said, "Yes, he has made an excellent start. However, I will be taking down most of the ancestral paintings, which will require that those walls be freshly painted or wallpapered. I intend to look into designers.

I have heard of a French lady, and we can all use any guidance we can afford from the French when it comes to fashion and design. Don't you agree, Charlotte? Although I understand she is very expensive—beautiful too! I do hope I can get her!"

Charlotte said nothing, but Arabella was outraged. "Our family goes back four hundred years. More than can be said for yours." Then she added, "My dear."

Bernadette was nonplussed. "Exactly, Arabella, and time they were laid to rest. Dusty, dirty old things anyway, and like my daddy, I prefer new and pristine. Well, I love some of your ancient furniture—antiques I think you call them—but that look can be overdone, can it not?"

Arabella chose to explain to the others. "My daughter-in-law doesn't understand lineage or the value of tradition and good taste."

She was about to continue with the put-down, but Bernadette finished for her. "Precisely, Arabella, me being the Irish bricklayer's daughter and all that. However, I do understand what it is to have sufficient resources at one's disposal for such an expensive project that I intend to take on."

Dinner was called, and conversation settled down somewhat. Once again, Bernadette changed about the place settings. This time, she placed Tony, of course, at the top of the table as lord of the manor and herself at the other end. However, all the guests were up at his end with a decided space between her and the rest of the company there assembled. She could tell he was angry, but she cared not and thought, *He should never have had them all here my first night home. Of course, here we go again. Is this really my home?*

Tony said, "My love, what has Higgins done with the seating? You are seated so far away from the rest of us."

She responded sweetly, "Oh, please don't blame him. I just thought you and your family and friends would want to catch up with one another, and since I don't give a jot about what you are all saying, I will finish my food and retire. I need my rest—in my condition. Or didn't you tell them, Tony?"

Bernadette noticed the looks that were passing across the other end of the table. She was once again back to being the Irish bricklayer's daughter—so far beneath them. Finally, dinner was over, and she led the ladies into the drawing room while the men stayed behind to finish their port.

The coffee was served amid an awkwardness that Bernadette knew that she herself had created. She started to feel rather immature and foolish. As hostess, she should be leading the conversation but had no idea what to say.

It was Charlotte who approached her. "I did hear the wonderful news and wish you every happiness."

Bernadette said, "Thank you. How are your girls? Oh, and Jeremy, of course. He didn't come with you tonight."

"Jeremy is living in London. It is more convenient for him."

Bernadette smiled, remembering her sister-in-law's bruised cheek. "I'm glad; you must be happy he is gone. Do your girls like sports? Tennis?"

"Rather! But I have two left feet."

"I could teach them. I think that's the only thing I am good at. I taught my nieces cartwheels. They're about your daughters' ages. Their father—my brother—was killed in the war."

Charlotte said, "Yes, I heard and am so very sorry. I think my girls would like that." She paused. "Bernadette, I know my mother is dreadful, and she dotes on Tony. Don't let her ruin your happy life. And as far as being the bricklayer's daughter, I'd rather be that than Sir Jeremy Sandringham's wife."

Bernadette was grateful for Charlotte's kindness. Finally, she felt there could be a friendship with Tony's sister and was about to question her more when Arabella shouted over, "Charlotte, come and sit by me. Marjorie has been telling me the most interesting story about the Arbuthnots."

Charlotte patted Bernadette's hand as she arose, a gesture not unnoticed by Lady Devereux, and left Bernadette seated alone just as the gentlemen joined them.

Tony still appeared annoyed at Bernadette, and when Arabella and Charlotte took their leave, she also excused herself as being very tired from the journey. The Fallsingtons, as usual, were staying over.

The night had been a disaster, except for Charlotte, and Bernadette had a splitting headache. It was not until the wee hours that she realized that Tony hadn't joined her. She still felt unwell, although not sick, as she had a few weeks beforehand. She was sweating, and her throat and muscles were sore. She grew afraid and thought, *I've caught it. That dreadful flu and without my mommy and daddy to care for me.* Then she remembered, *The baby! What about my baby?*

She tried to get up but was too weak to walk. She couldn't understand how this came from out of nowhere, and she was sure she would die, lying alone on the cool floor of her bedroom, waiting for someone to find her.

ﮩﻨﻫﮩ

It was Margaret who raised the alarm. Mrs. O'Leary came running, and the maids helped her to bed with some warm beef broth, while Mr. Higgins sent for Dr. Morris. Margaret was told to wait outside because of her condition, and no one could find the master.

Tommy Walker appeared and said his lordship had gone riding in the early morning with Cecil Fallsington, and Margaret shouted, "What! And left his wife lying on the floor?"

No one could understand it, and fortunately, Dr. Morris was there very quickly and confirmed the Spanish flu. He reassured Bernadette about the baby and told her she needed to fight this malaise very hard and get well. By then, Bernadette was becoming delirious and was shouting for her mommy and daddy but not for Tony, whom she felt had caused this. Of course, that was unreasonable, but at least for a while, that was what she truly believed.

Tony Devereux had not slept well. He felt that Bernadette had deliberately behaved very badly and didn't seem to appreciate anything he had done to the house, which was all just for her. And that talk about his ancestors and the paintings?

In his self-pity, he laughed about her ancestors, poor potato diggers living in a shack. For all her boasting about her father's wealth, that was what and where they came from. He found Cecil heading for the stables too. Cecil had developed quite a dislike for his wife, who couldn't even provide him with children, and both men went riding off together. They had been best friends since childhood, and Cecil also laughed about the Barrymores' poor beginnings—a matter that would later cause Lord Devereux to be very ashamed, as indeed he deserved to be.

When eventually both men returned, Dr. Morris was leaving. He looked outraged and said he would be back later. "Your wife is upstairs with the housekeeper. I can't allow her friend to stay with her in her condition. I hope you enjoyed your ride, your lordship. Your wife has succumbed to the Spanish flu."

Tony was shocked and completely ashamed and humiliated. He had slept alone on her first night home. He had left that morning without even checking on her. Why? Because he felt unappreciated, unworthy, his home dilapidated, and no matter what he did, it could never come close to the empire James Barrymore had built up with his bare hands.

He ran upstairs, two at a time, to find Bernadette sweating and coughing and Mrs. O'Leary trying to comfort her. Bernadette was begging for her daddy and mommy and was saying she wanted to go back to America.

Tony just stood there. How could this have happened? Bernadette shouted for him to leave. "Please, Daddy, get him out of here! Please, Daddy. Oh, Mommy, where are you?"

Mrs. O'Leary took him aside. "Where were you, your lordship? She is not really in her right mind and is blaming you for this malady. Please try to comfort her! We can't risk Margaret, and at least her ladyship seems to understand that."

Tony cautiously approached his wife. He felt so awkward and disloyal, the things he had been saying. "My darling, we will fight through this. What can I get you? May I sit with you at least?"

Mrs. O'Leary was standing by the door waiting for the onslaught, and it came.

"Yes, you can bring me my daddy and mommy and put me back on a ship to America, and then you and your rotten mother and ancestral paintings can bugger off! I hate you! Go away!"

But he refused to leave. "No, Bernadette. If you want me to go, you need to get well first. Then if you like, I will personally put you on a ship to America."

Of course, this was the wrong thing to say, and Bernadette started crying again for her daddy and mommy.

Mrs. O'Leary was about to suggest he leave her alone for a little while when Charlotte suddenly appeared. "Did I hear correctly, you idiot? Did you just tell your wife you were putting her on a ship to America?"

Tony said, "What are you doing here? And you don't understand the context in which I was speaking."

"Well," said Charlotte, "neither it seems did Bernadette. Here, I will stay with her; you go."

Bernadette seemed to rally around a little and said, "Charlotte, we are friends now, are we?"

Charlotte answered, "More than that, Bernadette. I am your big sister, and I will make you well again."

These words calmed Bernadette considerably, and Tony was quite relieved until she said, "I am so happy you came. Margaret cannot because of the baby. Will you tell that man to go away? He wants to put me on a ship, but I don't think I am well enough."

Tony tried to intervene. "Bernadette, please. I am not going to put you on a ship. Bernadette, I am sorry. I didn't know you were ill."

She responded, "Oh, that's why you left me to sleep on the floor. If you don't go away, I will scream and scream. Please, Charlotte!"

Charlotte ushered him out of the room, and Tony tried to make sense of what had just occurred. Bernadette seemed fine the previous night, with her ridiculous sitting alone at the table and nasty remarks. And since when were she and Charlotte such firm friends?

He found Margaret worriedly sitting in the hallway, who explained it was in case Bernadette needed anything.

Tony shouted, "Her head examined, spoiled, willful girl. She needs to grow up!"

He was speaking out of his own worry and shame. He felt everyone was looking at him as if he was to blame, but how did he know she spent the night on the floor? He said this to Dr. Morris upon a return visit a couple of days later, and he responded, "One would expect a husband might notice such an occurrence, your lordship. However, her ladyship is very fit and strong. A bit of an athlete, what? I already see an improvement. Don't you?"

Lord Devereux responded, "They won't allow me in there— my sister, Mrs. O'Leary, and Margaret sitting guarding her outside the door. Thank God my mother stayed away."

Dr. Morris responded, "Well, I think you should try harder.

Or what is this obsession she has about your family paintings? Mind you, there are an awful lot of them."

Tony made a decision. He gathered the male servants together, and under the direction of Mr. Higgins, they were told to take every one of them down and place them in the attics."

Mr. Higgins inquired, "The dowager viscountess too? And your lordship?"

"Yes, Higgins, all of them!"

The enterprise took hours to complete, and when it was confirmed that the task was done, Tony attempted entry into his wife's bedroom once again.

His heart was gladdened when he saw her sitting up and drinking tea, even though she was glaring at him. He motioned for his sister and Mrs. O'Leary to leave, and Bernadette said, "That thing you do with your hand. You are such a snob, and I hate you."

She was looking down into her teacup, which he took from her. "It is empty, your ladyship. It is quite a shame that you hate me since I am truly mad about you—or possibly just mad, like many of us upper-class snobs."

She couldn't stop the smile, although she didn't look at him, and he announced, "Dimples! I saw them, and you can't deny it!"

Bernadette said, "You left me on the floor to die, and then when I didn't, you told me you were putting me on the steamer to America."

Tony said, "Okay, the floor part. Obviously, I didn't know you were there, and I was feeling quite sorry for myself because you didn't like what I did for you in my home, your home. The steamer to America part was taken out of context."

Bernadette remembered him saying that to his sister when she was still very ill, and she said, "Didn't Charlotte call you an idiot when you said that before? I am sure I remember that."

"Yes, indeed she did. Do you still hate me, my love?"

"Yes," she said, but she was smiling, "unless you give me a bath like you did last Christmas Eve, and you need to sing to me too."

"If that is what it takes, I suppose so." He took off his coat and made to kiss her, but she stopped him.

"Not before I am clean. Then perhaps you may kiss me."

He ran the bath and gently bathed her, and for the first time, he noticed it, a little belly beginning to appear, and as he sang to her, his heart was singing too.

He dried her off and brushed her hair. "I need to look into that shower contraption." And then, out of nowhere, he said, "I said unkind things about your ancestors to Cecil. I am so sorry, but I need your forgiveness. I called them potato diggers living in a shack. Can you forgive me, Bernadette? That part has been eating me up."

Bernadette started laughing. "But so they were, Lord Devereux, which makes me so proud of my daddy. Is that all?"

"Well, I called you spoiled and willful and said you needed your head examined. Oh, and that you needed to grow up. That's everything I think. But I didn't mean a word because I don't want you to grow up. It might be nice if you could behave yourself when we have guests at dinner, but I suppose we can overlook that part, or at least put up with it. Oh, and I disapprove of that dress you had on. You knew I would, and that's why you wore it. Half-naked in front of other men."

"Tony, the lining was skin toned. And anyway, the only other man there was Cecil, who looks down his ugly nose at me. You never get jealous of me because you think you are better than me."

Tony sat down and pulled his wife on his lap. "You seriously don't believe that, do you, Bernadette? Michael O'Connor is in love with you. He saved you more than once, and I have to live with the fact that it wasn't me who did so but him. I watched you serve the handsome RAF officer at your perfume counter, and I was sick with jealousy. You are the most beautiful girl I have ever seen, and the older you get, the more exotic you become, with those eyes that draw a man in. I thank God every day that you are mine, and there is no way you are going on any ship to America. You need to fix up our home first anyway."

Bernadette sighed, thinking of all the ugly paintings. However, she enjoyed being called exotic. Then Tony led her outside the bedroom, in her very decent floral dressing gown and furry slippers, down the hallway and stairs, down to the great hall, and into the parlor and drawing room. "Well?" he said.

"What happened to them? Oh, Tony? Really?"

"Look at the state of the bloody walls," he said. "Time to call in that French woman or at the very least a wallpaper hanger!"

CHAPTER 18

Bernadette quickly recovered, and she and Margaret were allowing themselves to become excited about the babies. Bernadette had written to Madame Bouchard as soon as she felt a bit stronger. She checked the post every day and waited and hoped to hear back from her. She had read about her in *Ladies' Home Journal*, and although it seemed more likely that she would be turned over to a staff member or even turned down, Bernadette hoped her letter would inspire the beautiful French woman to come to her rescue.

She wrote that although she was Lady Bernadette Devereux, wife of Viscount Anthony Devereux, she was also an American from Boston. Her maiden name was Barrymore, and she had once sold Sir Leopold Blakeley perfume when she worked in Harrods.

Bernadette remembered the encounter because he had heard of her father. He was very handsome and charming and purchased an aquamarine atomizer to match his wife's eyes. He recognized her name, Barrymore, and Bernadette proudly told him her father was James Barrymore of Boston, Massachusetts. Sir Leopold told her he greatly admired her father. He was surprised to find her working in a department store, even Harrods, and Bernadette had told him it was a long story. He said to her that one day he would very much like to hear it and went on his way.

Bernadette told all this to Tony, and he accused her of being a flirt. "Tony, he was older, like fifty, but so debonair. I hope you are still debonair when you are fifty. You dress very nicely now and have an attractive and manly physique, but some men grow fat bellies as they get older, like Daddy."

Tony had responded, "You are starting to grow a fat belly yourself, my love. Do you finally feel more relaxed? You have passed that twelve-week mark my wonderful mother made you fear, and you are the picture of health."

"Tony, I thought I was exotic?"

He laughed. "Exotic health then."

The Devereuxes had settled down since that first terrible night and Bernadette's illness, and she was back to being her cheeky, bouncy self. However, she was so excited about this French woman. Tony was also watching daily for a response to his wife's letter.

Then finally, it came. It was brief but stated that Sir Leopold and Lady Amalie Blakeley would be pleased to call upon them at 11:00 a.m. on Saturday, October 11. Amalie had added, "I can't promise that I can help you, but it will be fun to see if we are a good fit."

Bernadette was thrown into a complete frenzy and, therefore, the house into an absolute uproar. Every surface was cleaned and polished, even as Bernadette lamented that she had no decent clothes to wear. And what does one wear to meet a renowned, exquisite French lady at eleven o'clock in the morning?

Bernadette saw the car coming and ran to get Tony. "He has a Silver Ghost too, Tony, only his is new. Now, remember, don't act like a snob. Be congenial and don't do that thing with your hand." She was flattening down his hair and straightening his tie, and she was wearing a brand-new skirt and blouse, cardigan, and shoes from Harrods. A necessary expenditure since she had nothing suitable to wear. Sir Leopold Blakeley drove to the front door and hopped out of his car. Mr. Higgins went to open the door for Lady Blakeley, but Sir Leopold motioned to him with his hand and opened her door himself.

Tony burst into laughter as Bernadette exclaimed, "I can't believe he did that thing with his hand! Well, I suppose you can carry on with it too. Oh my God, she is lovely; she is past forty and stunning. Oh, Tony, I hate my hair!"

Lady Amalie Blakeley received the letter from Viscountess Bernadette Devereux and was intrigued, as was her husband, Sir Leopold.

He said, "She told me that a multimillionaire's daughter working at the perfume counter in Harrods was a long story. It just got better! She is a viscountess as well?"

Amalie responded, "Yes, I remember you telling me about her. You also said she was adorable, and if this had been ten years ago, I would have been quite jealous. However, what would a lovely young girl want with an old man of fifty?"

Of course, Amalie was kidding her husband because even after twenty years of marriage, they were still very much in love. They rarely socialized other than with family and a few close friends. Now that the war was finally behind them, with their family coming through it unscathed, Amalie was highly interested in meeting this young woman and her viscount.

"Well," she said, "it will be a diversion, and you will discover the answer to your mystery of the adorable salesgirl who sold you perfume and an aquamarine atomizer."

The Devereuxes stood at the door to meet Bernadette's honored guests, and after introductions, they were shown into the parlor, which Bernadette believed to be the best of a bad lot. She offered them tea, and Sir Leopold said he would prefer cognac. Tony said he would join him and motioned to Mr. Higgins.

Amalie began, "Well, I can certainly understand your urgency with regard to a full home makeover, my dear, but tell me, what happened to all the paintings? There appear to be squares and rectangles all over the walls!"

Bernadette, known for her honesty, as was her special guest, said, "Lady Blakeley, they were all so ugly and depressing, and they gave me the Spanish flu, so my husband had them all removed. They are in the attics and not coming back down."

Sir Leopold laughed and said, "My goodness, Amalie, a kindred spirit! Lady Devereux, my wife took every one of my family portraits down early in our marriage. She called all my ancestors nasty and ugly, and now the house is adorned with portraits of the lovely Lady Blakeley instead."

Bernadette said, "Please, Sir Leopold and Lady Amalie, call me Bernadette. Lady Devereux is Tony's ghastly mother!"

Amalie laughed too when Bernadette whispered to her, "Is it true your husband commissioned a nude portrait of you years ago? That story is quite famous."

Amalie responded readily, "Yes, indeed he did. It was supposed to be quite personal, but for reasons I would rather forget, it was displayed for the whole household staff to view."

Tony was embarrassed and apologized to Leopold, who told him that his wife was very much like his, in the sense that she seemed to say whatever came into her head.

A fact further confirmed when Bernadette exclaimed, "I think that is so romantic. Tony would never do that because of his mother."

The conversation was lively, and Tony said, "My love, hardly something I would show to my mother. You make me sound like a prude, which I certainly am not. It might not be a bad idea."

Bernadette countered with, "No, really, he isn't a prude; he is a snob, however, and ever so posh, but he did floor an Irishman at my birthday barn dance in Boston for calling him an English murderer. I don't think Tony likes the Irish very much, and Daddy was quite frightful to him for the longest time. That's why Tony calls me 'my love,' Bernadette being a bit too Irish for him."

Amalie was charmed. "I will call you Cherie. Is that okay with you? I will make this ..." she searched for a word, which Tony provided.

"Ramshackle?"

"Yes, that will do, Tony. Now, before Cherie and I tour the entire house or at least what we will be renovating, Leo wants to hear the long story you referred to when you sold him perfume at Harrods."

Bernadette was permitted to call her guest Leo instead of Leopold and told the story of how she and Tony met in the foyer at the Ritz and how he proposed the very next day. "I was eighteen, and my daddy didn't like him because he thought he was impoverished English nobility, after my money, and none of Tony's family liked me, although his sister now does. Then Tony went to war and left me with his mother, who moved in from the dower house. She hates me, and my daddy was scared I got torpedoed, so he agreed to buy me a flat in Knightsbridge, and my daddy's agent came to England and got me a position in Harrods to keep me out of mischief. Then Tony's mother intercepted our letters ..."

She went through her story, and the other three sat silently listening, Tony with love, Leo with admiration, and Amalie with affection. They all could see how special she was, and Amalie could easily see why Tony was afraid to let her get away. She was lovely with those beautiful, brown, almond-shaped eyes, and her hair was magnificent. She had a curvaceous figure and just had no idea how to dress to accentuate all her wonderful attributes. Amalie had a new project and a unique, very dear little friend.

When Bernadette ended her tale, she said, "I hope you will stay for lunch. I got in oysters on the half shell, langoustines, filet of sole, and prime rib for the men."

"How can we resist?" said Amalie as Bernadette proceeded to show her around her house. "I don't like it at all, Amalie. Even my bedroom is blah. Tony did it, and I think I hurt his feelings."

Amalie was honest. "Everything that must be done will cost a considerable amount of money."

And Amalie laughed when Bernadette said, "I know, and Tony is working hard to build up his stables, but that will take a while. Daddy will pay for everything. He said to tell you to spare no expense."

Amalie was amused. "Leo's sister once said that to a French design team, and it was at Leo's expense. Everything in Blakefield Castle was burgundy and ugly. Cherie, you have waited many years to call this home your own. I will make it happen. I am very good with style, and I will also take you shopping. If you don't mind me asking, when is the little one due?"

Bernadette was thrilled that Amalie had noticed and told her February.

"Well, we best get to work then, and I will make my husband give you a discount. What sort of things do you like, such as wallpaper design?"

"Well, I would like my home to be modern and light. A few antiques, but I would like some new furniture. I like things very clean. This house is impossible to make clean.

"Okay, art deco design is brand-new, and art nouveau is still popular. Light and airy colors with some dramatic shades of teal or turquoise perhaps? What images do you like? Flowers, birds, anything in particular?"

"I like colorful parrots and peacocks."

"Okay, now let's go eat. Do you have a French chef?"

Bernadette rolled her eyes. "What do you think, Amalie?"

And so the day was a great success, and Bernadette had found an extraordinary new friend as well as a designer. The gentlemen got along well enough, and when Bernadette mused that it was because they were both posh snobs, Amalie laughed. Her new little friend was a godsend. After the war and all the sorrow and death, despair and depression, it was beautiful to see the light at the end of the long and desolate tunnel.

CHAPTER 19

And so the work began! Tony was grateful that he was not the man paying for it, since all of the main downstairs rooms, his wife's bedroom, the nursery, and three guest rooms were completely pulled apart. Also, Walker's cottage was in a shambles too. A conservatory was being constructed, and the invoices for everything were sent to Boston.

Tony expected many sarcastic comments from James Barrymore, but during his time in Boston, he began to look upon him almost as a father. His father had died when he was just a young boy, and therefore he had been the viscount most of his life. There was always sufficient money before the war, but the war changed everything, and men like him were somehow left behind as they fought in the trenches. Whereas others like James Barrymore and Sir Leopold Blakeley became even wealthier because of it. He wasn't bitter. Barrymore had lost his oldest son, and that was a horrific loss for a father to bear, but somehow that bereavement had lifted Tony into that position, and his father-in-law had even started calling him son.

The other Barrymore son, Sean, was too fond of good times, women, and drinking. He was charming and handsome, so women were drawn to him. Tony was almost certain that something happened between him and Margaret but found, if it did, he didn't want it confirmed to him—such was his respect for Walker. He knew his wife knew, but he chose not to ask her about it since she would quite candidly tell him. He still had nightmares about the story of Shona McPhee and her brothers at Bernadette's father's lake, and in a way, they lessened the ones he had about men being blown apart in France.

Bernadette and Margaret were going to Blakefield Castle for a week. The invitation sent Bernadette soaring to the heavens. Lady Blakeley omitted Lord Devereux in the invitation, but he understood Blakeley was mainly in London, and Amalie had sisters-in-law that she wanted Bernadette to meet. There was also a lady's maid that Amalie doted upon, and Margaret was very nervous about meeting her. He and Bernadette had been sleeping in his bedroom since it was not to be part of the renovation, and Bernadette had told him this was so he wouldn't ever want to sleep there again once her room was made beautiful. This delighted Tony, most especially when he remembered the last time he slept in there without her, and she liked to remind him how she spent the night on the floor.

The couple stayed in London a couple of times at Bernadette's flat. The place had remained untouched, although it was kept clean and fresh by the charwoman, who turned out in reality to be Mr. and Mrs. Parsley. Tony loved those little sojourns. They bought sausages and eggs from the butcher's shop and ate fish and chips for dinner. They would dine out, but he preferred the nights they stayed in. Bernadette had begun to call it their pied-à-terre, which was, of course, Lady Blakeley's influence. She had taken Bernadette shopping on several occasions for clothes and household furnishings, and the invoices from Harrods were sent to him since he had opened the account for her that Christmas Eve when he went to fetch her. He feigned shock at the amount spent during these shopping expeditions, but his home was beautiful, and his wife was glowing and as cheeky to him as ever. She was also developing a much improved and more expensive sense of style. Many women were beginning to cut their hair short, but Bernadette knew he would never allow that, and when he told her that he got lost in ecstasy when she kissed him all over and teased him with her hair, she was pleased enough to keep it long. Also, she pointed out that Lady Blakeley strongly advised her against it, and it seemed she had become his wife's style guru.

He drove Bernadette and Margaret to London King's Cross Station in his old Silver Ghost. He knew he would pick them up in his brand-new one but was keeping that a secret. He wasn't allowing Blakeley to be one up on him in that regard, most especially since Tony's title was hereditary and he was a member of the House of Lords. He heard that Blakeley was knighted due to his influential connections with the king.

Bernadette was excited as the car that was sent for them drove up to Blakefield Castle. The driver, a Scotsman called McBride, helped both women out, and Amalie Blakeley and a severe-looking woman in her fifties came out to greet them.

Margaret said, "Good grief that must be Bridgette! God help me," as she was led away with the French woman whose only intention was to put her at ease and to instruct her on how she too, as a special friend to Lady Devereux, could learn to rule Devereux House as she did Blakefield Castle. Bridgette was pleased Margaret was Irish, and they could therefore criticize the English to their hearts' content. It was all excellent fun since Margaret was married to an Englishman, and Bridgette affectionately referred to Sir Leopold as "the monsieur."

Bernadette became quickly enraptured by the house and the

beautiful gardens and woodland. Amalie told her she had a son, Leon, at Cambridge, where his father had attended university, but that he was determined to become a writer instead of going into finance, which somewhat irritated his father. He was coming down at the weekend to meet her. She also had a daughter, Cosette, and at sixteen, she wasn't yet out.

"I believe her father wants to keep her here with him always. They dote upon one another. You will meet Blanche and Cordelia, who are over from New York. They spend much of their time here, and my aunt and uncle March—oh, and how could I forget Malcolm McFadden, another American and our next-door neighbor. He is also my husband's business partner with regard to my line of fabrics and wallpaper."

Bernadette asked, "Isn't it really your business, Amalie? I mean, it's all your designs."

Amalie responded, "Yes indeed, but it seems that between both men and my lack of salary-negotiating skills, I am paid in cows. I now have a herd of them out in the pasture. What are your special talents, Bernadette?"

Bernadette thought for a moment. "Well, I am not artistic. I am very athletic. I can beat everyone at tennis, and I am very good at baseball and can hit the ball straight out of the park. I love doing gymnastics, and I taught my nieces cartwheels and handstands. If it wasn't for my baby, I could teach Cosette too."

Amalie said, "Well, you can teach her in the spring when your baby is already here, and you can also beat my husband at tennis. He is getting on a bit now, but he hates anyone beating him at anything and huffs about it for days, making every excuse. He still swims in his river, even when it is quite cold out. I feel neglectful not inviting Tony." Then Amalie was struck by an idea. "You shall stay for two weeks, and your husband can join you the second week. He can bring his man, Margaret's husband, and I will see to suitable sleeping arrangements for them both." Then she laughed. "Oh, I meant Walker and Margaret. Tony shall sleep with you—unless you prefer he doesn't?"

Bernadette was so pleased that Amalie talked openly with her and responded, "Oh, Amalie, I always prefer Tony to sleep with me, which is why we are leaving his bedroom ugly. Can I see your paintings?"

Amalie showed her one of her and Leopold together and said, "The others are dotted here and there. But you want to see the nude—am I correct?"

Of course, Bernadette agreed, and her new friend's beauty completely entranced her. "Oh, Amalie, your husband was so fortunate to win your heart. He is very handsome and all that, but your grace and charm are legendary. He's a little scary, I think. I'm surprised he allowed you to pose in the nude."

Amalie readily responded, "Oh, he never would have, but this was painted by my dear friend Imogen Armstrong. She has become well renowned and only paints those she feels are beautiful or handsome enough to deserve her services. Imogen is quite rich now. I will invite her next week as well. We will all have such a grand time, and we shall see what she makes of you and your viscount. I am certain she will be impressed enough by your appearance. Are you brave enough to do it?"

"Oh yes, Amalie, unless Tony disapproves, not that I ever listen to him. But if he doesn't want it, what would I do with it? I suppose I should wait until I have my figure back."

Amalie reassured her friend, "But yours is such a tiny belly, and you can always remember that you were with child when you had it done. Actually rather exciting. Your friend Margaret is quite a bit bigger, but you say you are due about the same time?"

Bernadette's eyes grew large as she confessed, "Oh, Amalie, it is such a problem!"

Amalie wasn't shocked by the tale of woe but said she would

need to think it over—the problem and the best way of addressing it, especially since the biological father was Bernadette's brother.

At dinner that night, Bernadette met the rest of the family: Cosette, who was pretty enough but nothing like her mother, and who played up to her father a bit too much; Blanche and Cordelia, who were a couple and not just friends; Malcolm, who was very good looking with a wonderful Texas drawl; and the Marches, who were quite eccentric, precisely as Bernadette imagined they would be.

Bernadette found Blanche and Leo a bit scary, and Amalie reassured her it was just an act and not to take them too seriously.

She was so pleased that she liked everyone and would meet Leon and Imogen the following week when Tony came. However, she was surprised that she couldn't quite warm up to Cosette. At sixteen, Cosette was too old to be showing petted lips to her father. It was almost as if she was trying to flirt with him or was in some competition with her mother, who she would never equal in charm, and clearly, her father doted on her mother. Bernadette noticed that this behavior somewhat upset Amalie and could fully understand why. Bernadette loved her father dearly but could no more imagine flirting with him than she could a billy goat.

During dessert, she asked, "Do you like sports, Cosette? If you do, I can teach you to become exceedingly good at them, especially tennis and gymnastics. Baseball too. I am very fond of anything athletic."

Cosette responded, "I'm not interested in becoming *exceedingly good*, and anyway, aren't you pregnant, or is that just a fat belly?"

Amalie told her daughter to mind her manners, but her father said nothing. Bernadette was aghast and said, "You know, Cosette, if you were one of my nieces, I would call you out on that remark and teach you manners. I'm surprised you are allowed at the grown-ups' table."

At first silence, then Blanche said, "Well said, Bernadette! It was about time, since someone is getting a little too big for her britches and should be sent back to the nursery."

Sir Leopold looked angry, and Bernadette wondered if there was a telephone so she could call Tony to come and fetch her, but he surprised her. "My apologies, Bernadette. Cosette, you are punished and henceforth will not be accompanying the adults at dinner until our guest has forgiven you, and I don't think she should for quite a long while."

Cosette arose and shouted, "Your fault, Bernadette!"

She had spoken her name with a phony Boston accent, and Bernadette readily responded, "It is *your ladyship* to you."

The girl ran out crying, and Bernadette said, "Gee whiz, I am sorry, but I will have Tony come and collect me. I won't take that from any child or person, whether a guest in their home or not."

Amalie was embarrassed and livid and said, "Leo, this is what comes of spoiling that girl. I am so angry, and I don't feel I can ever forgive her for her behavior this night toward my dear friend. Ladies, let us withdraw."

Bernadette was shaking, and Blanche took her hand and said, "It's okay, sweetie. Amie tells us she has christened you Cherie, and Cherie it will be. I know you shouldn't, but one tiny martini will settle your nerves. She is the most dreadful child, and my brother will have to do something about it."

Cordelia said, "Years ago, we christened Amalie Amie. We do that sort of thing. It's just a bit of fun. Please stay, Cherie. Amie was so excited to have you come visit."

Bernadette responded, "I am so honored by that, and I was so excited to come. Cosette is jealous of her mother—that much is obvious. Amalie's beauty and grace are legendary, as is the Blakeleys' love for one another. I read all about them in the *Ladies' Home Journal*. She will never be like her mother, and one day she will come to understand that. When she does, I expect she will become a much nicer person."

When the gentlemen joined them, Bernadette watched Sir Leopold check on his wife, after which Malcolm sat with her. It was evident to her that Malcolm loved Amalie, and it was no wonder since she was so beautiful and gracious. Bernadette suddenly realized Leopold was approaching her, and she grew wide-eyed with concern, but he smiled warmly at her.

He said, "I once saw a millionaire's daughter dutifully wait on unpleasant women, selling them perfume that would do nothing to improve their dispositions. It was as if she had no choice in the matter, yet she had no need to be there. I wish I could teach strength of character to my daughter. I am frightfully sorry about that business tonight. It was as if she decided to dislike you for no reason."

Bernadette thought, *Well, I have come this far, and I could still call Tony.* She said, "There was a reason. I watched her behavior with you, her father, and I saw how it hurt her mother. Amalie is the most beautiful woman I have ever beheld, and today I saw her nude too."

Leo blushed a little, and somehow that emboldened Bernadette. "Cosette knows she will never equal her mother in grace or beauty, and I thought that when she lashed out at me. It was like she read my mind. So we took a dislike to each other. I am only nine years older than her. I could easily be her big sister, and no girl should try to compete with her mother for her father's affection."

Amalie was watching the pair, and it seemed as if Leo was seeking guidance from her young friend. He very rarely spoke to other women, in her presence anyway, but Amalie felt no jealousy. She thought that some good would come of the conversation.

Leo was thoughtful, then said, "It was like that for Amalie; her parents died in an accident when she was nineteen. She came to England to live with her aunt and uncle. Her father loved her best, probably because Amalie so much resembled him, and although I never knew him, I know that he was a very vain and fastidious man who felt his wife was somehow beneath him. I believe Amalie sees this behavior as her punishment. I have no idea why I am telling you this, other than to ask if you think you can help my daughter and strengthen her relationship with her mother."

Bernadette said, "I can certainly try, since I find myself at loose ends awaiting this baby."

Leopold laughed and walked away to join Mr. March.

Amalie approached her. "I am intrigued, Cherie."

Bernadette simply said, "Leo asked me to help your daughter to become nicer. I said I would try. I think he believes that because I worked in Harrods for two years, I have some sort of strength of character, which is fine since you and I know it was a lot of fun in a way, and I did it because I hated Tony's mother. I still do."

Amalie laughed out loud and embraced her friend, and that was all that was said on the subject.

Bernadette was enjoying her week at Blakefield Castle. Amalie and her family had made her feel so welcome. She considered how different these people were compared to her husband's family and friends. She felt moved by her hosts' kindness and the friendly atmosphere of Blakefield Castle—so different from Devereux House, which was meant to be her home, and even after seven years of marriage, she still didn't feel it was completely that, even with all the paintings now up in the attics.

She was wandering alone in the rose garden, thinking of ideas for Devereux House. The gardens were next on her list to plan, and she wasn't sure how to go about it.

She suddenly heard a voice. It was Cosette, and she said, "I suppose I should apologize. I was very mean that night at dinner, but you see—"

Bernadette interrupted. "Cosette, let's put that part behind us. May I please come to see your room?"

Cosette seemed embarrassed and said, "You will hate it. It is childish, but I don't want to hurt Papa's feelings." And as they walked up the grand staircase, they passed Mrs. March, who greeted Bernadette kindly and gave Cosette a stern look.

Cosette said, "I hate her. I hate all of them except perhaps Malcolm. My mother dotes on Leon, and so do Blanche and Cordelia. Did you know they are lovers?"

Bernadette thought, *Oh dear, this might be harder than I imagined,* and said, "Cosette, you mustn't say that to anyone else. It is unkind and not your business anyway. I hate most of my husband's family and friends too, but we mustn't allow it to ruin our lives. Now show me your room."

Cosette laughed out loud and said, "Finally a kindred spirit!"

She opened her bedroom door, and Bernadette had to hold her breath. She too had been spoiled as a child and had a princess's bedroom—but this was ridiculous. There were dolls and stuffed animals galore, too many to count, and the décor was really for a very young child. This surprised Bernadette, given Amalie's impeccable taste.

"Cosette, do you hate your room?"

"My father likes it. He still buys me dolls and stuffed rabbits. My mother hates it too, but she doesn't say that to him or to me, but I can tell she does."

"Possibly, he is afraid to see his little girl grow up. I was eighteen when I got married. My father wasn't very pleased about it, but I stood my ground. Wouldn't you prefer a grown-up room and some grown-up dresses? Your mother is renowned for her sense of style, and I am sure she would love to help you. Perhaps she is reluctant to step between you and your father."

"Honestly, I love my mother, but I don't think she likes me. I think she hoped to have a stunningly beautiful daughter, or perhaps she is glad that she didn't. Did you see her nude? My father often sits in there admiring it. Also, they are quite old, but he is always kissing and fondling her. Malcolm is in love with her too, and Leon is an absolute mama's boy. I think she likes to be the center of attention."

"Cosette, do you think you are jealous of your mother? She is lovely and has many talents, but why don't we explore yours? What do you like?"

"Animals, all kinds, even the cows—dogs and cats, horses and goats. I want to become a veterinarian like Mr. Freeman, our local vet, but my parents would have a fit. I don't think I want to get married, unless to a veterinarian. Why did you marry so young anyway?"

Bernadette told Cosette her own story, and Cosette listened avidly. She said, "You are beautiful too, in a different way to my mother, but just as lovely really. Will you help me with my room?"

"All right, but first, let's get you dressed for dinner. I will fetch Margaret. She is very good with hair."

Bernadette found Margaret, who said, "Bridgette is showing me the ropes. I intend to utilize my new skills when we return to Devereux House—that is, if I still have a job after the baby comes so early. So what am I supposed to do for the spoiled brat?"

Bernadette said, "I actually feel quite sorry for her. Her room is decorated like a nursery for a six-year-old, and her dresses are childish too. She makes up to her father to make her mother jealous because she sees her mother as perfect. She said her mother doesn't like her, and, Margaret—I am not sure she does. Sir Leopold has asked me to help his daughter, but there isn't anything wrong with her. She just needs to be allowed to grow up. Let's go."

Margaret was appalled by the bedroom and said out loud, "No wonder you are so horrid! I'd be horrid too if I had to sleep in here. Let's get rid of some of this stuff—all of it possibly!"

∾⁓✺⁓∾

They cleared most everything out of the room—the stuffed animals, toys, and dolls. Already it looked so much better. They had the servants take everything away, and Cosette was smiling happily throughout the whole enterprise. Then she and Bernadette rehearsed her dinner conversation.

Bernadette said, "You have learned many things from your mother without even knowing it. Show her the affection and respect that you normally give to your father. Feel free to ignore him if you like. Let's see what happens. I am inviting you to my house after the baby is born. In the spring, you can help me plant my garden—well, I mean design it. You have a good knowledge of herbs and flowers."

Bernadette and Cosette walked a little late into dinner together. Cosette was wearing one of her less girlish dresses, and Margaret had put her hair up.

Bernadette announced, "I forgave her." And they both sat down.

The conversation returned to the usual pleasantries, and Cosette was smiling at her mother and ignoring her father. Both parents seemed a little confused, and then she announced, "Bernadette has invited me to stay with her during spring break. The baby will be here, and I can help her with it. She also needs my advice with her garden, as it seems it has gone to seed under the watchful eye of Arabella, the witch."

Bernadette burst into laughter, and then so did the others,

until Amalie said, trying to keep a straight face, "Cosette, you mustn't call her that when Lord Devereux comes to stay. It's his mother, after all."

Bernadette said, "Oh, he won't mind. I call her much worse things to her face, as she does me."

⌖

Cosette kept to her word, and Leopold later said to Bernadette, "What did you say to her? Threats? Cajoling?"

"No, Leo, I just realized she wanted her mother now. Daddy's little girl isn't so little, and she needs to learn women things that a man cannot teach her. She will find her way, and then she will return to you, but you need to let her fly, and Amalie needs to allow her fully into her heart."

Leopold was standing looking stunned at this little American who was still a young girl, setting him straight, and when Bernadette sensed this, she said, "Or there is always Harrods!"

And he burst into laughter.

There was a great deal of excitement when Tony and Walker arrived in a brand-new Rolls Royce Silver Ghost, and Bernadette would have jumped up and down if it weren't for the baby.

Shortly afterward, Imogen and Leon were picked up at the train station, and it was a jolly gathering for afternoon refreshments.

Bernadette whispered, "Oh, Tony, I so missed you. I couldn't spend another day apart. Can we promise that to each other?" And then she introduced him to everyone. "My husband, Viscount Anthony Devereux, Tony to his family and friends. And, Cosette, you promised me your opinion. Isn't he so handsome?"

Amalie couldn't hide her amazement as her daughter paced deliberately around Lord Devereux with a serious demeanor and then announced, "Yes, Bernadette, very well favored indeed!"

Tony shouted in pretend concern, "Oh no, you have not let my wife loose on your daughter?"

Bernadette answered, "They certainly have! And Cosette is coming to stay in the spring. I might not give her back."

Cosette was smiling happily. Bernadette was her mother's friend, but she was also her friend too, and she was really so much fun.

At dinner that night, Leon was gazing at Bernadette with such admiration that his father was reminded of McFadden in the early years. Clearly, his son was smitten, and he thought he had better speak with him and nip this in the bud. He was not in the mood for a lovelorn young man in his midst. His wife's little friend was very pretty and quite outrageous, but she was also a married woman and a pregnant one to boot. He recalled those days when Amalie almost drove him mad with jealousy—of her tête-à-têtes with McFadden and the times when she used to set him up at dinner, to the amusement of his sister and his guests. Sometimes she was still inclined to do so, but he was happy to pass the crown along to Viscount Devereux. He was considering this when he heard his wife say, "So, Tony, tell us how the house is coming along. Does your mother approve?"

Tony was responding that he wasn't too sure if she approved of the exotic birds now adorning his walls when Cosette interjected, "Lord Devereux, is your mother really a wicked witch?"

"It seems my wife has been telling tales" was his retort.

Amalie said, "Bernadette tells us it is necessary for her to sit at the other end of the table when you have guests, although fortunately your sister Charlotte now joins her there. We are all invited to this grand New Year's party you will be having, and I must admit we are so looking forward to it and to meeting your mother."

Blanche joined in. "Is it a very large dining room table? Perhaps then we can similarly divide ourselves for the occasion."

Tony said, "By now, you are quite getting to know my wife, in which case you should also know that you cannot rile me up. Bernadette is just jealous of my lineage. First time I heard of a New Year's party, however. My love?"

Bernadette said, "Yes, dearest, indeed, I am so very jealous! Four hundred years of really quite nasty and appalling ancestors, and then along came my handsome husband. What a relief for the House of Lords."

Cosette said, "I think it was so romantic the way you met in the foyer of the Ritz Hotel."

And finally, Tony had his moment. "Yes it was, Cosette. Bernadette had just arrived in London, intending to ensnare a peer of the realm, and lucky me, I walked right into her spider's web."

Leo added, "My wife hunted me down too! I was terrified of her, especially due to her hurling insults and looking down her little nose at me, but I couldn't get away—no choice but to marry her and have done with it."

Amalie feigned indignation and said, "Leo, how dare you? I was far too good for you, and, well, you knew it! It was quite the other way around, and you still don't deserve me."

All were laughing, and Tony said, "It was not so much Bernadette that scared me. She was just an eighteen-year-old waif. It was her father, James Barrymore, who terrified me. You will meet him at this New Year's party I am apparently hosting. Might terrify all of you too!"

And so the week passed quickly, and Bernadette was sad to leave. They were all so much fun, and she had made many new friends, her first real friends in England other than Margaret. Of course, she spoke to Imogen about a nude painting, and Imogen fixed the price so that Bernadette could afford it from her father's allowance that she had saved up during the war. Bernadette had reasoned that she had given Tony the miniature for his birthday; what better than to surprise him with a nude painting of his wife for Christmas? And thank goodness she didn't need to ask her father or Tony for the money she needed. Imogen promised not to make too much of her growing belly, and Amalie promised that none of them would speak of it to Tony, as it was to be a surprise. Bernadette could go with Margaret into London for a few sittings and use the excuse of Christmas shopping.

Leopold cautioned Amalie, "What if Tony disapproves of such a thing? Not all men are as open-minded as your husband."

Amalie had responded, "Then it will turn out to be such fun if he does. Although I would add, shame on him. Also, since when were you so open-minded? You've always told me that Bridgette and I have just beaten you down!"

❧

The car ride home wasn't so jolly. There was considerable tension in the air, and Walker was exceptionally quiet—even for him. Bernadette sat in the back with Margaret holding her hand. She could feel it as certainly as Margaret could. Something had happened or had been said, and she knew it was about time she spoke to her husband.

Tony broke the silence. "I got a letter from Daddy. He's bringing the whole lot over for the holidays, even O'Connor. They're all leaving early January, but he and your mother are staying on for the birth."

Bernadette and Margaret looked wide-eyed at each other—a sight not unnoticed by Tony in his rearview mirror.

Bernadette asked, "What, everyone? Nancy and the girls? What fun! Amalie and her family can meet them all, and Cosette can meet my nieces! We must see to all the guest rooms for New Year's eve! That's a lot of people to put up!"

Finally, Walker spoke up. "I understand your brother Sean is also coming, your ladyship."

There was something in the way he said it that made her grip Margaret's hand. But Bernadette ignored the comment and said, "Oh, and the Fallsingtons—they can meet them too, and of course your mother. Perhaps she will bring Lady Villan. What fun we all shall have!"

CHAPTER 20

It was Christmas evening, and a very pregnant Margaret assisted her pregnant mistress in finding something suitable to wear for dinner.

By now, the two friends had fallen into their new roles, which were mistress and lady's maid who confided utterly in each other, took tea together, and watched out for each other's welfare.

Bernadette had been quite surprised that Tony didn't speak to her about Margaret and Tommy after that dreadful drive home from the Blakeleys' in the autumn. Therefore, she too said nothing, and Margaret confirmed that neither had Tommy, although she felt he had built up a barrier of silence between them.

"I know he thinks something is fishy, but he doesn't say a thing. Meanwhile, I feel my time is coming very soon, although I keep saying February."

Bernadette responded, "And so you must carry on saying that. I keep thinking Tony is going to ask me about it, and I am dreading that; however, since he has already spoiled Christmas Day for me, I will just tell him to go to hell if he does."

Margaret couldn't help but laugh. The painting, it seemed, had been an utter failure, and Bernadette was so funny when she was angry with her husband.

"I told you, Bernadette. It was a bit risky. Remember Lady Blakeley's husband commissioned her nude, and even then, she told us he was regretful of it. Now, what are you going to do with it?"

Bernadette had already decided that. There are enough rooms in this mausoleum. I will speak to Amalie about fixing up one of the guest rooms as my private quarters. That way, I can hang the painting there. I might even build up my own collection of art—all nudes. Also, Tony didn't ask Imogen for a portrait of me with my clothes on! He thinks I am not worthy of the honor—me being the Irish bricklayer's daughter. Did you know his mother sent her butler Dankworth over to collect the painting of her and Tony? I told him to take them. He can take Tony too. Oh dear, nothing fits me!"

Margaret said, "Me neither, and I really could have done without the honor of the dinner invitation, given Tommy and me tonight. It will be so much fun—believe that if you will!"

Just then, Tony appeared and dismissed Margaret. Bernadette said, "Oh, that wave of the hand thing. Don't you dare do that to me, or I will punch you! Remember, it was last Boxing Day that I left you. One year ago tomorrow, and I can certainly do so again!"

Tony lay down casually on top of the bed. "What? And miss the great Lady Blakeley and her tribe for your New Year's Eve party? Anyway, my love, you waddle too much to climb aboard ship. You might fall over."

Bernadette responded, "Yes, you are right. I will wait until January fifth when everyone but Daddy and Mommy are returning to Boston. Michael will lend me his arm and look after me. I will take my painting with me, and you can hang all of your ugly ancestors back up on the walls, because this time I will not return."

Tony was exasperated; Bernadette had been behaving like a spoiled child almost throughout her entire pregnancy. The painting was undoubtedly tastefully done, and his wife, of course, was lovely. Imogen had brought out her eyes to perfection, and Bernadette was wearing a secretive little smile that showed off her dimples. She was wearing very little else except some strategically draped silk scarves. If she had chosen to wear a bit more clothing, he would have been so proud to hang the painting above the fire in the great hall, pride of place, but what could he actually do with such a risqué painting of Viscountess Lady Devereux? He also knew, or at least felt, that Margaret was about to go into labor any day, and then all of his reassurances to Walker will have been in vain. *It might be Christmas Day,* he thought, *but since my wife is already in a snit, I may as well ask her what I should have asked months ago.*

Bernadette was pulling dresses out of her closet and throwing them on the floor. She felt about to burst into tears. She felt so fat and ungainly, and her husband liked to tease her about her waddling. She had been so excited when he ripped off the brown paper the painting had been wrapped in, and he was excited too—until he realized that she was naked, and then he seemed disappointed. He certainly disapproved of it. That much was quite evident, and Bernadette was deeply hurt, although determined not to show that to him.

"Kindly get out of my room. I need to get dressed for dinner. Unless, of course, you prefer that I stay in my room since you have the usual Christmas dinner guests."

He responded, "Actually, only five—my mother, Georgiana, Cecil and Marjorie, oh and Walker. I am counting my sister

Charlotte in with your guests, which, including your nieces, number I believe ten."

Bernadette was livid with Arabella for once again inviting Lady Villan, most especially with her being over seven months pregnant, with her baby due mid-February. She also thought Tony was behaving very badly toward her, and it was becoming increasingly difficult to hold back her tears.

Then Tony quite shocked her. "Bernadette, I need to ask you this now, seeing the sheer size of Margaret. This is a little awkward, to say the least, but—"

Bernadette interrupted him. "Then, since it is so awkward and you are supposed to be a gentleman, can't it wait until tomorrow or another day before I leave you forever on January fifth?"

He stood up and said, "I expect so," and he turned and just walked out the door. Bernadette felt as if she was the one being punished for Margaret's indiscretions.

Margaret returned and helped Bernadette with her hair. She was about to take out the diamond and emerald tiara. Bernadette said, "I'm not wearing that thing. I'm not wearing my earrings or necklace either. I wonder why he always gives me emeralds. Well, I suppose possibly Granny had green eyes or something or other, since they are all out of the family vault. I am wearing Daddy's pearls instead. They are real pearls, all the way to my waist, and knowing Daddy, they cost a fortune. Don't you love yours too, Margaret? Come on, help me put a sheet around the painting. I have a feeling his lordship will be sleeping in his own room tonight, and I have no wish to offend him."

This done, both women waddled downstairs arm in arm. Margaret said, "I am sure Mr. Higgins is expecting you to change the place settings again this evening. He was absolutely tickled pink with the gold watch and chain you gave him, and Mrs. O'Leary, the diamond broach. No wonder they love you, Bernadette."

Bernadette responded, "Well, oftentimes servants can be such snobs, yet they were always so lovely to me. I mean real servants, Margaret. You are not a servant and never will be. It is just an excuse to keep us together. And we will always be together, come what may—babies and all. I need to move you into the main house until the birth. I will get Dr. Morris to say it is a necessity. He has been on our side with this. I think everyone hated Arabella so much; that is why they are so good to me."

These words touched Margaret since she wasn't very sure of her position, and she kissed Bernadette's cheek in response to them.

Mr. Higgins was expecting his mistress to appear in the dining room as she did, with Margaret in tow, and as she proceeded to switch around the place cards, he thanked her again for such a generous gift.

Bernadette brushed it off by saying that many back payments were included in it as she kissed his cheek, and he blushed.

As the two friends entered the drawing room—Margaret a little hesitantly—Tony was standing talking to his father-in-law, Cecil, and, for some unknown reason, Lady Villan.

Bernadette ignored them as Michael and Sean stood up to offer the two pregnant ladies their seats on the sofa, and Bernadette kissed them both on the cheek before taking hers.

Arabella exclaimed, "Bernadette, how you have grown! Isn't it about time you excuse yourself when there are guests?"

Even Lady Villan and Marjorie Fallsington were taken aback by the dowager viscountess's comment, as were the others. However, in the case of these two ladies, their shock was tinged with envy. Neither woman had children, and it seemed quite likely that neither ever would.

Bernadette ignored the remark. She was used to her remarks, and it was only rarely that Tony had his mother there for dinner. Instead, she said, "Arabella, I will allow you to come for my

New Year's Eve party. You will be able to meet the magnificent Lady Amalie Blakeley and her family. They are such amusing and intelligent company. I have rarely been impressed by anyone as I have been by them—indeed, if ever! Of course, even the English members of her party are half Spanish, and Lady Blakeley is French. There are also Americans, and I must say, Arabella, the gentlemen are as handsome as the women are charming. It will be quite a treat for you."

Arabella responded, "Do you think such an endeavor is wise in your condition, my dear?"

Eugenie surprised everyone by responding to the last remark, "Lady Devereux, my daughter is as healthy and strong as she is beautiful. She will be excellent, and all who love her will be there to support her. It is very generous that she invited you and your special guest."

Arabella said, "What special guest, Mrs. Barrymore? I am afraid I don't understand."

Eugenie said, "I have been twice to stay in my daughter's home, and each time, you seem to come along with your young blonde friend. Lady Villan, is it? Do you have children? Lady Villan?"

Eugenie spoke so sweetly, and Georgiana just answered, "No," as all were called in to dinner.

Tony shook his head once again at the seating arrangement. James Barrymore was seated at the other end of the table with his daughter and wife on either side of him. Next to Bernadette was Michael and then Nancy and her girls and Charlotte. Sean was next to Margaret, and he thought, *Not such a wise decision, my love.* He noticed that the youngest girl, Nanette, had her aunt's dimples and her vivaciousness and sparkle, and she was the only one who smiled at him as they were seated. Tony had his mother on one side of him, and for some twisted reason, Georgiana was seated to the right of him. The Fallsingtons were next in his lineup, with Walker at the end.

The dining room table, when fully extended, could seat thirty-six, and although he couldn't remember the last time it was fully extended, it seemed on this occasion it was. He realized that Bernadette was hurt by his reaction to the painting. She misunderstood him as usual. It was beautiful, but where would he hang it? She also wasn't wearing the diamond and emerald necklace and earrings he had given her. She was wearing her father's pearls. She certainly wasn't displaying much sparkle that evening, and he knew he was the cause. He asked himself, *What kind of man would hurt his dearest little, very pregnant wife on Christmas Day?* He knew the answer. *A man terrified of what lies ahead. A woman can die giving birth. It happens often enough.* He then fully understood his reaction to her painting. It had nothing to do with where to hang it. The house had enough rooms to make one private. It was just that he was struck with the sudden fear that he would be sitting looking at the beautiful painting in the years ahead, and she would be gone forever.

He needed so much to tell her so. He felt it just couldn't wait. She was trying to be jolly with her usual quirky sense of humor, but somehow it stabbed him in the heart because he could see right through it. The footmen were serving out the soup when he stood and excused himself. "Please, everyone, carry on. There is a matter of some urgency that I forgot to mention to my wife. We will return to our seats momentarily."

He walked over and helped Bernadette out of her chair, and when they left the room, she said, "Have you lost your mind, Lord Devereux? What urgent matter are you referring to, and it better not have anything to do with the Walkers."

He said, "Who? Oh yes. No, it doesn't."

He led her into his study, a room she was barely ever in, closed the door, sat down, and pulled her onto his lap. "God, you have gotten heavy," he said, really without thinking.

Bernadette replied, "Have you brought me in here to insult me?" And she started crying the tears she was holding back all day.

He began, "Bernadette, my love, the love of my life, I love your painting. It is the most beautiful thing I will ever own."

Bernadette said, "Then why did you act like you didn't like it?"

Tony answered simply, "My love, in less than two months, you will be bringing our child into the world, and I was suddenly struck with the fear that … well, I don't know how quite to say it. The fear that I will sit gazing at that painting for the rest of my life, and you will be in heaven looking down upon me."

Bernadette stopped crying and said incredulously, "Is that it?"

He said, "No, there is more. I need to be with you—when the time comes. I can't be downstairs pacing the floor. I need to hold your hand and reassure you that all will be well."

Bernadette felt loved more than anyone else in the world and said, "Tony, isn't that a little unusual? Also, it sounds as if I might be the one reassuring you. I don't know, Tony. It is kind of—well, I don't know, but I do know that giving birth isn't pretty."

"Nevertheless, promise me you won't let them throw me out."

Bernadette hugged him and kissed both of his hands and said, "I promise."

When they both walked back into dinner, Bernadette said, "Tony made me promise him something. So I did."

She was wearing a secret little smile, and Margaret knew she would find out later. Several folks at Bernadette's end of the table knew that too, and dinner progressed quite happily after that, as did the rest of the evening.

Tony took the sheet off the painting and carried it into Bernadette's room as she lay exhausted in bed. "I think we shall hang it in here, our private oasis, and anyway, at least certain parts of you are hidden. It is you— the painting, isn't it? You've grown a bit since then."

Bernadette turned around and said, "Gee whiz, I can't wait to have this baby. I am so uncomfortable, and it's all your fault."

Tony turned over too, thinking about Walker, and smiled in the knowledge of the joy he felt in absolutely knowing that was the case.

CHAPTER 21

Boxing Day and a telegram arrived. It was from Blanche, and it said that Bridgette was down with the Spanish flu. Consequently, they couldn't possibly leave her to come to Bernadette's party.

Bernadette was disappointed but not terribly so. She was more worried about Bridgette and the rest of the family, most especially Amalie's welfare.

Fortunately, like Tony and Bernadette, Bridgette recovered, and Amalie joyfully wrote to Bernadette and promised they would all come after the babies were born. It was time now for both women to take it easy. She added that she had given Margaret and her situation a great deal of thought but somehow couldn't get beyond the fact that Margaret's baby would be Bernadette's niece or nephew and, of course, James Barrymore's grandchild. She added, *We must consider both Margaret and the baby's welfare before Mr. Walker's, but all will become clear to us after the birth.*

Bernadette knew exactly what she meant. The baby's grandfather was extremely wealthy. Walker was a valet.

Margaret went into labor on January 2, and the whole Barrymore family was still there. At 2:00 a.m. on January 3, she gave birth to a healthy, nine-pound baby boy. Tommy Walker had waited with the other men downstairs, but after his first glimpse of his son, he left the house, appearing upset. Eugenie, who had attended the birth with Dr. Morris, Nancy, and Bernadette, who held Margaret's hand throughout, was not surprised by this occurrence. She had worried about it for many months, and even for an infant, his resemblance to her son Sean was remarkable. She was the baby's grandmother.

Eloise, who had been both Leon and Cosette's nanny, was employed for the position at Devereux House and had been sent for "a few weeks early," and Eugenie told her daughter to go to her room and rest since her time was not so far away.

Bernadette was lying down when Tony came in to see her. He had been up all night like the rest of the family, and the men had been drinking. Bernadette prepared herself for the inquisition. He looked angry, and she felt he had no right to be so.

"You've known from the start, haven't you, Bernadette?"

"I knew it was possible, only a possibility, and that was all."

Tony looked outraged. "Possibility? Bernadette, when it comes to babies and a man's wife, there can be no possibilities or even probabilities. It should be a certainty. You were with her. How did this happen?"

Bernadette felt sick, and she was so tired, but the anger welled up in her, as it seemed that her husband was indeed blaming her for Margaret's infidelity. "I am her friend, Tony, not her guard dog and—"

He interrupted her. "No, Bernadette, you are her mistress— or were. It seems you are full of secrets and surprises."

Bernadette was outraged and so very hurt. She wasn't sure what he meant, but she felt her heart break as she shouted, "Daddy!" And this time, she knew he would come to her.

It was Eugenie who first appeared. She looked tired and very concerned and told Tony to leave her daughter to rest. "We are all overtired and should have a sleep before anything further is said."

Tony seemed to settle down and was about to usher Eugenie

out of the door when James Barrymore appeared. "No, not in here, Tony. My daughter's mother will stay with her. Go find somewhere else to rest and to sober up."

That was all he said, but the man was nobody's fool and had decided that although there was much to be said, it would be said later in the day, and he would not have his daughter upset by her English husband's accusations and anger.

Tony obeyed the order given him by his father-in-law, but he felt that the Barrymores had completely taken over his home and his wife. He felt sick for Walker and sicker still for how he spoke to Bernadette in her condition, so he too strode out of the house. Only he made his way to the dower house, where his mother was happy to comfort him and set him up for a nice sleep in one of her guest rooms.

❧

Hours later, the family started to come back to life. It had been a long and dreadful night and day, and it was already late afternoon. Eugenie was first awake and was running a bath for her daughter. "You will feel better after a nice, warm bath. Margaret is fine, and Nancy is with her. The nanny, Eloise, has arrived, and is taking care of the baby."

"Mommy, I want to go see Margaret first. I need to reassure her. No matter what happens now, I will be by her side, as indeed she was by mine for more than two years when the Devereuxes ignored my very existence."

Eugenie agreed that she should, and before her bath, Bernadette went to reassure her friend. "You look grand, Margaret, and you're lucky. You have the birth behind you and a bonnie baby boy to love you, as indeed we Barrymores all love you, especially me."

Margaret seemed relieved by her friend's words. Bernadette was indeed her friend and not her mistress, and she said, "I am calling him Thomas Junior, although I have no idea where Thomas Senior has taken himself. It is funny, Bernadette, but the very first time you hold your baby—it is like you know that one way or another, everything will turn out just fine."

Margaret seemed so serene, and Bernadette was glad of it. She was despondent and disappointed in Tony but quipped, "Well, you might have no idea about your husband, but mine is at the dower house with his mother and Lady Villan nursing his wounds. He is putting his nose in where it doesn't belong and has even made insinuations about me. However, the Barrymores are here, and one way or another, as you say, everything will be fine. I am jealous, however, that you have it all over with, and I hear as birthing goes, yours wasn't so bad."

Margaret said, "I'll be up and about to see to you, Bernadette. And imagine me having a nanny too!"

Bernadette left her to take her bath and encountered her freshened-up husband already in her room, having asked Eugenie for some time alone with his wife.

"Why are you here, Tony? Did your mother throw you out? Please go away. I can't bear to look at you and your insinuations. I am taking a bath. My time is just around the corner, and I have my parents to care for me now. You are no longer needed. We will be away soon enough, but I cannot travel in my condition."

Tony noticed she called her mother and father her parents and not the usual mommy and daddy. He had hurt her yet again. He wasn't insinuating anything about her, and he already knew this secret. He just never wanted to be told it. He had allowed Bernadette to carry the burden alone.

"Bernadette, I was not insinuating anything. I was rather drunk and outraged for Walker, who has been so good to me."

Bernadette just gave him an incredulous look and proceeded into her bathroom and closed the door.

When she emerged, he was sitting on her bed. She knew deep

inside that Tony was terrified about the birth. She had seen it in him since he told her on Christmas Day, but she was hurt and angry, and he needed to be told a few home truths.

"Tony, I see you are still here. I really don't understand why you need a man to look after you anyway. My father has gotten along fine without one. And as far as him being good to you. Where would I have been if it wasn't for Margaret during that terrible war? You and your mother took nothing to do with my whereabouts or welfare. You buggered off to fight for king and country as soon as the war was declared, without any thought for your young, American, twenty-year-old wife with no friends or family to see to her. Well, actually, I did have. My daddy saw to me from all the way across the Atlantic. Were you never home on leave? Did you never in all that time wonder what had happened to me? No, you preferred to imagine the worst. I was living in a flat in London and having a jolly time seeing other men. Tony, it's over. I give you back free and clear to your mother and the likes of Lady Villan. I am too good for you and ..."

She stopped. He was sitting with his head bowed down, and she thought, *Four years in the trenches, Bernadette. What are you trying to do to the man?*

So she went to him and sat down beside him. "I didn't mean any of that, but, Tony, I intend to stand by Margaret, come what may, and whatever that means to you."

He surprised her. "I just want this to be over with, my love. I am almost jealous of Walker since at least he knows his wife survived. Although, of course, I have the certainty that he never had, poor chap. I wonder what he will do."

Bernadette said, "Tony, that is up to him. Are all Englishmen like you? I promised you I would be fine, but I am not so sure if you will be, and I can't have you passing out in the birthing room. I might have to go back on my promise."

He just said, "There are people everywhere in this house.

Thank God most of them leave on the fifth. Can we just have dinner in our room tonight?"

Bernadette said, "My thoughts entirely."

Things settled down after most of the visitors left, and there was some sort of discussion between James Barrymore, Tony, and Tommy Walker. Bernadette found that she really didn't want to know about it, at least at present, and during the next month, she kept up her correspondence with Amalie. She told her that Tony was so nervous that he was making her afraid.

On February 9, a car drove up, driven by Blanche, which included Cordelia, Amalie, and most importantly, Bridgette, who took complete control of the birthing room and of even Dr. Morris.

Bernadette's labor began on the evening of February 11, and Bridgette quickly and decidedly threw Lord Devereux out, saying, "No men in the birthing room. Go down and join your father-in-law. I do not need you hovering around your sweet wife as she endeavors to bring your child into this world!"

Bridgette called it the shortest labor ever, and at 12:01 a.m. on February 12, Bernadette gave birth to a ten-pound baby boy. His hair was black, his eyes were blue, and his father and grandfather were quite drunk when they both came in together to meet him. Bernadette was sitting up proudly. Her mother had tied her hair with a pretty blue ribbon, and she was beaming.

Tony barely noticed the boy in his cradle, in his relief to see how well Bernadette looked. It was finally over, and she had survived, as had her dimples, since she was smiling at him. That was until his father-in-law, who was holding the baby, exclaimed, "By all the saints in Ireland, this one even looks like an Englishman. Daughter, where is all his Irish blood?"

Tony then turned to take his boy and said in awe, "I have a son! A handsome one at that! Actually, quite a chubby son, Bernadette, for a newborn baby. All those sausages. No wonder you were waddling."

Bernadette said, "Well, I won't be waddling now, and I will soon be beating you at tennis, Lord Devereux. Don't you both want to know his name? I have decided. It is Louis James Devereux, the Right Honorable. I think that's the correct title."

Tony liked the name but couldn't help but say, "Don't I get a mention?"

And Bernadette said, to her father's burst of laughter, "You've already had a mention, many times, dear husband, when I was in labor!"

CHAPTER 22

It was a beautiful morning in May 1920. Both baby boys were thriving, and Eloise was an absolute delight, just as Amalie had promised.

Margaret had never moved out of her room in the main house, near the babies' nursery, and Tommy was still living in the cottage. He paid little attention to Margaret's baby, as he referred to him, and even less attention to Margaret. However, since they barely crossed paths, there was no atmosphere between them. Tommy seemed devoted to Tony, and Margaret was devoted to Bernadette.

There was finally a family meeting that included Tommy, Tony, Margaret, and the Barrymores. James announced his intention of legally adopting Tommy as his grandson without any declarations about his parentage. Sean would not be a part of the boy's life, and he would be reared in England with his cousin Louis.

Bernadette and Margaret stared at each other wide-eyed and tried not to show their happiness overmuch, but Tony was quiet, and Tommy just said, "Is that it? Well, I suppose so. No giving up on being the grandson of the great James Barrymore, and who am I to ask it? He has my name, and I will treat him as my own, or at least I will when Margaret decides to move back into the cottage and be a wife to me."

Later that day, Bernadette said to Margaret, "Well, it seems that Tommy wants you back. Isn't that good news?"

But Margaret responded, "I need to be near the babies to help Eloise. They are too much for her alone, and the dowager is on your husband's case about you carrying little Louis around with you everywhere. I best stick around for a while—in the main house, I mean."

Tony came by the newly planted rose garden where Bernadette was sitting, as usual, holding his son. He watched them for a little while before he spoke. He wondered if there was ever such a devoted mother, in his social class at any rate, and smiled at how this unexpected occurrence seemed to irritate his mother, "Granny," as Bernadette had named her. The Barrymores were given the titles of Nana and Papa, and of course, he was Daddy.

"A letter from Sir Leopold. He is confirming that I am agreeable to his daughter spending the summer here to help out with the birthing and the foals. He seems to think this will get the idea of becoming a veterinarian out of her head."

Bernadette responded, "No, it won't. Cosette can never compete with her mother in grace or beauty, but she is spirited and has her own personality. She is seventeen years old and still not out, and I understand that she refuses ever to be out. Her dream is to work with animals, and I will bet money that she isn't at all squeamish. At any rate, they are all coming on the twenty-seventh, and I am so proud of my beautiful house and my beautiful son and my handsome husband that I must show you all off. However, we must get in some practice on our tennis courts beforehand. I already know I can beat you, but I must also beat Leon. Leo and Malcolm will be that bit easier, being in their forties and even fifties—that's if they come."

Tony said, "Don't think I overlooked the handsome young Leon staring at my wife. A bit young for you, my dear."

Bernadette smiled smugly at him, and he sat down and took his son from her, smiling as she tried to rearrange the way he was holding him.

He said lovingly, "You know my love, you are a smashing little mommy." And then, "So we have the Blakeleys for a week, Cosette for the summer. Any plans on your parents going back to Boston?"

Bernadette had been expecting this. "Well, Tony, here's the thing. Daddy is semi-retired, and Sean has been ordered to toe the line with the threat of Michael taking over the business. He is already second in command. Also, what with baby Tommy and everything, Sean seems to have sobered up—somewhat anyway."

Tony said, "And?"

Bernadette closed her eyes tight. "Wouldn't it be just wonderful if you and me and baby makes three could go to Boston in the fall for the holidays? Thanksgiving and Christmas and all of that lovely snow. I can teach you to ice-skate, and we can go coasting too. I am very good at both, and Daddy has horse-drawn sleighs. Oh, *please*?"

He surprised her because he already knew of the invitation. "Why not? So when are they leaving?"

"August, I think, and we can go in October since I want to be there for Halloween. We do it much better in the States, and little Louis and Tommy can be cowboys. I was thinking of you and me as Anthony, of course, and Cleopatra."

"Cleopatra? We will see about that, my love, and I am not wearing a toga. At any rate, what about the Walkers?"

"Oh, Walker can come too … I mean, if that is all right with you and if he wants to. Margaret and baby Tommy are coming anyway, and Sean is in Nevada, some new venture of Daddy's."

Tony smiled. "Bernadette, my love, I'm afraid I have to tell you this. I know how to ice-skate and am rather good at it too, and coasting is easy if you know how to steer. However, I draw the line at cartwheels. Can you still do them now with your girlish figure back again?"

"Of course I can, Tony, and I have told you many times I am athletic. It was obvious that I would soon be beautiful again, just like my painting. I am glad that little Louis was inside me when Imogen painted it. Okay, I will do a couple of cartwheels for you, but I need to tie up my skirt. No one is looking, right?"

Tony watched proudly, holding his sleeping, contented baby as his adorable wife easily performed four of them in quick succession.

She then took back the baby, as always complaining about her hair, and he said, "Thank God I met you, Bernadette. Thank God you were standing in the hotel lobby when I walked in with your best friend, Cecil. Thank God you smiled at me and not at him. I've never regretted it, even during the dark days of the war."

Bernadette was smiling with those dimples he loved so very much. "Tony, I would love to relive that moment and have done so many times in my mind. Only, when I relive it, I am wearing a nicer dress, and my hair is fixed up, and my face isn't red from blushing at you."

He laughed and said, "No, you were perfect the way you were, and, my love, you are still perfect. Now let's get little Louis back to the nursery and check on the mares. I will take you riding too and show you my special place."

Bernadette said with mock severity, "Is that where you used to take the lovely Georgiana?"

And he answered, "Not telling."

Finally, the big day arrived, and Bernadette was, as usual, carrying her baby as she inspected each room to ensure everything was perfect. They were coming for the whole weekend—Amalie, Blanche, Cordelia, Leon, and of course, Cosette, who would be staying on. Mrs. March decided to come too, and also Bridgette to see to her mistress and to how Eloise and Margaret were coping with the babies.

Bernadette's guests were all looking forward to meeting Arabella the witch—a moniker that stuck to her after Cosette first coined the phrase.

Bernadette had sent formal dinner invitations to the dowager viscountess and the Fallsingtons, and she was determined to have a most enjoyable weekend, even despite her mother-in-law's acceptance, which included her bringing a special guest—Lady Georgiana Villan.

After being shown to their rooms to freshen up, everyone gathered in the newly completed conservatory, where Bernadette excitedly took the ladies aside. "My silk harem pants have been delivered, and they are so beautiful! Three pairs—ocean blue, aquamarine, and fuchsia—and I am wearing one pair to dinner tonight. I can't wait to see Arabella's face. Oh, and my satin pumps too. The toes are so pointy that they curl up. And matching headbands. They are all the rage and so jolly. I seriously doubt Tony and his mother will find them jolly, however." Bernadette put on a pretend worried frown. "Oh dear—how worrisome."

They all laughed, and Blanche said, "Please let us have fun with the seating, Cherie. This Fallsington chap and his wife sound a delight, and now you tell us we shall also be meeting Lady Villan."

"Yes," said Bernadette. "It appears that my mother-in-law is up to her usual mischief. I can hardly believe she has the nerve to bring that woman here yet again, but I extended the invitation to her. What else could I possibly do? Anyway, I have opened the table to its full length. It seats thirty-six. I will put Tony and his people at one end and us at the other. I fear there will be quite a distance between both parties so we might have to shout at one another."

It was a beautiful spring evening, and the table was laid out delightfully. The crystal was gleaming in the candlelight, and Amalie had brought an abundance of fresh flowers from her garden.

Bernadette laid out her shocking new clothes in Amalie's room, and when Tony appeared to get dressed for dinner, he asked, "Where's Margaret? Aren't you getting dressed to greet your visitors?"

Tony put on his usual white tie and cutaway and asked again, "Bernadette, what is going on? When are you getting ready?"

She remembered his remark from their wedding night and said, "Ready for what, Lord Devereux?"

However, he didn't laugh, and she told him to go downstairs, and she would find Margaret. There was a problem with a fastener on her dress or some such thing.

So he left her to it, and Bernadette ran along to Amalie's room, where all the ladies were awaiting her. When she got dressed, she modeled for them like the girls in Harrods, and Henrietta March surprised them all when she said, "I wish I were ten years younger, and I would purchase a pair of those myself! I find I rather like them—so chic and stylish."

And Blanche said, "Just ten years, Henrietta?"

Cosette helped Bernadette rearrange the table, and Cosette giggled at the large space that separated the guests in the middle of the very long dining room table. Dinner was to be delayed a little, with some made-up excuse, since Cordelia was showing Higgins how to make her famous martinis.

Cordelia said, "Two glasses, and your mother-in-law will be soused!"

Bernadette walked into the drawing room and said brightly, "I am so sorry I was delayed. Tony, have you introduced everyone?"

He stared at her in amazement, trying to find the right words, but his mother beat him to it.

"Bernadette, what on earth are you wearing? You look ridiculous. You really cannot be serious, my dear. Tony, what are your thoughts on this indecent mode of apparel?"

Eugenie was about to pounce again on her daughter's mother-in-law, which wouldn't be the first time, but Amalie saved the day by saying, "Cherie, you look magnificent. Come and kiss me. Is this the latest thing?"

Bernadette said, "Arabella, your wig is crooked," as she walked over to join her guests.

The older woman touched her hair as Cosette started giggling, and James burst into laughter. Bernadette looked at Tony with a sassy smile but was not surprised to find him glaring at her.

Blanche whispered, "Well, this seems to be off to a good start."

Cordelia's martinis were flowing, and dinner was delayed due to a problem with the poached salmon. Henrietta March, on her second drink, joined Arabella on the sofa. "We have found your daughter-in-law to be such a delight, and so kind of her to invite my great-niece for the summer. You must be so very proud of your new grandson."

Arabella answered, "She carries him around far too much.

The boy is becoming quite spoiled. However, I understand her sort often do that type of thing."

Eugenie heard this. "What sort would that be, Lady Devereux? The loving mother sort?"

And to the utter shock of everyone who was just expecting a bit of fun, Arabella responded, "No, that's not what I meant, Mrs. Barrymore. My son is a viscount—a member of the House of Lords. He picked up his wife—your daughter—in a hotel lobby, for goodness sake. She spent much of the war gadding about in London—up to goodness knows what—and now she has ensured that she will keep her place in a family well above her station by seemingly providing my son with an heir."

Everyone went silent, and James Barrymore looked about to explode. All turned to Tony, who was in a state of shock himself, but all he could manage was, "That's enough, Mother. Enough said. I think you have voiced your opinion of my wife loud enough now for all of our guests and even the servants to hear."

They were finally called into dinner, and Bernadette felt sick to her stomach. She expected the usual sarcastic Irish bricklayer remarks, but the wicked woman just actually cast aspersions upon her grandson's parentage. She thought, *"Seemingly providing my son with an heir," and Tony stands there with that stuck-up expression. He is correct; nothing must ever rile him if that comment did not.*

Tony attempted to lighten the conversation by saying, "So, my love, are you the genie from a magic lamp tonight? Am I to be granted three wishes?"

He approached her to take his arm. She did so only because Georgiana looked disappointed in the gesture since she must have so enjoyed Bernadette's put-down.

Bernadette said, "No, they are not for you tonight, Lord Devereux, and I am not your love. I am keeping them for another more deserving individual."

Tony would have laughed at the seating arrangement, had it

not been for his mother's remark. It was way beyond her usual insults to his wife, and he was seething. James Barrymore was glaring down the table at him, but he would need to deal with his mother later—alone.

Tony once again had Georgiana seated on his right side and his mother on his left, and of course, the Fallsingtons were assigned seats on his side of the table. He said to no one in particular, "Please forgive my wife's childish behavior with regard to the seating arrangements. I believe she is proving a point of some kind, although I am loathed to know what that point might be."

No one answered him, and Georgiana, still basking in the glow of Bernadette's put-down, said, "Oh, Tony darling, you must take me upstairs to look in upon the baby. Does he look at all like you?"

Bernadette was almost speechless at such rudeness and was still considering the correct response when Tony said, "Of course, you haven't yet met the little fellow. He is not so little. However, he likes his food, as does his mother. Quite a handful but a handsome little chap."

He smiled at Bernadette, but everyone knew this was a foolish response to such a backhanded request, which should have been turned over to his wife.

All could see the hurt and anger in Bernadette's eyes, and Blanche patted her knee to calm her. Then, quite unexpectedly, Arabella shocked everyone by saying, "Yes, why don't you both go up together after dinner. The nursery has just been done over by Bernadette's guest, Lady Blakeley. My daughter-in-law has more money than good taste, as you may well already know. Of course, money doesn't buy class or breeding, and I am afraid she is very much lacking in both of these qualities. This was made clear tonight by her mode of dress."

Bernadette ignored this particularly rude remark, even from

Arabella, who seemed in fine form that night, probably with the intention of humiliating her son's wife in front of her new friends.

Instead, she said, "Lady Villan, I'm afraid I cannot allow you to go upstairs with my husband or to see my baby." And then she casually turned to the others and said, "These oysters are so fresh. They are delicious, and I must compliment Cook. As my husband just announced, I have a very healthy appetite, and this dish is my special favorite."

Bernadette's guests continued eating, ignoring Lady Villan and the dowager's angry expressions at the other end of the table. Cordelia said, "I do so prefer fish and shellfish to game and red meat."

They all laughed when James said a nice, thick steak was more to his taste, and Blanche added, "Washed down with a large whiskey."

Bernadette's guests were deliberately snubbing Lady Villan, so much so that even Cecil Fallsington made no secret of his amusement with regard to it. He disliked Georgiana and knew what she was about. He also knew at one time Tony's mother was trying to arrange a match between Tony and a much younger Georgiana, but Tony would have none of it. Therefore, he couldn't quite understand why she appeared so often at Devereux House—mooning over Tony in front of his wife.

Cecil surprised Bernadette when he said, "Georgiana, you have been spending a lot of time in Hampshire this past year or so. At a bit of a loose end—so to speak? Surely there is much more amusement to be had in London?"

Bernadette, for the first time ever, felt grateful for Cecil's intervention, and she added, "I absolutely agree with you, Cecil, especially since I spent so much time *gadding about* in it. However, I suspect Lady Villan is ever hopeful of spending time with my husband. I understand they were great friends in their youth."

Arabella then did a hat trick, the martinis having entirely

gone to her head. "Much more than that, Cecil, and well you know it. They were practically betrothed before he took leave of his senses and up and married the bricklayer's daughter. Georgiana tirelessly nursed my son when he had the Spanish flu. Meanwhile, his wife was off doing goodness knows what in Boston, without a worry or a care."

Bernadette had no idea whether any of this was true. Still, it would certainly explain Georgiana's dislike of her, even Arabella's, although she had just put it down in the past to them being such frightful snobs. Tony should have told her all of this. Had he done so, she certainly would not have allowed her to join them yet again for dinner. She felt a little silly in so doing. It was like they all knew something she didn't, and she turned to her new friends and parents and said, "I really must apologize to you all. I am as surprised as you must be as to why this woman would even be sitting at my table—for that matter, even Tony's mother, with how she has spoken to me this night. Please promise you will stay the whole weekend. We must help Cosette settle in, and I promise neither of these persons will join us tomorrow night, nor during the rest of the weekend. Cecil and Marjorie, you are welcome to stay and may even join us at our side of the table for dinner tomorrow night. Cook is serving her specialty, filet of tenderloin. It is scrumptious. However, Tony might prefer to dine at the dower house."

Bernadette expected Tony to be angry, ashamed, or shocked, but he carried on eating and said, "What pleasant conversation for the dinner table, my love."

Bernadette felt there was something not quite right in the way he said it, and she wanted to shake him and ask him why he was acting so cold. For the first time ever, she began to wonder if there was still something between them—this vile woman and her husband. She thought that surely the others were thinking the same thing. She felt humiliated and not sure what to do or say next. She didn't want her parents to intervene, and it was as if they sensed it, since they said nothing.

She felt young and inexperienced in the behavior and mannerisms of Tony's upper-class family and friends. She wanted to run away—all the way back to Boston. They were happy there. She considered leaving the table when Leon spoke up and broke the awkward silence.

"Bernadette, it's such a beautiful, sunny evening. Fancy a drive in my new Buick? My father bought it for me for my twenty-first birthday and had it shipped over from the States. Pater is a total motor enthusiast, so is Malcolm, and they've been purchasing motor cars since before they had proper engines! Always trying to outdo one another if you ask me."

Bernadette looked from Amalie to Blanche, then to her father and mother, and they all nodded.

Cosette shouted, "I want to come too!"

But Leon said, "Not a chance, Cos."

Eugenie said, "The rest of us ladies will withdraw. Marjorie, you are welcome to join us. However, not you, Arabella, and certainly not you, Lady Villan. I think the correct thing is for both of you to leave my daughter's table at once."

Tony was about to tell his wife that she was not allowed to go gadding about the countryside with this young man, but he was stopped in his tracks by Georgiana, who stood up in her indignation and said, "How dare you address me in that manner." However, as she stood, a note she must have forgotten in her anger fell from her lap to the floor. Bernadette spotted it immediately, and although Georgiana hurriedly tried to retrieve it, she was no match for Bernadette's speed and precision.

Bernadette picked up the note, which Georgiana tried to grab from her, but Leon, who had been sitting next to Bernadette, stood up and grabbed Bernadette's hand, and they both ran out of the dining room, laughing as they went on their way.

Tony sat for a few seconds in shock about what had just occurred, then got up and followed them. However, they were already driving down the long drive, and his wife was laughing and throwing her arms in the air.

He had done nothing wrong, yet he felt he had again lost her, and when he walked back inside, as expected, James Barrymore was waiting for him. All he said was, "That note better not say anything incriminating, son, because if it does, by God, I will ruin you."

Tony responded, "I have done nothing to be ashamed of, and I am growing tired of your threats." He then picked up his car keys and stormed out of his house as his guests gathered for drinks in the conservatory.

Mr. Higgins gave the dowager viscountess and Lady Villan their wraps, and they were forced to walk to the dower house, a distance of just under a mile, since no one offered to drive them.

Eugenie began to apologize to her daughter's guests, even the Fallsingtons, but it seemed everyone agreed with Blanche's statement.

"Eugenie, I can't remember when I had such an interesting evening. Well, perhaps years ago with my brother and dear little Amie." Then she added, "James, I'm a pretty good judge of character. Your son-in-law is merely guilty of not knowing how to handle his mother and successfully get rid of the strumpet. Nothing more than that. Your daughter reminds me a bit of Amie when she was younger, and remember, Bernadette allowed that woman to come in the first place. Still, I am sure we are all in one mind as to wondering what the silly strumpet wrote in her note."

Everyone agreed, and James Barrymore even lightened up. "This just might be the end of Arabella's nasty remarks, or she can tell them to herself in the dower house, with no one there to listen to her. I hope she enjoys her walk home."

Amalie said, "I am afraid Blanche is right. I did often put

poor Leo through the wringer, but I love him so much. Tony and Bernadette are mad about each other. We can all see it. However—and Blanche will agree with me here—there must be some reason Arabella is such a nasty woman. A reason why she so hates your beautiful daughter. Perhaps we will find it out if we probe deep enough. As for Lady Villan, I suppose a woman scorned?"

Cecil said, "As Tony's best friend and confidant, I can reassure you that he was mad about Bernadette from the moment he first laid his eyes upon her. I was there, so were you, James and Eugenie, and it was plain for us all to see. He was twenty-eight at the time, and he and Georgiana are of similar age. Had he wanted her, I am sure he would have gotten around to proposing long before that. I don't remember that he ever admired her at all. However, she was constantly putting herself forward—thus, she married Lord Villan, probably for his money, but not until after she painfully watched Bernadette walk down the aisle."

Marjorie actually spoke up. "I watched her. There was hatred in her eyes. Then the war came, and everything changed for everyone, and there was no time for petty jealousies and thoughts of revenge. My advice to Bernadette is to rid her from her life."

All agreed, and Cordelia added thoughtfully, "Amie dearest, what is this about probing into the dowager's hatred of our Cherie? Blanche, is our dear sister planning to get us all in trouble again? Will we be exploring the attics?"

Everyone laughed, and the martinis were refreshed as they all waited to see who would arrive home first and in which car Bernadette would arrive.

Leon drove for a while, at first in silence, until he noticed tears running down Bernadette's lovely cheeks. He said, "Bernadette, they are just a couple of nasty old women. They are jealous of your beauty and vitality and how you light up the room. I think it is about time your husband banished both of them from your home, even his mother, if she can't learn to behave herself."

Bernadette responded, "Leon, I feel so stupid. I extended my invitation to Lady Villan tonight. I thought it would be a lark, especially since Lady Devereux is always pushing her at Tony. I thought he didn't like her at all. Possibly I misread everything. You heard Lady Devereux say that they were practically betrothed. Why did Tony never mention that? What was he hiding? I am afraid to read the note, but I know I must. Will you stop the car, and we can read it together? I mean, in case it reveals something terrible?"

Leon pulled the car over. "Bernadette, before we read it, do you have any reason to think he has been unfaithful to you?"

The words stung, but she bravely answered, "For most of our married life, we have been estranged. First, the war, when his mother intercepted our correspondence with one another, and we never saw or heard from each other for three years. Then I left him on Boxing Day 1918. He had just returned from France, and I left him and went back to Boston. I left him, and that woman was there the night I did. He came for me but not until five months later. So, although I never thought so before, he has had plenty of opportunities."

Leon said, "Well, Bernadette, brace yourself." And she handed it to him to read to her.

Tony,

I need to see you alone. To talk to you and discuss how we can be together. I still believe we were made for each other, even if that means meeting only in secret. Let's go riding tomorrow morning. Your wife will be with her friends, and you should be able to slip away. We could meet at the stables, possibly at 9 a.m.? No need to answer; a nod will suffice, and I will wait for you. Tony, you know I will wait for you forever, hoping one day you will come to your senses and our passion may finally be fulfilled.

Ever yours, Georgiana

Bernadette felt as if her heart had stopped beating. She grabbed the letter, which didn't prove one thing or another. "Leon, drive up the road a bit. Tony showed me this spot the other day and told me it was his special place. I want to investigate."

Leon started the engine, and Bernadette couldn't help but laugh when he asked, "Are we looking for clues in the grass?"

It was a beautiful spot, a clearing amid the trees that were in full foliage, but now it didn't feel very special to Bernadette, as when Tony took her there just a few days earlier. They had tethered the horses that day and sat on the grass as they chatted happily, laughing at this thing or that. Bernadette remembered him saying, "Not telling," when she asked if he had taken Georgiana there.

She sat down with Leon, and they re-read the note. Leon was reassuring Bernadette that it contained nothing incriminating when they suddenly heard a voice—Tony's voice. He said, "Leon, I need to talk to my wife alone. We will see you back at the house."

Leon had no choice but to stand up and take his leave, and Bernadette stood too, kissed him on the cheek, and thanked him for being a friend when she so dearly needed one.

Tony sat down on the grass, taking Bernadette's hand, and asked her to join him there. "Let me see the note, Bernadette. I have nothing to fear or be ashamed of. That woman means absolutely nothing to me—quite the reverse. Even when we were young, my mother always put us together, and I disliked so many things about her. She made me cringe. She still makes me cringe, and after tonight, I am done with being a gentleman about it."

Bernadette still held on to the note. "First of all, what about her made you cringe? I am not sure if I believe you. She is quite beautiful, I think, even at her age, which must be close to yours. I am sure she was pretty ten years ago—or more like twenty years ago …"

She smiled when she corrected her rival's age, and Tony saw the dimples he adored. He turned to make sure Leon had left and took Bernadette in his arms. "Why do you not understand how much I am in love with you? I am sorry if I cannot be gregarious like your Irish admirers. I cannot show on my face what I feel inside. I love your strange little outfit. It suits you. God, Bernadette, I love everything about you, even your dinner arrangements. I don't mind if you choose not to sit with me at dinner, as long as you are always beside me in bed."

Bernadette liked him saying that to her and knew he was telling the truth. The mask he often wore hid so many of his emotions—but that was just who he was, the man she loved. She would never want to change anything about him, except perhaps his mother. Nevertheless, she was curious. "What made you cringe? You must tell me if you want the note."

Tony shook his head and said, "All right. Her voice is shrill. She is too tall and thin, with big feet, and her bones stick out, or at least they did the one time I ever kissed her when I was eighteen. She smelled sour, like stale sweat, and I felt sick afterward. I never kissed her again, but still, she pursued me. Then years later, having gotten rid of her, my mother and my wife began inviting her to my home."

Bernadette smiled smugly, enjoying her arch-rival being described in such a demeaning manner, and Tony continued, "Then I met the girl who would become my wife. I knew it the moment I saw her, and when I kissed her, her womanly scent made me mad with desire. A desire only she could ever satisfy in me. Her hair is wild and romantic and so wonderfully soft and sensual when she runs it down my body. Her curves are so womanly. Her skin is so soft. Her eyes so alluring, and then those dimples. Did I forget toes? Toes I will one day eat for my supper. My beautiful wife, do you still doubt me?"

Bernadette was glad that Lady Villan dropped the letter. She felt so adored. So much better in every womanly way than the woman who tried to steal her husband from her. She handed Tony the note, and he read it.

"Vile woman" was all he said as he ripped it up and turned and passionately kissed his wife.

When he drew back and smiled at her, he said, "Dimples."

Bernadette smiled and said, "Can I have the pieces back? I want to show it to Margaret. Also, Amalie and Cordelia—"

He interrupted her. "Fat chance," he said, helping her to her feet. "Now, my love, let that be the end of Lady Georgiana Villan."

When they were driving back to the house, Bernadette asked, "Why does your mother hate me so? I thought when she sent me your letters and our wedding photographs, it was a peace offering—sort of—but it wasn't, was it?"

He replied, "I've often wondered about that. Not at first, she so strongly objected to our marriage, but it seems to have almost gotten worse. I thought after the baby ..."

"Maybe it's just because she feels you could have done better. But you don't believe what she says about me gadding about?

Tony laughed. "What—a good Irish Catholic girl? Not a chance! And there is no one better than you or who even comes close. Before I walked into the Ritz that night, I thought I would remain single. No woman ever really caught my fancy. Then I saw you. You turned and looked at me, and my heart did a somersault. I smiled at you, and you smiled back. That's when I noticed your dimples, and, my love, your dimples just finished me off."

"I was mortified when Daddy introduced himself to you. I heard the concierge call you Lord Devereux, and I knew that was exactly why my daddy did so."

Tony again laughed. "Yes, I remember your shocked expression. I wondered why. That was until your father bought me a drink in the bar. He thought I was an impoverished sod with a title in need of some hard cash. I was sure that's what you had been taught to believe about English gentry. He threatened to ruin me tonight, on my way out the door to find you."

Bernadette said, "Oh, that's just Daddy's natural charm. He loves me dearly, and I am sure he meant it too. He was so angry when I told him I would marry you. He said I was too young. He called you *as smooth as silk*. That's because nothing ever riles you up, I suppose."

As they turned into the long driveway, Tony said, "Actually, you continually rile me up, one way or another, but I'm a public school boy. I was taught never to show my emotions. Surely by now you see through the act, but I hope you will keep my secret."

Bernadette said, "Of course, I will! I love when you look down your nose at people, even me at times."

Tony helped his wife out of the car and said, "I see Leon is back. I'm sure they've all interrogated him. Poor chap. I intend to thrash him at tennis tomorrow. Revenge for him fancying my wife!"

When Tony and Bernadette walked inside, they came upon Mr. Higgins, who informed them that their guests were enjoying refreshments in the conservatory. From the laughter and chatter, Tony asked if they were running out of vermouth. Mr. Higgins reassured him that the supply of gin and vermouth should last a while longer, but by necessity, he would need to arrange for some to be delivered the following day.

The atmosphere was jolly when the couple walked back in, hand-in-hand, and James Barrymore was reassured that he had no reason to ruin his son-in-law after all.

Bernadette took her glass of martini and joined the ladies. "Oh, he hates Georgiana. He said the most unkind things about her, even that she made him cringe. Did Leon tell you all what the note said? Tony ripped it up and said, 'Vile woman.'"

Once reassured that everyone was in on the note's contents, Bernadette said, "Can you believe the nerve? Anyway, beyond that, the tennis tournament is tomorrow afternoon, so I thought that in the morning, you could help me explore some of the forgotten rooms on the third floor. Margaret can help us too. I am searching for clues about Arabella. I always found it too creepy to go up there myself, and then there are also the attics."

The ladies laughed, and Blanche said, "Our Amie loves a good mystery. I'm all for it!"

Amalie stated, "Well, Cosette is going with Tony to help out with the new foals, and I believe one of the mares is close to her time. I am all for it. Aunt Henrietta?"

Henrietta and Eugenie stated their intention of sitting in the garden. Leon and James were going to the stables, too, so it was decided Bernadette, Margaret, Blanche, Cordelia, and Amalie were going on a fact-finding expedition immediately after breakfast.

When they retired, Tony asked, "What was all the planning I heard? You should save your strength for the tennis tournament. Three matches might be too much for you, my love."

"Nonsense," she said as she watched her husband get undressed.

He was rubbing his right shoulder, and she suddenly felt so tender toward him. It wasn't yet two years since the end of the war, and he never spoke about it, except perhaps to Walker. She said, "Tony, I'm so sorry that you didn't receive my letters and my photographs. I can't even bear to think of how you must have felt when they brought the post and there was never anything for you. I wish I wasn't so stupid and posted the letters myself. I wish I had gone to see you in Sussex after you were injured. I don't understand why your mother wanted you to be sad. Why is she so unhappy, Tony? The thought occurs to me that she must be very bitter to resent her son's happiness."

He didn't answer her, just shook his head as he climbed into bed, and Bernadette gently made love to him as she spoke so very tenderly of her love for him. He drifted off to sleep, and he was smiling. She decided that she must try to find a way to make peace with Arabella or even to understand her. No matter what evil she did, Tony always forgave or somehow overlooked her behavior toward his wife; even in front of others, she never relented. One answer was to bar her from Devereux House completely, but wouldn't that drive a wedge between her and Tony?

Then there were the paintings. He had them all taken down. His whole family history was removed and erased because his wife called them ugly and nasty. Who was she to speak so of his ancestors? That behavior was as nasty as his mother's. And he put so much effort into fixing up the house for her, and she had it completely redone, at her father's expense and without a thought for Tony's feelings.

Sleep evaded Bernadette that night, and as she lay softly crying, Tony awakened and said, "That was beautiful tonight, my love. Thank you for loving me so much, but why are you crying? Don't listen to my mother. I know I don't."

She said, "It's not that. I am used to that. Although questioning Louis's parentage was a new low. No, it's just that you are too good for me. I come from a family of poor farmers who couldn't even feed their families. They were my ancestors. No magnificent paintings of them, although my father partially remedied the situation with the huge one of himself in his office. I made you take all of yours down, and I would like to choose some of the nicest to put back up again. That was childish of me. I'm a spoiled, willful child."

Tony laughed and pulled her in his arms, kissing the top of her head. "Do you honestly think I didn't already know that, sweet Bernadette? I wouldn't have you any other way."

She responded, "Me neither. I mean about you. I love your stuck-up, superior expression." Then she realized he was already fast asleep again.

CHAPTER 23

The ladies were all wearing aprons from the kitchen. The men had left very early and had taken Cosette with them. It seemed likely that Marigold would foal that day, and Cosette was so excited to be there, as indeed was Leon.

Margaret said, "Bernadette, you can't take the baby upstairs. It is filthy up there. No one ever goes there. So Bernadette relented and reluctantly handed baby Louis to Bridgette.

Bridgette was enjoying her time with Margaret and, of course, Eloise, who she had known for so many years, and she found it quite lovely the way Lady Devereux wanted to carry her baby boy with her everywhere. Certainly, her mistress, Amalie, was never quite as motherly as that. Few of the wealthy classes were, and the lower orders had little choice in the matter.

Bernadette announced her intention of bringing a few of the paintings back downstairs, and they found so many of them leaning up against the walls of one of the guest rooms on the third floor, where the wallpaper was partially hanging off the walls. In other rooms, there were boxes of photographs and letters, old-fashioned top hat boxes, gentlemen's gloves, and silver-handled canes. A tour around the various rooms revealed more and more items of men's apparel and accessories, and it was as if someone had just stood at the doorway and thrown these items inside, since there was no order or arrangement to anything.

First, they sorted through the paintings. Of course, they were dusty and dirty, and these were not the ones hanging before the renovation and redecoration, or at least not that Bernadette could recall.

Cordelia shouted, "Come see this one. It is a very young Arabella. She looks to be no more than seventeen or eighteen. She was quite lovely."

Bernadette said, "There was another that she took to the dower house along with the one of Tony, but she was much older in it. Oh yes, she was lovely. I wonder what happened to her. I am bringing this one down, I think."

Blanche said, "If you're sure Tony won't be upset about it. I mean, why is it in here with all these much older paintings?"

Amalie said, "The rest are ugly—no wait. Is this Tony's father? Who is this other man? This is more recent than the others; well, I mean, possibly painted around thirty years ago. The clothes look like the 1890s, and why are both men in the painting? They are certainly handsome. Tony looks like his father. It is easily discernible that this man is his parent."

First, Blanche looked at Cordelia in complete understanding. Then the penny dropped with Amalie and finally Margaret, and then they all looked at Bernadette, who just said, "Oh dear."

The ladies asked the obvious question, "Does Tony ever talk about his father? We've never heard him mentioned."

Bernadette said, "Only that he died when he was very young, so he has been the viscount most of his life. He didn't seem to remember him much. I thought maybe life with Arabella caused him an early death. Should I take that painting downstairs too?"

Blanche said, "Not a chance unless you want to start another war."

Amalie grew wide-eyed, and Blanche and Cordelia reflected that she had never changed since she was a young woman. She said, "Bernadette, the truth lies in those boxes of letters and photographs."

Despite feeling utterly disloyal, Bernadette immediately returned to the room with the boxes, followed close behind by the others.

Each took a pile, and soon the truth was made clear to them. Tony's father's name was Edward, and the other man was Peter Forsyth. It seemed he was a house guest for many years, and there were many photographs of him and both men together. There were none of Arabella—none of Charlotte and Tony—none of any person other than these two men.

Cordelia said, "Bernadette, I don't think you should read the letters. I believe we all know what they must contain. Poor Arabella. Just a young girl used to provide heirs, her life treated as if it was of no consequence."

Blanche said, "Then along came the lovely, vivacious Bernadette Barrymore. Rich beyond belief, adored by her father, and, worse still, worshiped by Arabella's only joy, her handsome son, Tony."

Cordelia mused, "It was not that she didn't want her son's happiness. It was more like she despised yours. She was once young and beautiful, of no doubt excellent lineage, and married off to a man who openly displayed his love of another man—to her at any rate. How awful her life must have been. Sorry to say it, but I'm glad he died young. His treachery was quite appalling."

Margaret spoke up. "Well, we all know he would have no other choice than to lead this double life. It was just unfortunate for Arabella that she was chosen to play the role of ... well ..."

Bernadette continued for her. "The role of a young wife,

who was never truly a wife, was never truly loved or cared for. She was married off to a man who despised her so much that he didn't even attempt to hide his indiscretions. I, too, am glad he died young and Tony didn't have to grow up in that atmosphere. Poor Charlotte. She was older. Tony might not even know any of this, and if he does, why didn't he dispose of all of these things? This is his house, after all. I want all of it disposed of now. No wonder Arabella is full of hate. Poor woman."

She picked up a stack of letters—they each did—and they were love letters. There were also diaries, which appeared to be written in code.

Bernadette said thoughtfully, "I bet my daddy knows about this. I am sure he does since he had Tony investigated before our marriage. He is excellent at that sort of thing. It makes me respect Daddy even more than I did before. His discretion, I mean and … ladies, what should I do? I sure didn't expect this."

Amalie said wisely and through her own experience with her husband's past family life, "You will have to tell him, or it will eat you up. It will stand between you. He may accuse you, but he'll get over it. These items should have been cleared out long ago. I don't understand why they were not."

Margaret said, "I bet that is part of it! Arabella's hatred. She thinks you have known all along. You know how cheeky and sassy you can be, Bernadette. Perhaps she saw that as ridicule since she believed you knew all of this. But you didn't know. Tony never told you."

Bernadette said, "He once accused me of keeping secrets when all along …"

Blanche was looking out of the dusty window, which she had cleaned somewhat with her handkerchief. "They are all on their way back. Remember, luncheon and then the tennis tournament. It might be hard, Cherie, but do you think you can keep quiet about this until we have a chance to discuss it further? We don't need to leave until Monday, so we have all day tomorrow to put our heads together for the best strategy. We ladies can all go riding—you too, Margaret, since Bridgette is here with Eloise and the babies will be well cared for."

As they made their way downstairs, Amalie thoughtfully repeated, "Honesty is always the best policy, although seldom do men think of it as such—husbands at any rate."

~~~

Bernadette was donning her tennis whites when Tony entered her room. "Did Marigold have her baby yet? Poor thing."

He said, "No, but Cosette certainly seems to have a way with horses. I promised to tell her father. I think the girl should be allowed to follow her dreams. Too many young women are led to believe their only course of action for the future is a successful marriage. By the way, I saw Blanche looking out of a third-floor window. Why were you up there, my love?"

Bernadette felt she had been caught being a naughty girl, as she often was in her youth, and answered defensively, "Sometimes I find it irritating when you call me 'my love.' It sounds almost demeaning or that you can't bear to say my name. Lots of men call their wives darling, honey, or even sweetheart. My brother James used to call Nancy sunshine."

Tony said, "Well, I should indeed try to follow the Barrymore men's example by all means … sunshine."

"Don't call me that. It was just a for instance. Call me by my name."

He said, "Okay, Bernadette, what were you all doing on the third floor? Snooping, I presume?"

Bernadette responded, "Why? Am I not allowed up there? I considered fixing the rooms up, but there is so much junk to go through—paintings, photographs, and old letters. I wouldn't know where to begin."

She was almost sorry she said it, but he had irritated her with his high-handed manner of speech. She flounced into the bathroom to fix her hair, and he came to the door and watched her.

He thought, *She has such beautiful hair and shapely legs. My wife is perfection.* But he didn't say that. "That skirt is rather short, in fact too short to be worn playing tennis, flashing around your legs and your knickers. I think you should change it. By the way, did you find anything interesting? Among the photographs and letters that weren't addressed to you?"

This was too much, and Bernadette was livid. She now knew that he knew precisely what secrets the third floor contained, and she said, "You know what, Lord Devereux, *go to hell!*" And she grabbed her tennis racket and stomped out of her room, clad in what her husband considered indecent apparel, although he had never said that before when she wore it.

Luncheon was being served, but Bernadette hurried hers and then challenged Leon to a match.

Of course, he was enthusiastic, and by the time the others strolled out to watch, they were already well into play.

Tony watched as Bernadette once again performed her little dances when she made a great serve or won a long volley. She did her little dance if she won a game, and then finally, after a match well played by both participants, Bernadette won by a point and did her little dance again. Leon shook her hand and then bowed and kissed it in mock gallantry, and Bernadette was laughing. Tony thought her such a lovely creature and so full of devilment and fun. He was so very much in love with everything about her. Then he recalled how sweet and tender she was to him the previous night. It made his morning quite perfect, remembering the things she did and said, but now he wondered, *Was that some sort of pity party, son of a man such as my father, shared now with all of her friends?*

He said, "Okay, Bernadette, are you ready for another match?"

Bernadette responded, "Tony, may I be allowed to catch my breath first?" His challenge confused her. He had been watching and knew she had just finished three sets.

"Okay," he said. "Ten minutes and a cool glass of lemonade. Best leave out the gin, however."

Bernadette rolled her eyes at her friends and whispered, "He saw Blanche, and then he irritated me, and although I didn't admit to anything, he knows. What's more, he knows all about his father. He didn't say it, but I could tell."

James Barrymore had gone upstairs for a nap after such an early start to his day, and Henrietta and Eugenie were drinking tea and dozing off in the conservatory. Therefore, the spectators for the next match were just Amalie, Blanche, Cordelia, Cosette, and Leon, the Fallsingtons having left that morning.

Bernadette was tired from her game, but her husband was quite fresh, and she almost hated him when she missed his very first serve.

The match was completed in record time. Lord Anthony Devereux showed not one bit of mercy to his lovely wife, and she barely won even one or two points until the match was over in two sets. The score was 6–2 for Tony in the first set and 6–1 for Tony in the second set. No one cheered, and before she ran away, he saw great big tears running down his lovely wife's cheeks, the cheeks with the dimples that were not displayed even once to him during the match. Moreover, she looked almost in tears on several occasions during each set. There were certainly no little dances either.

The spectators stood up and walked away immediately after the match, and Leon shouted, "What a rotter!" as he walked away too.

Tony stood for a moment. *What did I just do? Humiliate my sweet wife for discovering secrets that were not kept very secret. I should have cleared out those rooms years ago. I just couldn't face it. Now I have hurt my little love so very badly. She will never want to play with me again. I can't say I blame her. She will probably never want to speak to me again either.*

Bernadette felt she wanted to run away and never return, but it was time to feed her baby, and he came first. She changed into her dressing gown and nightdress. She couldn't bear to face the others after that humiliating defeat. She fetched Louis and settled down with him on her bed, and as she began nursing him, Tony came in looking very ashamed of himself—not that she cared. She carried on feeding her baby and was singing a little song to him as she completely ignored her husband.

He said, "My little darling, my love, my beautiful Bernadette. You were tired. You played so well against Leon and beat him soundly. I watched you lovingly, your little dance, your lovely, shapely legs, all the while hoping for a peek at your knickers when you went full out for one of those hard-to-reach balls, which you invariably hit and hit hard. I did it deliberately. Not because I am better—well, although you know that I am better—but you were tired, and I knew it. You are still nursing our baby, and I'm an absolute cad."

He lay down next to her on the bed, with sad blue eyes—and was that a petted lip?

"So," she said, "why did you do it? And why should I ever forgive you or even speak to you again?"

By now, they both had petted lips.

He said, "To prove I'm a man."

Bernadette looked at him, amazed. "Do you honestly think I don't know that? Tony, you are being ridiculous."

"I mean, I know what you must have discovered this afternoon. I wanted you to discover it because I was too embarrassed to say it to you. Of course, now, as it turns out, half of Hertfordshire knows about my shameful secret too. I used to think they were best friends. I was very young, and I liked Peter Forsyth. He was kind and a lot of fun. So was my father. My mother was miserable, and that's how I saw her, so I preferred my father and Peter."

She threw Peter out when my father died from cancer. Peter cared for him when he was ill, and I believe they truly loved one another—right or wrong. I knew somehow you would understand. I mean, your new friends are so very open-minded, but I was afraid you would think I was like him—and I'm not."

All of Bernadette's anger melted away; her poor husband felt he had something to prove to her that afternoon. Didn't he understand her unconditional love of him?

"What happened to Peter?"

"When he left, I was a seven-year-old viscount, and I couldn't do anything about it. I did track him down when I was fresh out of Oxford. It had played on my mind for years. I gave him a few of my father's things and some money. He was living rather modestly in a small flat in Kensington. I promised him the painting and the photographs and letters. My mother threw a fit, and I never got around to it. And then I met and fell in love with you. The war came—so many excuses, so there they still sit."

Bernadette asked, "Is he still alive?"

Tony said, "I believe so. No, that's a lie. I know so."

Bernadette said, "I'm glad. Please invite him for dinner tomorrow, with Blanche and Cordelia and Amalie still here. None of this is his fault. If anything, it is your maternal grandparents' fault for not taking better care of their daughter and finding her a man who could love her."

Tony said, "Are you serious? What about Daddy?"

Bernadette said, "Knowing him, he already knows all about it. He had you fully investigated, you know—thoroughly, before he would allow me to marry you, but I would have married you anyway."

Tony laughed, relieved.

"He can take the painting and the photographs and letters, which belong to him. Does he live alone?"

"Yes, quite alone. I will ring him on the telephone. Believe it or not, he had one installed. I will go and fetch him. He will be surprised, to say the least. He asks about you."

Bernadette said, "So you visit him, Peter Forsyth?"

"Yes, although I should visit him more often. He talks about my father, and my mother never does."

Bernadette felt so sad and rather stupid. How could she not know this? "Oh, Tony, why didn't you tell me? Although I suppose I can see why you didn't. I understand your mother better now—but she is still horrid. I think you should tell her he is coming to dinner, if of course he accepts your invitation, and let this be the end of secrets."

Tony's face softened. "All along, I could have told you. I should have known you wouldn't judge him or me."

"Well, I do judge him somewhat. What he did to your mother? No, forget that. It was wrong of him to treat her so badly, but it is not my place to judge. I want to hang her painting, the one when she was just a girl, in the drawing room with pride of place. And then we should get one done of us both together. Perhaps we should take her to Boston."

Tony said, "You can't be serious. One last question. Last night. The way you came to me. What was that about? Had you already made your discovery? Proving something to yourself? I mean about me and my manliness?"

Bernadette took his hand and kissed it. "I watched you rubbing your shoulder, and it occurred to me that you had gone through hell for four years and were only back for less than two. I was filled with so much love for you. So the answer is no—I hadn't yet made my discovery."

Tony smiled happily, and Bernadette said, "Now, here, take your son and burp him."

Which of course he did.

Bernadette jumped up to tidy herself in the bathroom and laughed when she heard her husband shout, "Not again! All over my tennis jersey! Mommy! Come clean up your son!"

Bernadette peaked out the door and said, "Daddy! Serves you right, and you can take care of it."

CHAPTER 24

Peter Forsyth was utterly elated and gladly accepted the invitation. It had been so many years since he stepped inside Devereux House.

Tony was to pick him up at 9:00 a.m. so that he could spend a few hours sifting through what he wanted, and Tony would have his men deliver these things to his flat in Kensington.

Then there was to be a tennis doubles match with Bernadette and Leon facing Tony and Cosette. Tony pretty much knew how that would go—two-against-one sort of thing, since Cosette was really quite hopeless.

And finally dinner with his guests from Hertfordshire, whom Peter would already have met at the tennis match as a spectator. Arabella had declined Bernadette's invitation, much to everyone's extreme pleasure.

With this in mind, Bernadette extended the invitation to remain overnight, so Mr. Forsyth could have more time to go through the contents of the previously forgotten third-floor rooms, and the servants could have longer to get everything packed up.

Peter Forsyth was a man of around sixty, and Amalie and Bernadette agreed that he was quite swoon worthy, with his piercing blue eyes and silver-gray hair. He was immaculately dressed in the height of fashion from twenty years ago, and Bernadette took to him straight away.

Everyone, even James Barrymore, was polite and respectful and on their very best behavior, as if they could sense this was important to Tony.

Henrietta even said to Eugenie, her newfound friend, "Perhaps we might enjoy our dinner this evening."

And Eugenie responded, "Provided my daughter doesn't start playing around with the seating arrangements, and Arabella doesn't turn up unexpectedly."

They both agreed as they made their way to the tennis court. Mr. Forsyth had spent the morning going through the third-floor rooms, and all knew that this must have been nostalgic for him, bringing back so many happy memories—and some not so much so.

He was charming company, and his manners were impeccable. As he settled down to watch the match, he sensed kindred spirits in Blanche and Cordelia, and this served to relax him, as did Tony's charming wife, so full of fun and laughter. He sipped his cool lemonade with a splash of gin—now a Devereux House specialty, and Bernadette included a sprig of mint from the garden, just to add that certain something.

Of course Bernadette and Leon won a resounding victory, since Cosette could barely hit the ball. Tony would shout, "Your ball, Cosette!" And they all watched it fly right past her as she swung her racket in the air.

Tony's torture lasted for three long sets, and when his side was finally beaten, his wife added cartwheels to her victory dance. Everyone was laughing, and Cosette also demonstrated her new skill, which still needed a considerable amount of practice.

As they all gathered for dinner later on, there was a sense of peace about the table, and Bernadette—who did not feel the need to tamper with the table placements and had several of the leaves taken out of it—declared, "My darling husband, have you noticed how tranquil it is without Arabella?"

Amalie added, "I find I feel quite relaxed amid the intimate place settings. Mr. Forsyth, may I ask about your interests? I am creative, and Bernadette is athletic; that is how we new friends define ourselves."

Before he responded, Cosette said, "And Uncle Tony's mother is an evil witch."

Tony said, "Hey, wait a minute, Cosette. When did I become your uncle?" And she informed him that she decided it the moment they teamed up for tennis. "We really must do that again and beat Bernadette and Leon. We almost did today!"

Peter Forsyth asked his fellow guests to call him by his first name, and it seemed to Bernadette that he fit in very nicely. He said he was a writer. He had published a number of books but was no Nathaniel Hawthorne, whom he said was his favorite author.

Bernadette said she would buy all his books when next she went into town. "Are they tragic romances? Or do they have happy endings?"

Peter Forsyth described his work as "dark romances," and Bernadette and Amalie both wanted the titles, since this sounded so very intriguing.

Just then, the pleasant dinner conversation was interrupted by news from the stables that Marigold was about to foal.

Tony, James, Leon, and Cosette abandoned their dinner at that point, and Peter Forsyth enjoyed the remainder of his dinner in the company of his charming dinner companions.

The following day, Bernadette sadly waved goodbye to her guests, and the following month, her parents.

Cosette left to go back to school, by which time she felt like a little sister to Bernadette, who was again carrying baby Louis around with her as she wandered aimlessly around the house and gardens. She was supposed to be mistress, but it occurred to her that everything ran just fine without her.

One morning, she confessed to Margaret, "I think I'm bored. I mean not with Louis—of course not! Not with Tony either. Well, maybe with Tony. He's not romantic anymore."

Margaret said, "Bernadette, I think I know what you mean. It's not so much that we miss the war. How could we? It was a terrible time. But life was raw. We worked hard and dreamed big, and now we just … well, we are wives and mothers. Why don't you go stay at your flat for a few days? A week even? That will probably get Tony's attention. As far as my Tommy is concerned, well, I just can't wait to be off to Boston. Four whole months, and I am not guaranteeing that I am coming back. You go. I will take care of baby Louis, and Eloise loves him dearly. Shake Tony up a bit. You've been too pleasant these past weeks, and I prefer when you are sassy and cheeky."

Bernadette responded, "That is exactly what I will do. He can't stop me. It's my flat. Do you still have the spare key? Oh, he will be so angry with me—or maybe he won't. He can have his mother back for dinner. I am still considering taking her to Boston and marrying her off to a desperate old Irish widower. That would be a perfect end to the story!"

Bernadette grabbed her carpet bag. "I don't need to bring much. I am just going to be plain Miss Barrymore and sit in the park and maybe do some shopping. I wonder why Tony never wanted a portrait painted of him and me. He has mentioned it, but by the time he gets around to it, I will be a wrinkled old woman with no teeth and hair on my chin."

Margaret said, "That sounds more like the old Bernadette. Oh, there will be fireworks tonight, and yes, I still have the key!"

❦

Tony returned home from the stables and came up to change for dinner, expecting his wife to be doing the same. Instead, he found her sitting with her coat on and a carpet bag at her feet.

He immediately became concerned. "What's going on Bernadette? Are you going somewhere?"

"Yes," she said, attempting to sound calm. "Well, you know that Louis is done nursing now, so Margaret and Eloise will be looking after him for a few days. I am going to spend a little time, possibly a week, in my flat in Knightsbridge."

Tony couldn't quite believe his ears. "On your own? Are you so fed up with me? Regardless, Bernadette—fed up or not—the answer is no. You cannot go to London on your own, and I'm too busy right now to accompany you."

Bernadette responded, "Actually, I didn't ask you to come. I am going alone. I want to find out if I will miss you. Also, you will be able to find out if you miss me. An inspired idea, I think. I won't be gone long because of the baby, and as you know, you abandoned me for years, and I made out just fine. My turn to abandon you for a little while. You can have your mother over for tea."

Tony stood there, at a loss for words. He was incredulous. "No, Bernadette. The answer is absolutely not! Whatever nonsense this is, forget it. Now, are you getting dressed for dinner?"

If Bernadette felt a little bad about doing this to her husband without warning, the feeling passed with those orders, and such perfect timing when she looked out the window, and there was Leon.

"No, I am not running away with Leon! No, God forbid! He

is dropping me off at my flat on his way out to meet up with some university friends. Oh yes, just like you used to do."

Bernadette grabbed her bag and said, "Don't worry about money. Daddy gave me some before he left. He knows you are not the most generous man in the world."

Tony stood in front of the doorway and said, "I mean it, Bernadette. Stop this nonsense!"

Bernadette responded, "Am I now a prisoner, Tony? Years spent as the abandoned wife, now to be followed up with being locked in my room? Kindly step aside."

Tony started to think this was some kind of game, a joke that they would laugh about later in bed. He stepped aside, his brow furrowed, and as Bernadette walked past him and ran down the stairs, she shouted, "I'll be back in a week or so!" She jumped into Leon Blakeley's Buick Roadster. She was laughing, and then she was gone.

He angrily shouted, "Margaret!"

This she expected. "Yes, your lordship. What can I do for you?"

"Margaret, what is going on? And don't pretend you don't know."

"Well, you see, your lordship, her ladyship just needed a wee break away from her responsibilities."

Tony exploded. "What responsibilities, Margaret? All she does is carry her baby around and do cartwheels!"

Margaret expected hurt and anger, but that remark was just plain nasty, so she said, "Precisely, your lordship. You just hit the nail on the head," and she walked away.

Tony was livid. Even so, he knew that remark was a bit below the belt. He thought of calling Margaret back and saying he didn't really mean that quite as it sounded, but he was quickly stopped in his tracks by the appearance of his mother at the front door.

"Did I just see what I thought I saw? Your wife driving away with that young man who came to dinner? What's going on, Tony? Has the bricklayer's daughter finally left you? And her child? I would never allow her access—"

Tony cut her off. "Mother, please calm down. Bernadette has just gone on a little holiday, and Leon Blakeley is merely dropping her off at her flat."

He was still at the top of the stairs, and his mother started climbing toward him. "A little holiday? You allowed that? Have you lost your mind?"

The drawing room door was wide open, and from her position on the stairs, she could see inside, and the huge painting of her, painted as a young girl, before life took every ounce of joy away from her. She said, "What is the meaning of this? Who hung up that painting?"

"Oh," he said, "that would be Bernadette. She said you were very beautiful and wanted to hang it there."

Arabella wasn't sure what to say. "Is this some kind of cruel prank? I don't understand. And why have you not had her portrait done by now?"

He said, "I have, or rather she had it done for me. For Christmas. I pretended I didn't like it at first. There seems to be quite a strain of unpleasantness, cruelty even, that goes along with the Devereux name."

"Show it to me!" It was a command.

"Okay." He led his mother into his wife's abandoned bedroom to view the half-naked portrait of Bernadette.

His mother stood and viewed it very carefully, employing the use of the monocle that was hanging amid the multitude of pearls around her neck. Finally, she said, "Very well done. Looks just like her. Or at least the parts I have seen."

Tony said, "My, my, mother, that was almost a compliment."

Arabella said, "Well, she is pretty enough, not aristocratic, not in the slightest—but I suppose if you like that type of woman."

Tony laughed. "Well, it would seem that I do. She wants you to come to Boston with us. Almost four months if she has her way. Halloween through Louis's first birthday in February. Well, that is if we are still married by then."

Arabella tutted, "Nonsense! However, I might just take her up on that, even though I am sure it is just to show off the Irish bricklayer's house."

"Mansion actually, Mother, and you have never seen the like of it before. Made me feel like the impoverished viscount her father thought me to be, and that I did in essence eventually become after the war, if not for him."

"Well, I will think about it. When are you going for her? She can't stay in London by herself. She is too used to being looked after now."

"I thought perhaps midnight? She will be quite nervous by then. I am sure of it. And even if she doesn't miss me, she'll miss our baby. As a matter of fact, she'll be missing me too."

Arabella actually laughed as she walked away and said, "I may come for dinner tomorrow night. If she is back by then."

⸎

Leon offered to see Bernadette into her flat, but that didn't feel right to her, so she just let him take her to buy sausages, bread, and tea and a bottle of wine and bid him farewell. She mounted the stairs and turned the key in the door she had come home to so many nights in the past but that now felt so alien to her. Alien without Tony. She had grown used to once again having him beside her.

Bernadette believed she would enjoy a few days away, while at the same time making her husband suffer, but she had no sooner lit the fire, eaten her sausages, and drank her tea when she started to cry.

The flat was strange without Tony. They used to come here sometimes before the baby was born—a romantic retreat. And she said aloud, "For goodness sake, Bernadette. You lived here for two whole years. All by yourself!"

She wandered into the bedroom and opened her closet. Her work clothes were still hanging where she left them, relics from the past. The fashion photographs were still pinned to the wall—old-fashioned by now, of course.

She went back out to the living room and sat by the fire. She poured out a glass of her wine, and it was really very bad. However, it would need to be good enough; she was not about to go back outside to the shops. She looked out the window, willing the Silver Ghost to appear.

On her second glass, she said, "Bernadette, what type of husband would have just let you go and get driven off by another man?"

It had gone ten o'clock, and she decided to get ready for bed. By now on her third glass, she closed the bottle and put it away, saying, "No more, Bernadette." Then she started to cry again. She wanted her baby, she wanted Tony, and she wanted to go home.

However, she thought, *I can't go back for at least three days, unless he comes for me, and if he doesn't come for me, what does that mean? That he is glad I left?* Then she said aloud, "Well, he can't have my baby," and then she started to cry yet again. Why did she do this? It was stupid. She was no longer the girl who lived here and worked at Harrods during the war. She was Lady Devereux or, more importantly, Tony's wife and baby Louis's mother.

She lay on the sofa by the fire. The flat felt so strange to her. It was her past but no longer her present. She knew she should go to bed, but she so wanted to go home. Midnight—clearly he wasn't coming, and she had one last look out the window before finally retiring for the awful night that lay ahead of her. But there it was! The Silver Ghost, and Tony was stepping out of it, carrying flowers. She burst into tears once again and went running down the stairs in her bare feet. As he entered the doorway to the flats, she quite literally jumped upon him in her joy and started kissing and kissing him in her relief.

It was a better welcome than he could ever have expected, and he said, "How is your holiday going so far, my love?"

Bernadette was pulling him by the hand upstairs, and he said, "You'll have dirty feet running around the street like that, and you know how much I enjoy your toes."

Bernadette blushed and said, "I want to go home, Tony. I missed you and Louis. Tony, I missed you so very much. How did I manage all of those years?"

He said, "Let's put them behind us now, my sweet Bernadette. Let's pack away your shop girl clothes and buy some nice new furniture and a new bed, especially a new bed, and this will be our special retreat, but only together—always together. Deal? So why did you leave me? You seem to have missed me an awful lot for such a short space of time away." He looked at his watch. "Not quite six hours actually?"

Bernadette poured her husband a glass of wine, and he cringed as he drank it.

She said, "I don't have a purpose. The house runs itself, and the servants are so kind, and everyone looks after me. I'm useless. You know I am. Boring and useless."

He expected this sort of response. It was typical Bernadette— typical of the woman he was mad about. He said, "Okay, I have been giving this some thought. I need some help at the stables, especially now with Cosette gone. I paid her three pounds a week. You didn't know that, did you? I will pay you three pounds and ten shillings, and if you like, we can make you a carrier so that you can carry little Louis around on your back, something like your ancestors used to do in the fields."

Bernadette playfully hit him. "I want four pounds and ten

shillings, and I will work no more than three hours a day—without Louis on my back. Oh and Saturdays and Sundays off."

Tony said, "Lady Devereux, you drive a hard bargain, but what are you going to do with all that money?"

"I will save it up so I can buy you something very special."

"Another nude?" he asked.

"No, a shower contraption. If we can find one in this country. Or else Daddy can send it."

Tony was laughing and peeking down his wife's dressing gown, which she was pulling shut. "Okay, I'll make it five pounds for a measly three hours of work a day, and two whole days off a week. However, there is a caveat."

Bernadette could easily guess what that was going to be and said coquettishly, "What would that be, master?"

He said, "Exactly. I think you know. Your master will require some very special services from you."

Bernadette happily kissed him. "I will be happy to provide these special services free of charge, beginning right now—after I have washed my feet."

Tony said, "No, your ladyship. That will be my pleasure."

It was raining hard when Bernadette awoke the next morning, and she was immensely relieved not to be there alone. She took Tony a cup of tea and one sausage with a slice of toast, then jumped back in bed beside him.

She said, "Sorry, I only bought half a pound, and I ate the rest last night. You can have half of mine if you like."

Tony said, "You are such a funny little thing. Look at the damn weather. They could find us in here starved to death."

Bernadette said, "Well, I have half a loaf left and some tea. Oh and the wine."

He pulled her to him and said, "Remind me never to allow you to select from the wine menu, my love. Let's stay in bed a while longer, at least until the rain lets off a bit."

He dozed back off until Bernadette awakened him an hour later and said she was hungry.

Tony got up, threw on some clothes, and went out for some food with the money Bernadette brought with her from her father. He came back an hour or so later with a roast of best beef, a bag of potatoes, and brussels sprouts—also eggs, bacon, sausages, and a selection of cakes from the corner bakery. He also brought back a couple of bottles of decent wine.

Bernadette started, of course, with the cakes, and Tony said, "The shops are starting to come back to normal somewhat. The prices though are outrageous. Good thing my wife is rich! I called home. Before you ask, our son is just fine. I told them we'd be back in a few days, since we needed to go shopping for the flat."

Bernadette was delirious. Perhaps this was what she really wanted, some time alone with her husband.

She cooked up the roast of beef, and he laughed at the skills that she kept well hidden at Devereux House. "Perhaps we could give our cook the sack and have you take over?"

He was funny and romantic, and they shared ideas and made lists of what was needed to make the flat into their own special retreat. Bernadette said she had learned a lot from Lady Blakeley, but this would be all their own design based on their mutual love of color and comfort. They also decided that the nude would be moved to the flat, most especially with baby Louis becoming more aware of his surroundings.

Tony said, "By the way, I showed it to my mother. She said the parts she recognized were an excellent likeness. She even said you were pretty, 'if one likes that sort of girl.' I told her that you are exactly the sort of girl I like. Oh and she might come to Boston. Not sure how I feel about that actually, or how your parents will feel, but if she doesn't behave herself, they can always ship her back to England."

This was all interesting news to Bernadette, but she asked,

"Tony, what does your mother mean by 'that sort of girl'? It sounds demeaning."

He said, "Oh, that's easy. The type of girl that men desire not only for her beauty and shapely curves but also her sensuality. As the fortunate man you chose as your lover, I will always feel blessed to be the lucky recipient and only man with whom you will ever share such passion and desire. At least I hope that will ever be the case."

Bernadette stopped in her task of peeling potatoes. "Tony, that is so very romantic, but I don't think she meant that—although I did like hearing you say it. Were you filled with desire when you saw me the very first time at the Ritz?"

He laughed and came up behind her, lifting her skirt. "Not until I saw your dimples. Seriously though, my mother didn't understand that was what she meant, although truly it was. She may have been a beauty in her day, but she never had what you so casually possess. So the answer is yes—from the moment you looked at me, I knew. I knew I had to make you mine and that no other woman could ever satisfy the depth of desire I felt. I was driven quite mad with it."

He became serious. "All those years apart, you must have been asked out by other men—pursued even. Weren't you ever tempted?"

"No never, not even once. Even though I hadn't heard from you in so many years, I still cherished the desire that once you returned, if you ever did, you would fall for me all over again. I honored my vows and gladly did so. It was no sacrifice. I only ever wanted you and ever so badly. Thus I came to the train station, and it broke my heart when you walked away with your mother."

Tony said, "I was so shocked to see you there, looking magnificent except for your silly little hat. I didn't know what it meant—you being there—having received no correspondence from you. I came to your flat. I couldn't help myself from doing so. I made my mother give me your address, and I came to you, albeit full of doubt and suspicion. I couldn't stay away, and when you undressed me and wrapped your naked body around me, I knew you still loved me—there had been no other man."

Bernadette asked, dreading the answer as she turned around and looked him straight in the eye, "What about you, Tony? The girls in Harrods said that men have needs and that most likely their men were having relationships with women in France or Belgium. They said I was fortunate not to have a man to worry about, and I just smiled and agreed with them."

Tony laughed. "Is that what they said? Well, there are men who are not quite as discerning as me. There of course were opportunities. When I stopped receiving your letters, like a fool, I stopped going home on leave. I know now how stupid that was, that I should have made a point to find you. For all of the lack of any correspondence, I found that I couldn't even consider another woman. I wanted to—some sort of twisted punishment—but I couldn't find a girl who was anything like you, and I found I couldn't consider anything less."

He turned her back around, and Bernadette said, "Standing at the kitchen sink? This is a first, Lord Devereux!"

It was a perfect sojourn. It was just what was needed to reboot their marriage after so many visitors and so much entertaining. Upon their return home, Bernadette immediately ran upstairs to take her baby—who was crying—from Eloise, who was carrying him around in the nursery. Eloise said he was teething, but he stopped crying as soon as his mommy took him in her arms, and Bernadette laughed merrily at her happy life. She carried him downstairs to see his daddy, only to find Arabella seated in the parlor and Tony standing at the doorway. Before they saw her, she heard Arabella say, "You let that girl wrap you around her little finger. You go chasing after her like a love sick schoolboy. I told you to go fetch her home—not to hang around for days, making up to her."

Bernadette stopped in her tracks and was about to return upstairs, but then her baby said, "Daddy." It was clear as a bell and his very first easily discernible word. She changed her mind and proceeded downstairs.

She heard Tony say, "Mother, we just got back. Were you here awaiting our return to cause trouble? Were you so bored?"

Bernadette breezed into the parlor. She did not greet her mother-in-law but said to Tony, "Somebody just said his first word."

As if on cue, baby Louis said it again, "Daddy," and he put his arms out to his father.

It was the first real connection he made with his father, and Tony's face lit up as he took his son into his arms and said, "Yes, Louis, that's me. Goodness sake, you are an armful. Your mommy takes such good care of you. You're a lucky boy. Daddy's a lucky boy as well. Mommy takes good care of him too."

Bernadette felt triumphant and so much love for her husband and son—actually for so many wonderful people in her life. And although her intention was initially to berate and insult Arabella, she could suddenly see it in her eyes. The sadness and jealousy. She was a woman who was only ever loved by one person, her son, and her daughter-in-law had taken the greatest part of that love away. She was no longer content just to call Bernadette names; she was now starting on Tony.

Bernadette decided enough was enough. "Arabella, would you like to hold your grandson?"

The older woman hesitantly put out her arms in agreement. He was such a beautiful baby and so like his father. She had deliberately shut him out of her heart, the way the boy's mother constantly carried him about and doted upon him, but as she took her grandson in her arms, he laughed up at her and repeated, "Daddy."

Bernadette watched and wondered about her reaction, which was, "Goodness no, Louis. I'm Granny."

The baby put his hands on his granny's cheeks, and quite amazingly, she kissed them.

Bernadette had the feeling of holding her breath, and unbeknownst to her, so did Tony.

Arabella sat for a few minutes fussing with her grandson and then handed him back to his mother saying, "Goodness, child! What do you feed him? He's growing too heavy for you to be carrying him around—but I know you'll do whatever suits you."

Arabella stood up. "With your permission, I will dine with you both tonight. I am considering this trip to Boston and would like to hear more about it, and of course this mansion of your father's."

Bernadette realized Arabella was talking to her and not to Tony. "You are most welcome to come, Arabella. I will be glad to tell you all about Boston."

The older woman responded, "Oh, I am sure of it, Bernadette," and she left—Tony having spoken not one word during this almost congenial exchange between his mother and his wife.

༄

The house was soon in a complete uproar. How does one pack for a four-month trip abroad?

Bernadette and Margaret saw to everything possible—right down to presents for all the servants, to be stored with Mr. Higgins until Christmas. And there was a frenzy of shopping and packing, which kept Lord Devereux at the stables as often as possible, just to get away from all the chaos.

He had a good team, and they were given early holiday bonuses with the promise of another if the horses were well taken care of. He had buyers already, and his foreman and estate manager were to send him weekly reports. Several of his mares were again in foal, and he would be back long before their time was upon them.

Cosette would be returning in the spring, and her father, Sir Leopold, had finally given his permission for her to apply to the Royal Veterinary College, where she was one of the first females ever to be accepted as a student. She was to begin her first semester in August 1921 and had negotiated a wage of five pounds per week from her employer, Lord Devereux, which she was saving up for her course requirement of books on equestrian anatomy and physiology, which she wanted to make her specialty. Of course, her father could easily pay for all of this, but both he and her mother were so very proud of the woman she was becoming, independent and with her own mind—so different from the girl they first introduced to Lord and Lady Devereux. The acquaintance had most definitely brought out the intelligent young woman, previously hidden deep inside of their daughter.

Since his wife never picked up her wages from him, Lord Devereux had money enough to pay such exorbitant remuneration. Bernadette loved to ride, and she rode most mornings with her husband to view the estate. However, she only actually worked for him three days and then stated that she would even prefer Mr. Montague to him as an employer—so she resigned or "quit," as she put it. Lord Devereux was relieved about this and wondered how she ever kept her position at Harrods with all of her cheekiness and willfulness. She had an argument against every task he assigned to her.

Bernadette received letters from her mother and informed the others that her parents were going all out to impress the dowager viscountess. Of course, as she said to Margaret, "I don't really know why they feel they have to do so, considering what she was used to in this dusty old house."

Margaret said, "Well, it is very beautiful now, Bernadette. I am sure she wishes she could move back in."

Bernadette laughed. "Well, that will never happen after the last time, and anyway, while we are away, Tony is having the dower house painted up a bit. He is also fixing up my flat—our romantic getaway. It was all supposed to be a surprise, but I persuaded Lady Blakeley to get involved, and she is making Sir Leo give him a deep discount."

Margaret said, "Won't they be in New York this Christmas?"

"Yes, and I have invited them all to stay for a few days over the holidays. Of course I haven't told Daddy and Mommy yet, but I am sure they won't mind, since Mr. and Mrs. March will be there too. Oh, and of course Blanche and Cordelia—unless they all go to Mrs. March's daughter's house in Long Island instead. Or she can come too, with her husband and daughter. Her name is Annabelle, and I am told she is very charming. Do you think that is too many people? Well, perhaps only some of them will come. And it will only be for a few days, after all."

Margaret laughed and left to get on with her packing. They were leaving on October 9, plenty of time for Bernadette to make the arrangements for the Halloween party she was planning in Boston. She was planning on dressing up as Cleopatra, with Tony as her Anthony—that was, if she could persuade him to wear the toga she had found in London. Otherwise, it would still be

Cleopatra, but her Anthony would be dressed as Lord Anthony Devereux—Tony to his family and friends.

The dowager viscountess had only traveled abroad one time before—on her ill-fated honeymoon to Lake Como. She was excited about the whole enterprise and amazed that she was included in her daughter-in-law's plans. Tony had told her it had nothing to do with him and even said after her treatment of his wife, he could never have expected such forgiveness.

There had been so much unpleasantness between them for so many years, and although Bernadette was still as cheeky as ever—spoiled beyond belief by her husband, who took over very nicely from her father in that regard—Arabella was well aware she was the person most at fault, due to her cruel treatment of the girl. She could admit it now—to herself at least. Sheer jealousy. And when she most expected ridicule—the whole sordid truth of her miserable marriage revealed after all these years—Bernadette never uttered a word on the subject. It wasn't through awkwardness either, or even through kindness, unless of course it was the reason she was taking her along to Boston for such an extended visit—that indeed was an act of kindness. Arabella cringed about all the name-calling and the terrible things she had done to try to break up her son's happy marriage. Yet now it seemed it had somehow been forgiven, and by those whom she once felt were beneath her and whom she treated with such contempt.

Arabella reflected upon her past deeds, the worst of which had been the letters she kept from a young couple so much in love, most particularly during the very worst of times. Yet through it all, they were both steadfast in their love for each other.

She looked at the clock. Just after 10:00 a.m., and Tony was taking her shopping along with Bernadette and Margaret. Arabella couldn't help but laugh. All of her disdain of the Irish, and now there were more of them in her life than Englishmen and women! Many of her friends had deserted her, or died, or moved to the continent for a more temperate climate. She pondered, *Well, now I have new friends—and a family who should have cut me off long ago with my vindictive behavior. I will do better in the future. It will not be easy, since my daughter-in-law so exasperates me. However, I intend to surprise the Barrymores. They will be expecting a different dowager viscountess than the one I intend to be—even if it kills me, which it may well do!* And she laughed out loud at her own foolishness.

CHAPTER 25

It was smooth sailing all the way to Boston, and the party of five adults and two babies, together with their nanny, arrived safe and sound.

The dowager countess was, of course, given the best guest room in the Barrymore mansion, and Tony and Bernadette stopped by to see if she was comfortable enough and to take her downstairs for tea and refreshments.

Tony said, "So what do you think, Mother? Is the room adequate for your comforts?"

Arabella scoffed and mumbled something about excessive and extravagant expenditure and how the shower contraption in her bathroom was unhealthy. However, she was soon settled in her beautiful bedroom suite, as were all of Bernadette's party, newly arrived from England. Margaret was once again in a guest room with her husband, Louis and baby Tommy were sharing the newly refurbished nursery, and Tony was sharing Bernadette's childhood bedroom, which had been done over the previous year for a married couple.

Bernadette's nieces were still staying in the house with their mother, Nancy, and were quite grown up from when they were in England the previous Christmas. The eldest, Emma, was graduating from high school in the spring.

It seemed to Bernadette so very many years ago since she and her parents made that fateful voyage for her eighteenth birthday. That was right after her graduation too. She graduated on June 5, 1912. Set sail for England the following day. Celebrated her eighteenth birthday aboard ship. Arrived at the Ritz Hotel on June 12 and became a married woman less than two months later, on August 3.

The Barrymores frequently had guests for dinner, and not surprisingly, James's friend Seamus O'Hanlon was a frequent visitor. He had been widowed three years previously, and it seemed to Bernadette that he was in search of a wife and companionship. She could hardly believe that Arabella was actually flirting with him, indeed if that was what one could call it, after all the Irish bricklayer's daughter remarks—after all the insults about the Irish.

Tony found the whole thing quite amusing, so did Margaret, but somehow, Bernadette did not.

She looked around the table that fateful night. There was Margaret, her best friend and the mother of her parents' oldest grandson—by six weeks. How on earth did that come about? Louis was their grandson. Tommy should be Walker's son and nothing more, and meanwhile, Tony was talking on and on about Cosette and how young women were beginning to make their way in the world. He was speaking encouragingly to her nieces, who clearly adored him, and Bernadette felt like some dimwit— married fresh out of the schoolroom. Some girls were academic; some like Amalie were creative and artistic. Bernadette was athletic, and really, how could a woman—now a twenty-six-year-old woman—be described as athletic? Who cared? She thought, *I will be married for nine years next August. I have only actually been living with my husband less than half of our married life, and he is sitting encouraging my nieces not to be like me—never to be like me.*

Margaret had told her that morning—she was joking about it, and Bernadette laughed—Tony's comment about her carrying around her baby and doing cartwheels. It was apparently all she was good for. Bernadette knew it was self-pity, but somehow she just couldn't sit there any longer listening to his sound advice to her nieces.

She said, "Or the alternative is to marry young, hope your husband is nice to you, have babies, and stay evermore in the background."

Tony looked at her questioningly. They all looked at her, but only her parents did so with understanding. James and Eugenie Barrymore—dearest to her in the world along with her baby, because, in that moment, she hated Tony. He didn't wear the toga; of course he didn't. Her Halloween party was a flop since her English family had no idea how to celebrate it, and coming up next was Thanksgiving—another un-English holiday.

She stood up and said, "Excuse me," and when Tony looked concerned, she said, "I just need to check on Louis."

The reaction, as she expected, was, "My wife, the best little mommy in the world."

So condescending, she thought, but she smiled sweetly at him, although she would have preferred to slap his face, and went on her way out the door. She went through the kitchen and grabbed her old coat and hat. She donned her muddy riding boots, which Walker had promised to polish up for her but apparently forgot to do so, and went out to the stables. It was mid-November, so it was dark outside, but she didn't care. She saddled up a stallion, her father's and one she was quite unused to, and went on her way. She thought, *I'll just ride around the house, stay close by since I can see by the porch lights.* Her only intention was to irritate Tony, as he was irritating her with his dinner conversation.

There was talk of snow, but none had yet fallen. However, the sky looked rather strange, and it seemed to her that Tony didn't even know she had gone out. "Or care," she said aloud. Then suddenly a snow squall surrounded her. She had seen them before in Boston but had never encountered one when upon a horse, and here she was riding an unfamiliar horse, not able to see her hands in front of her, which by now were like ice, since she forgot her gloves. As she tried to keep the horse steady, hoping the squall would quickly pass, there was a crash of thunder. *Thunder snow,* she thought as the horse reared in fright, and Bernadette's frozen hands couldn't keep a hold of the bridle. Down she fell, and as she landed, she hit her head on a rock that was lying in the middle of the open lawn, a place where it shouldn't have been. Her last thought before she passed out was her bedroom carpet the night she fell ill with Spanish flu. *Is this the same night?* The horse rode away, and the squall passed, but Bernadette was unaware of all of this in her deep, dreamless sleep, in the cold darkness of a mid-November night.

Eventually, Tony made a remark about Bernadette most likely having fallen asleep beside Louis, and Margaret agreed that it was not so terribly unusual if she did. He had drunk more than his usual that night. It was a fine, smooth cognac, and it had quite gone to his head before he realized it.

James nodded at Michael O'Connor, who knew exactly what that meant, and Tony said he was going upstairs to awaken his sweet wife. He said to the others, "She is the loveliest creature in the world, and so smart too! I am the luckiest man alive to have found her before any other man did."

The others laughed as he left them, since they had rarely seen Lord Devereux in his cups.

Five minutes later, he reappeared. He looked completely sober but terrified. "She's not there! Eloise said she never went upstairs! I am sick of her pulling these stunts to terrify me. Where the hell did she go?"

He looked frantic and was about to go outside to search for

her when suddenly Michael appeared with Bernadette in his arms. Her hair was bloody, and she was clearly unconscious. He said, "I will carry her upstairs. Tony, follow me up, and then I will go for Dr. Finnegan. Eugenie and James ran upstairs too, as did Margaret, and the ladies chased the men out as they undressed her. She almost appeared to be dead, her breathing so shallow. Eugenie was in a state of angst, and so was Margaret, regretting her stupid words that very morning. She of all people should have known what Bernadette was like—willful and impetuous. She was screaming, "This is all my fault!" And finally Arabella appeared and took control.

"Everyone, calm down. She is not dead. Her breathing is shallow, but she is alive. However, it appears that she hit her head. What was she doing out riding anyway at this time of night? Margaret, why is this your fault?"

Tony had reappeared and was trying to look calm, although his heart was racing. He couldn't lose her now, but a blow to the head could be fatal. Internal bleeding. He also turned to Margaret for an explanation.

Margaret thought, *I'm done for now anyway, so why not tell the truth to Lord Devereux and his dear mother.* "We were talking about hidden talents. Stupid really, but I remembered his lordship's words the night she ran away to her flat. I said them, and she laughed, but I could tell she was hurt, and I tried to take them back, but contrary to what you might believe, your lordship, Bernadette is not stupid."

Tony grew angry. "What are you talking about, Margaret? What words? When did I ever belittle my wife's intelligence?"

Margaret looked him straight in the eye and said, "With respect, your lordship, you were doing it all through dinner with your talk about women and careers and how they should aim for the sky, follow their dreams. Didn't you notice that every word was like a knife in her heart, since she married you at eighteen?

By the way, the remark was the one about her responsibilities, and may God forgive me for suddenly remembering it tonight. If she dies, it will be my fault. Mine and yours, your lordship. Oh, and Lady Devereux—I suppose we can count you in too."

James seemed ready to explode, but Arabella interrupted him. "What was the remark you made, Tony?"

He knew straight away what it was but said, "I don't really remember. I was angry. I went after her that same night and—"

Margaret said, "The basic gist was that all she did was carry her baby around and do cartwheels. When his lordship is upset with my best friend and mistress, he says things and then feels guilty and confesses them to her, and she always forgives him—like the potato digger's remark, or the fact that she needed her head examined. Odd remark, that one, when you look at that poor wee soul now. Oh and, your lordship, feel free to give me the sack, because if my friend doesn't make it through ..."

She began to cry, and it seemed everyone was crying. James was about to swing for Tony but got quite a surprise, as they all did, when his mother slapped his face and said, "Pull yourself together, Tony!" Then she turned to Dr. Finnegan. "Can you save her? Will she be all right? Can't you awaken her?"

The good doctor said, "It is in the hands of God, your ladyship. With a head injury, she will either awaken just fine, or awaken confused, with complete memory loss, or, God forbid, never awaken at all."

That night, the whole household kept vigil, and still she slept on. In the early morning, Eloise brought in baby Louis. "Your lordship," she said, "I thought perhaps baby Louis could awaken her ladyship. She loves him so. She won't want to leave him."

The baby's crying awakened those who had dozed off, and once again, it seemed that everyone was crying, and even Arabella had tears in her eyes. Dr. Finnegan had told them the longer she slept, the less likely she would awaken.

Tony was sick inside, and his face showed it all so clearly. He was as white as a sheet and said to his father-in-law, "If my wife doesn't make it, sir, please look after our child."

James Barrymore sensed what his son-in-law meant but asked anyway, "If my daughter dies, you plan to kill yourself? Is that what you are telling me?"

Tony answered flatly, "So many times, I have gotten everything wrong, said everything the wrong way, but I never took her for granted because I always knew she was my very soul and I could never live without her. In France, I so longed for her, and the time the grenade exploded in front of me, I just stood for a few seconds. I wanted to die. I thought I had lost her. Then I remembered a man telling me—you met him actually, Peter Forsyth—where there is life, there is hope. So I ran as fast as I could, and Bernadette kissed my scars from the shrapnel that I couldn't completely escape, so many times that I am quite glad that I have them. I have always known that should she die first, I would die soon after, not of a broken heart, although my heart would certainly be broken. My preferred method will be a gun to my head."

Bernadette had slowly awakened during this speech, possibly to the sound of her baby crying. She felt groggy, and her head hurt, but generally she was okay, and hearing her husband say all of this, she made an oath to herself and to the good Lord above that she would never try to punish him again for not loving her enough. She was loved more than any other woman on earth. He would have died for her.

She decided to ease his mind, his wonderful mind, and she opened her eyes and asked, "Did everyone see that snow squall last night? I couldn't see a foot in front of me. Oh boy, do I have a headache! Daddy, what was in that lemonade?"

At first, everyone just stared at her—scared to hope that she was perfectly fine. And then she said, "That was meant to be a joke. I'm so sorry, Tony. I am sorry, everyone. And, Arabella?"

Arabella said, "You gave us quite a fright, young lady. We will have no more of your nonsense!"

And Tony, wiping the tears from his eyes, said, "Mother, what do you expect from an Irish bricklayer's daughter? I suppose I will need to learn to keep my mouth shut in the future."

He was kissing his wife's hands and then laid his head on her breast as she stroked his head like a child. Her Tony, her public schoolboy looking down his nose at everyone, but not so much that morning.

Arabella said, "Well, hold on to your hats because I have special news of my own to share with everyone—now that my daughter-in-law has decided to recover. Mr. O'Hanlon has asked for my hand in marriage, and I have accepted him. He is quite the charmer. It's in the Irish blood, but you already know that—about the Irish, I mean. Anyway, I am tired of living alone and getting on everyone's nerves. We will be married on Christmas Eve, and my daughter-in-law will arrange everything. In fact, she will be my matron of honor. You will be getting rid of me, Bernadette. I am not returning to England with you and Tony."

Bernadette was astonished and burst into laughter, even though it made her head hurt. She had once made a remark to Margaret that this could absolutely be the end of the story.

"Where's Margaret?" she asked.

"Out of a job," Margaret responded, stepping forward, but she was laughing because she knew everything was going to be just fine now.

Tony said, "I might not sack her, but I might need to address what I am paying her. But, Mother, this marriage business at your age. I am not sure that I approve of it. We will need to discuss this in private."

"You can discuss whatever you like, Tony, but my decision

has been made. I am jumping ship and joining the Irish contingent of the family. As I said to Seamus, if you can't beat them, join them—and my dear boy, your wife has me well and truly beaten."

After duly congratulating the dowager viscountess, while at the same time realizing that their daughter's loss would be their gain, since Seamus was a frequent dinner guest, James and Eugenie Barrymore told Tony to step aside, as it was their turn to embrace their daughter. And as they took her in their arms, James said, "No matter what that clod of a husband says, always remember that you are the most special girl in the world. James Barrymore's beloved daughter and that English coxcomb's beloved wife.

The two most important men in Bernadette's life gave each other a bear hug after that, and Eugenie and Arabella embraced too.

Margaret was standing holding Louis, who was breaking his heart, reaching for his mommy, and Bernadette said, "Oh, Margaret. Please help me get up and dressed so I can carry baby Louis around and do some cartwheels for his lordship."

Tony turned to her, looking concerned, and she said, "Actually, dearest husband, I don't feel up to cartwheels today. Perhaps tomorrow?"

He was about to apologize for his stupid remark, but Bernadette shushed him and said, "I love you all so very dearly, and I have never felt so loved in my entire spoiled and willful life. I am almost glad I fell off Daddy's horse, but you must all go now and rest. Tony and me and baby makes three need to have a nice little nap together, and, Tony, you look quite sickly. I hope you aren't catching a cold."

The snow had started falling in earnest, and Bernadette said, "Gee whiz, I can't wait until the lake freezes up. I'm certain I am a much better skater than my Tony thinks he is. After all, dearest, how often did you ever get to skate in Hampshire? It is never cold enough for the lakes to freeze!"

Tony sleepily responded, "I'm sorry to say this, my love, because I know how happy this will make you, but I have never ice-skated before in my life. I'm afraid I lied about that part—just to ruffle your feathers a bit. I'm not sure I want to learn, actually, at this stage in my life—most especially with you as my instructor. However, I am sure you will persuade me, and my guess is that you are exceedingly good at it and will be showing off unmercifully."

Bernadette laughed out loud, as did Tony, and soon even baby Louis was laughing, because it would be a shame to miss being part of such a perfect, happy moment in time.

Ingram Content Group UK Ltd.
Milton Keynes UK
UKHW011826040423
419625UK00001B/167